PHILIP ROONEY

CAPTAIN BOYCOTT

Marjorie Greenan

ANVIL BOOKS

Anvil Books Ltd., Tralee, County Kerry
Republic of Ireland

First published by the Talbot Press 1946
This edition by Anvil Books 1966

Made and printed in the Republic of Ireland
by Browne and Nolan Limited, The Richview Press, Dublin
Set in Linotype Times

CHAPTER ONE

THE May twilight was already deepening to dusk, and all the country from hill to lake was still and empty under the evening sky. Here, in the wide, low levels of Gortnacarrig bog, the land brooded in silence under the shadow of the coming night. The only sound was made by the hurrying footfalls of the man who took his way alone through all that empty land.

Where the narrow lane dwindled to a narrower cattle-track he began to step out more hurriedly. The bog sucked muddily now about his feet as he followed the twisting path through a maze of turf pits brimming with the oily blackness of stagnant water, and that soft, squelching sound seemed to heighten rather than break the silence.

And then, in the far distance, a single shot rang out in the stillness and rolled, echoing, under the empty sky.

"Cinders of Hell!" said Watty Connell softly into that shattered silence. "And me so far from home." His corrosive, cynical mouth twisted in a grin of soured humour. "Is it landlord or snipe yon lad's after—or bailiffs?"

He added one more long inch to his stride, but not fearfully. He had as little fear in him as the next man, or the man after that, had this bailiff to Captain Boycott, the Land Agent to the Earl of Erne's Mayo estates. And yet he had good cause for fear. Two bad harvests had brought poverty and a hunger that was near to famine amongst Boycott's farms on the shores of Lough Mask; and on the heels of poverty and unpaid rent had come process and notice-to-quit.

That very day Watty Connell had served more than twenty notices. He remembered now the secret, hard look on the faces of the men who had received the notices. Somehow their grim silence had seemed more dangerous than the wild threats and frenzied curses that had greeted him in other years.

'Twas easy enough to find the cause of the trouble, of the

new dogged spirit, Watty told himself. The cause was there for any man to see: Land Leaguers and speech-makers promising the tenants that never again would they be evicted and flung out wholesale from their cabins. Promising them that there would be no evictions this winter coming, and urging them not to starve while there was a harvest that could be held and eaten.

Wild promises! Watty strode on, his massive head sunk into bowed shoulders. And worse than wild promises, indeed! Over in the Joyce country and back west in the Partry mountains there were whispers and rumours that the Ribbon Lodges and Whiteboy Societies were forming again. And didn't Sergeant Dempsey of The Neale tell Captain Boycott himself, not more than a week ago, that the Government had certain knowledge of how the Fenians were drilling and swearing-in men again? Fenians here in Mayo—where there hadn't been trace or tidings of the like even in the worst days back in '67.

Ah! Well! Fenian or Moonlighter. 'Twas all in the day's work, Watty told himself. And he had done this day's work without guard or escort, policeman or dragoon. Twenty notices served, and one more to serve. He would serve this last notice in his own way—and that way would have in it its own sharp tang of satisfaction.

He strode forward into the twilight, a squat, massive, toughened man of middle years, with a strong jowl blue and stubbled from lack of shaving, and wary eyes set deeply under a grizzled thatch of brow.

Over the last lift of ground at the bog's rim he came on his short man's wide and rolling stride. Where the lift of land commanded a view of Lough Mask shore he came to a halt and stooped forward, peering into the shadows.

Shadow had deepened here, although all the higher ground was still bright in the afterglow. The lake lay shining like a mirror, bright with retained and reflected light in a dim frame of woodland. A stone's throw away a rivulet poured into the lake, a cold white line of water marking the thrust of the live stream into the still lake.

Beyond that clear cold spearhead of water, in the shadowy undergrowth, a figure moved. Watty Connell was certain of that now. He could see the moving man, a tall man slinking stealthily in the gloom, on his shoulder the elongated shape of what seemed a long-barrelled fowling piece.

Carefully Watty eased one of the brace of pistols in his belt. Even now he was not touched by fear, but the memory of that single shot was fresh in his memory.

"Yourself, down there," he called. "Come up till we have a look at you."

The man in the shadows took his own time to answer. He stood still in the deep shade and spoke down softly to the girl who was hidden from the watcher on the road above by the slanting bole of a tree.

"'Tis all right," he said softly. "It's only Watty Connell. You've no need to care what he thinks."

The girl moved back into the shadows, and now he could see no more than the pale blur of her face under dark wings of hair.

"Watty is it?" Her voice was no louder than his own. "Is it have him see me—and have his tongue clacking and gossiping about me the length and breadth of the parish. No! I'll away off home through the wood. There's no need for him to see me . . ."

There was no need—no need at all. And yet, not for the first time or the hundredth time, Hugh Davin found himself rebelling against all this semi-secrecy, these cloaked meetings, this hidden love-making.

"Let him talk," he said, on a rising note of anger. "Let him talk from end to end of the county, if he's so minded . . . 'tis time and past time for your father and mother to know . . ."

The bailiff's voice came booming down to them again, rising in impatience. Anne Killian paused, poised, ready to move away.

"Hugh! Hugh!" she entreated, and that clear, cool voice of hers, now as ever, soothed his impatience. "Let us not make trouble where there's trouble enough, God knows."

He could not see, but he could sense, the live, bright curve of her mouth as she laughed softly. He did not protest, as he had often protested before, against the furtiveness and secrecy of their meetings. Too often, of late, he had noticed that his protests brought a shadow of trouble to her eyes. He would not darken the light mood that was on her now.

"And won't we be meeting again to-night—at the dancing . . .? "

The tall man could wait no longer. He came out of the shadows into the light, and he was not slinking. He was not slinking indeed. He carried himself with a tall man's smooth and far-reaching stride. He carried himself with an easy air that was not stealthy nor touched with fear. Over his shoulder slanted a fishing-pole, a single spar of trimmed ash.

"Yourself, Watty," he said lightly.

His was a strong, tenor voice, not loud but with a clear ringing note to it. A voice with a chord of humour in it, and now that humour was nicely flavoured with malice.

"'Twas rabbits the lad yonder was shooting. Martin Brannigan, the Captain's groom—I saw him."

He let the fishing rod drop in the grass and leaned against the wall that had given the bailiff shelter. Without haste he began to fill his wooden pipe, leaving Watty Connell to consider the full import of that malicious remark.

And Watty Connell took his own deliberate time in considering the remark—and the man who made it.

It wasn't that he disliked Hugh Davin. He had no cause to dislike the man. But Davin was almost a stranger, not more than twelve months in the district; and Watty's trade made him cautious in dealing with men whom he did not know well.

If this new schoolmaster was like old Master Kearney now, a twisty, whiskey-drinking old devil, the bosom friend of Sergeant Dempsey and all the Constables in The Neale barracks, and a man not above having a quiet drink and a quieter chat with Boycott's bailiff, it would be easy to know what to expect from him. But Davin, Watty decided, was a deal sharper and deeper than the old master. He was friendly enough with policeman and bailiff, to be sure, but he spent no long hours of hearty drinking with them in Martin Egan's pub. Just friendly enough, Watty thought sourly, to make sure that he wouldn't be noted by the Sergeant as a disaffected person and so, maybe, lose his schoolmastering job. But deep enough—the bailiff's mouth twisted in a quirk of cynical understanding—deep enough not to get too friendly and make enemies for himself with the Land Leaguers and the speech-makers.

Ah! Well! Watty Connell could be nicely tolerant of vices that matched his own. 'Twas a hard game, this business of living, and a man was well entitled to play the game his own way. Still and all, 'twould do no great harm to see on what side of the ditch young Davin stood. He'd find that out some day—in his own way and his own time.

"You see a hell of a lot for a man that talks so little," he said at length. He set himself squarely against the wall in the tall man's shadow. "An' tell me this now. For one that fishes so much, do you ever put a hook in a fish?"

Hugh Davin had a sound excuse for delaying his reply to that question, a question which might imply much or nothing. The flame, twice quenched, was at last burning steadily over the bowl of his pipe, and his whole interest seemed centred on the kindling tobacco, as why should it not be?

He stooped over his cupped hands, and the light spilled softly upwards in a revealing wave over his intent face. Yet that light revealed little. Slender and fine-boned his face was, with a tight jaw and a firm chin. His eyes were deeply and darkly set under a strong, surely drawn arch of brow; but his eyes, lifting from the flame, looked out now over that twilit land with an air of lazy interest that would, ever and always, be a fine screen for his thoughts—when his needed screening. And the line of his mouth was now no more than whimsical, a broad and mobile mouth, full-lipped enough for passion or for tenderness, but firm enough for caution and an iron reticence.

"Catching fish isn't the best part of fishing, Watty," he

replied easily. "Fishing keeps me out of trouble—and trouble's easy come by these days."

His pipe was drawing freely now. The drifting smoke veiled his face and his expression. He leaned over to look more closely at the pistol which the bailiff still held in his hand.

"You have your own way of keeping trouble at a distance, Watty. That's a handy tool."

"'Tis and it isn't." Watty tucked away the pistol with the other of the brace in his belt. "Myself, now, I'd as soon have the ould blunderbuss any day. A grand, handy tool that same blunderbuss. The noise of it, itself, was half the battle. And the way 'twould scatter a half-pound of slugs and tinpinny nails into a suspicious bush would do your heart good. 'Twould so. But sure the Captain favours the wee yokes. And he's a man that does be to have his own way."

He buttoned up his coat and patted the pistols into place.

"Ah! Well! We all have our own notions. An' if it pleasures the big man to fill the house above with fancy guns, hasn't he the good right to do it."

He flashed a calculating glance at the younger man and added casually, or not so casually:

"And maybe he'll have the need for them too. Both him and me."

Hugh Davin made no reply to that probing remark. Trailing his fishing rod, he fell into step beside the bailiff and together they faced the slope that lifted from the shadowy levels of the lake shore to the higher ground along the Kilmaine road where, in the bright afterglow, the mail-car from The Neale was slowly breasting the hill.

It was a high, deep-welled side-car that had once been painted scarlet but which was now faded to a rusty shade. On the driving seat the driver humped dolefully into the upturned collar of his coat. Flanking him were two armed policemen. The larger policeman sighted the men on the roadside and raised his voice in sonorous command.

"Amby Nolan! D'you hear me, Ambrose!" he roared into the ear of the driver. "You will halt to allow me to dismount. After which you will proceed slowly down the road, remaining always under my direct and personal supervision: that is to say within sight and hailing distance. When summoned by me . . ."

Old Amby brought his nag violently to a halt. He shrank deeper into the shelter of his coat collar.

"Erra, Sergeant! Can't you lave the chat for the journey back," he protested hoarsely. "I'd as lief take my chance without the protection an' be shot, if shot I am to be. For if so be I'm another half-hour late with the post for Lough Mask House, 'tisn't shot I'll be but skinned alive by Captain Boycott."

With immense dignity Sergeant Dempsey descended from the car. A fine, upstanding man he was, topping six feet of broad-shouldered massiveness now gone slightly to flesh. His moustache bristled in a great inverted horseshoe against a broad and florid face. His forage cap sat at a rakishly elegant angle over an eye that looked out upon the world with infinite self-satisfaction.

"You will remember that you are a servant of the Crown, Ambrose—although in a humble and unimportant position—and you will remember that it is the duty of a servant of the Crown to render aid, comfort, and loyal assistance to the members and officers of Her Majesty's Royal Irish Constabulary."

He was a man with a fine imposing voice and a liking for the boom of that voice. For a moment now he paused, savouring the rich round echoes of his voice; then he came striding widely down the road, the butt of his carbine tucked under his oxter. In mid-stride he caught Watty Connell's eye, and not even his self-esteem was quite proof against that bright, sardonic stare. It was to Hugh Davin he spoke, and his voice, now as ever when he came face to face with this tall man, was not friendly.

"The paid servants of the Crown, Master Davin," he said ponderously, "are slow at times to remember what's expected from them."

For all his pomposity there was no mistaking the antagonism in his voice. The colour deepened in his face, and the flick of his hand as he brought the carbine muzzle up to the "trail" position was marked enough to engage Watty Connell's attention. Thoughtfully Watty's eye slid to Hugh Davin's face, but that face told him nothing.

"D'you tell me, Sergeant," Hugh said blandly. "Well so! Sure every man will do his part when the time comes."

For a moment longer Dempsey continued to stare down his adversary, but Davin's eye did not fall before him.

"That time has come," he announced with evident satisfaction. "I was laughed at when I promised trouble; but the trouble has come . . ."

"Not hereabouts, Sergeant," Hugh said quickly. "Not in The Neale district?"

Davin, old Watty pondered, was very prompt in making that remark—or protest. He tucked away the thought for further consideration. He eyed the Sergeant cynically.

"Dambut! For a fine figure of a man, Sergeant, you have a taste in gossip like a tailor's widow. What the hell is frightening you now?" he asked.

With dignity Dempsey shortened his grip on the carbine and moved it into a more comfortable if less official position. He signalled the car to return.

"'Tisn't me has the reason to be frightened, me good man." He had little liking for the bailiff and no great reason to hide his dislike. "But it might interest you to know that Major Scott's bailiff, Hussey, that's missing this three weeks, was found to-day—in a bog-hole at Tourmakeady. In a bog-hole, Mister Bailiff Connell, with a half-hundred-weight of stones tied in a bag to his feet."

The post-car had come pacing back. He turned to mount it. Over his shoulder he scattered a parting broadside.

"'Tisn't for me to force the security and protection of the Law on any man. But if I were in some men's shoes, I'd not be slow looking for proper police protection and escort." Ponderously he swung himself on to the car. "And I'd have a care not to go too much alone—or in any company I couldn't trust and depend my life on."

In silence Watty Connell watched him go, his soured, cynical mouth twisted in its own grin of derision.

"There's a herring-gutted fish-eater for you," he said with contempt. "He gets a few shillings special pay for every day he's on protection duty, and he can't abide me because I persuade the Captain that himself and myself are better protection for our own two selves than any peeler."

He rubbed his hand raspingly along his chin and looked guilelessly into the darkened sky.

"Divil a much he thinks of you either, Master. He has a class of a set on you, so he has," he said mildly. He paused for an instant and went on blandly: "To listen to him and to watch him, you'd think that it was how he was suspicioning you of something." The dry, goading voice went on, probing: "Maybe, it's a thing he doesn't know that you have the Captain's leave to fish, and that he had the idea 'twas poaching you were."

He sucked at his pipe, hollowing his unshaven jaws under their craggy bosses of cheek-bone.

"Or you might have a bad friend, Master, that was whispering the false word in the Sergeant's ear?"

For the second time that evening Hugh Davin's pipe saved him from the necessity of making an immediate reply. He blew vigorously through the stem and knocked out the bowl with unnecessary violence. Casually he parried the bailiff's probing questions. He would not allow his secret, and the secret of fifty others, to be so easily surprised.

"His own reasons he'd have, Watty," he said easily enough. "If a peeler ever has reasons."

"Aye, so!" The bailiff chuckled deeply, a rumbling belly laugh. "A quare breed! Still an' all, 'tis odd the way he has the set on you. 'Tisn't the poaching now—for you're a fair-to-middling honest man. An' 'tisn't the drinking—for be all accounts you'll not go far past the third tailor of malt. And they tell me in The Neale that the Sergeant has the promise of a strong farmer's daughter and a stocking of sovereigns up in the County Roscommon, so 'tisn't a girl . . ."

"A great chance I'd have against the fine uniform and the stripes, Watty."

It was easy to say that lightly, but his mood was not light. He watched the post-car go bowling out of sight. For a moment he forgot the sergeant. The picture of Anne Killian which the bailiff's casual words had called up, took warm and living shape in his mind. He could see now, in that swift memory, the glowing pallor of her face, the white forehead, broad and low under smooth, sleek wings of dark hair. The bright, live line of her mouth, her woman's mouth, was sharp in his memory. And now, as ever, he could see her eyes in his own mind's eye, brown and ardent and deeply lit—and sometimes, in those latter days, shadowed by trouble.

The memory of those troubled eyes stayed with him. He stared unseeingly down the empty road, his own gaze dark and brooding, his mouth not warm with humour now but pinched with thought. Watty Connell considered that thoughtful face with interest

"Dambut, Master," said he, "a body would think you were mourning George Hussey. Myself now, maybe I have reason and plenty to do that . . ."

His words seemed to pull Hugh Davin back from dark thoughts to thoughts that were even darker. He threw up his head, as if aware for the first time of the emptiness of that shadowed road.

"The fools," he said deeply, out of some sudden impulse. "To let themselves be forced into that . . ."

He broke off sharply, conscious of Connell's appraising stare. His face lightened. He hunched his shoulders in a swift gesture, as if shaking off a sudden chill.

"Bad work, Watty," he said lightly, and his mouth was at its old trick of masking his real humour again. "Pitching a bailiff into a bog-hole settles nothing."

"Barring the bailiff," the other countered dryly. "It settled George Hussey."

And he, too, turned to look down the Lake Road. The post-car had long since vanished from view over the rise of Carnagower Bridge. All the land was empty again, empty and drained of colour. Far and wide before them Lough Mask lay cold and gleaming in the greying light. Beyond the steely waters, far and far away, the mountains ranged, Benlevi and Maamtrasna, the giant Partrys and Nephin's towering self, misted against the fading sky. All the wide spread of land and water was held now in that desolate moment when day is done and the first clear starshine has yet to come.

The chill of that grey and desolate moment touched Connell now. Even yet he was not afraid, but the cold loneliness of the evening had laid its chilling finger on him. He shivered a little in the first rising wind of the evening and upturned the collar of his coat. No! He had no fear of George Hussey's killers in him; but he would not refuse company down the lonely road.

In that moment a new thought struck him: Here to his hand was a chance of putting Davin's doubtful friendship to the test, of forcing him to say on which side he stood.

" Maybe the Sergeant was right and all," he said. " Maybe I might do no harm if I had a man with me on the way home."

He was watching Hugh Davin steadily now.

" I have one small job to do above at Killower," he went on deliberately. " And I'll be glad of your company if 'twouldn't demean you in the eyes of your friends to be seen walking my road."

A straight request, that, asking for an answer straightly and promptly. Hugh Davin did not delay over-long in making his reply—and his decision. For a moment only he hesitated, and even in that moment his face did not betray him. The black and curving bar of brow that was drawn so firmly over his dark eyes lifted in one faint movement of derisive understanding.

" One road or another, Watty," he agreed, " 'Tis all one to me—so long as I travel it my own way at my own gait."

CHAPTER TWO

THE silence that had brooded over Gortnacarrig did not lie so heavily on the lawns of Lough Mask House, but here, too, had fallen a stillness that magnified all the small sounds of evening, the far, faint voices of the men at work in the Castle field, the rumbling of cart-wheels on some hidden lakeside road.

A constrained silence had fallen on the man and woman who had been walking on the lawn which fell away in a smooth sweep to the trees by the lake shore. In silence they had now returned to the gracefully curving fan of steps before the house door, the woman to resume her seat in the high chair set on the topmost step, the man to stand behind her, concealing his gathering anger as best he could. And he did not do that well.

"It's a question of money," Charles Boycott said angrily, picking up the discussion again at the point where it had almost become argument. "The two bad seasons have hit me just as hard as they've hit the tenants on the bog farms."

He moved restlessly behind his mother's chair, not looking at her, but sharply aware of the unyielding set of her shapely, greying head, of the cold firmness of her mouth. He moved away from her and paced to the narrow limits of the step. Even in that narrow space he contrived to move with a military precision of stride, pacing firmly back and forward, his hands linked behind his straight back. He had not lost the soldierly bearing of his Captaincy in the Inniskillings. His long-waisted coat and wide-breasted waistcoat set off his broad shoulders and tapering waist. His head was carried high and well, a bullet-round, massive head, with a vigorous sweep of reddish hair grizzling already at the temples, the face high-boned and high-coloured, a strong setting for hot, intolerant eyes and an iron mouth.

"I've poured money, hand over fist, into my own farms," he stormed in an echoing, vibrant voice. "Every ha'penny of Erne's miserable salary, every penny of my own money . . ."

"And now my money," his mother reminded him quietly.

She had a beautiful voice, musical and clear as a bell note but cold, too, as the clang of a bell.

"No, Charles! What little money I have will not go, not one penny of it, to improving Henry Erne's property. If it were your own land . . ."

Her firmness dulled the anger in him, and his voice was no more than surly when he answered her.

"The land's as good as mine. I hold my own farms on a fine long lease," he protested. "A better lease than any man in the country. Erne treated me well."

To that Caroline Boycott made no answer at all. She had placed a work-basket on the arm of her chair and was now bending over it. She must, her son thought suddenly, with an interest that was not usual in him, have been exquisitely beautiful back in the days, five and thirty years ago when, after a whirlwind courtship, she had married Lieutenant Malcolm Boycott of the 49th, then stationed at Galway. Even now, in advancing middle years, her face still showed the fine clarity of line and perfect modelling that had made Caroline Blake the loveliest of Galway's lovely girls. Age had not flawed the fineness of her skin, but it had robbed her face of warmth. And her eyes were cold too.

Cold, her son thought, with a preoccupation in another's affairs that was strange to him. And coldest of all at any mention of Henry Lord Erne.

And that in itself was strange; for Erne had been an officer in Malcolm Boycott's regiment and a friend of the youthful Lieutenant and his bride away back in the days when the red-haired Scots subaltern had married the Galway beauty. Nor had Erne forgotten his old friendships; for, five years ago, when Charles Boycott had sold out his commission in the Inniskillings and tried, most unsuccessfully, to farm a wild estate on Achill Island, Henry Erne had remembered his old-time friends and had appointed Malcolm Boycott's son to the agency of his Mayo estates.

It was strange, puzzling. But Charles Boycott was never one to waste time and effort in profitless speculation about matters outside his immediate concern. Now, as ever, his mind swung back to consideration of his own present problem.

"Well! If you can't see your way to help," he said, "there's no more to be said. I'll just have to do my best and cut down expenses still further. For if I'm not to lose everything, I must find some money."

Carefully the woman matched colour to colour from amongst the stuffs in her basket. The colours were rich and bright, and against them her hands glowed with a pale ivory tint of their own.

"You could marry money, Charles," she said softly. "A wife with a dowry would make you free of Henry Erne. Make you independent. As it is"—she lifted a pale hand in a small gesture of contempt—"as it is, you're little better than a glorified tenant-at-will of Erne's. A wife with money . . ."

"Easy talking . . ."

"Why not? It could be easily managed. You are young." She leaned back to look at him, admiringly, and in that instant there was warmth in her smile. "Young and personable. And, aside from your present difficulties, quite comfortably circumstanced . . ."

"You might find it hard enough to convince mothers of dowried young women of that," Boycott protested gruffly. He was suddenly embarrassed as a gawky schoolboy. "Ladies with dowries are hard to please."

If Caroline Boycott noticed his discomfort she gave no sign that she had done so. Placidly she patted away the coloured stuffs in her basket and went on in a matter-of-fact tone.

"You can leave that in my hands, Charles." Again that quick, warm smile touched her mouth fleetingly. "I can prolong my visit here for another two or three months. There's quite a lot I can do. Entertaining for you . . ."

She was silent for a long, thoughtful moment.

"Alice French and Olive Burke, Charles," she continued, as if carrying on a discussion already begun. "Both charming girls."

In that quiet remark was an uplifting note of enquiry, but her son chose to ignore the implied question. Vaguely he felt his discomfort grow. They were charming girls, true enough. But was charming the term to describe them? John French's small, dark daughter and the tall Burke girl. Pretty girls, handsome girls. But charm? The memory of them did not stir his blood or quicken his mind. And surely a man wanted that —and more.

Uneasily he moved away again from the woman's chair and began to pace to and fro before the quiet house. He did not turn to look at the house but the picture of it was clear and bright in his mind: a strong, square house, bold and harsh of line, looking out westward over lake and lawn to the far-off hills. The shadow of the ruined castle beyond fell on it and the tall, too-near trees darkened it; but it was a warm, secure house for all that, quiet in the evening light.

Some day he would bring a wife here. And some day the quiet house would be loud with the voices of children. But this chilled, planned business of choosing a wife and dowry...

He stopped short in mid-stride with a jerky, clumsy suddenness as if he had found himself hedged in and trapped. His mind, forceful and direct, baulked at this twisting network of thought.

"There seems little other choice left to me," he said with an anger that he did not fully understand. "Little else, except I listen to Erne's complaints and raise the rents again." He laughed shortly. "More rent for him—more salary for me."

"You can't do that, Charles." For the first time there was a real note of feeling in Caroline Boycott's voice, a note of alarm. "That would be madness. It'd drive the tenants to every devilry, to murder . . ."

"They're welcome to try. That wouldn't stop me if there was one small hope in Hades of getting the extra money from them, on my own farms or on Erne's. But there isn't. Not a man of them but's a full gale behind with his rent already—and half-starving into the bargain."

He expelled his breath in a gusty sigh of ill-temper and essayed a smile that was soured and ill-humoured.

"There's nothing for it but this wealthy wife of yours."

At that he relapsed into moody silence which the woman wisely made no effort to break. Moodily he stood before the open doorway and let his eye roam over the far limits of that wide spread of land and lake, idly but not blindly.

Not blindly; for his idle eye was idly held by the far, flying shape of a car blackly drawn against the sky as the horse was whipped to a spanking trot along the road which swept in a high curve above the lake shore before passing the entrance gate to Lough Mask House.

Far away, where the sun had fallen behind the purple reef of the Partry Mountains, the line of peak and swelling hill was drawn surely and sharply against the soft sky, a clear keen line edged with light. Already shadow was softly flowing into the bowl of the plain, and field and woodland were dissolving into formless dusk. But the lake still held steadfast in its quiet centre the pale light of the sky. And the high sweep of the road above the shining water was yet bright in the afterglow. Idly Boycott watched the car wheel blackly against that curve of lighted land and come bowling up the drive to his house.

With no foreshadowing at all of the storm that was already darkening about him, he walked briskly down the steps and across the wide bay of gravel to where the car had stopped.

. . . .

Sergeant Dempsey had already climbed down from his seat on the car and was standing to attention. He saluted briskly, but with an over-emphatic flourish that stirred Boycott to irritation.

"You have a fine time car-driving round the country, Sergeant," he snapped in unreasonable anger. "I'm hanged if I know why they don't find some work for you fellows to do."

The Sergeant drew himself up a shade stiffly; his chin came up a little, the jaw tightening. But the habit of discipline was strong in him.

"Consequent on information received with regard to the

troubled state of the country, in particular in and about the districts of Partry and Tourmakeady," he explained grandly, "and pursuant to the special powers invested in me as Sergeant and Acting-Head-Constable, I took it upon myself to place the post-car under police protection." He remained rigidly at attention, but his speech eased a little. "A bad business that, over west, Captain—the murder of George Hussey."

"Damned bad," Captain Boycott agreed. He reached up to the driver for the locked leather mail-satchel which he tucked under his arm. "Bad surely! But if Major Scott chooses to employ a fool as a bailiff, where else can he expect to find him in the end, but in a bog-hole?" He looked the policeman straight in the eye. "This is no country for fools, Sergeant."

That jibe eased his ill-humour a little, and he was smiling to himself as he watched the Sergeant mount the car again and bowl away. He opened the leather case and riffled through the packet of letters. He passed to his mother those addressed to her, and from his own mail he drew out one inscribed in the scrawled, uneven handwriting of Lord Erne.

With no great interest he began to read the letter; then, slowly, a shadow of amazement darkened his face.

"Well! I'm . . . I'm . . ."

He broke off and laid his hand on his mother's shoulder.

"Listen to this! It's the most amazing thing . . .

"Just listen. It's from Erne." He turned back the sheets and began to read. As he read, his voice, without deliberate intent, took on a faint mimicry of Henry Erne's languid, intolerant tone:

"'I am taking advantage of your mother being with you, my dear Charles, to ask that you and she will extend the hospitality of Lough Mask House to a very dear and charming young friend of mine . . .'"

"A young and charming friend of Henry Erne," Caroline Boycott said coldly. "Does the man think . . . ?"

"A moment, mother." Her son went on reading. "He makes it clear enough who the girl is; he's by the way of being guardian to her. She's Wynne's daughter, Hubert Wynne, who used be racing and stud manager of Erne's place in Sussex many years back. Her mother . . ."

"I knew her mother. Who did not?" The contempt in Caroline Boycott's voice was edged as a knife. "Violet Martin of Baronscourt. Five-and-twenty years ago she made a fool of herself about Henry Erne, and ended up by marrying one of his stable-boy cronies."

"Mother!" The man did not attempt to hide his astonishment—and his distaste. This is hardly the time," he rapped out, "to unearth old scandals about a poor lady who died" —he glanced down at the letter—" who died less than a year ago."

The hard note in his voice warned the woman that even she could not press Charles Boycott too hard or too far. She sat still for a moment staring down unseeingly at the letter which she had taken and crumpled in her hands. A little gust of anger shook her. Even yet the memory of those days, thirty-five long years ago, when Henry Erne had thrown her over with a cool and callous finality, had power to hurt and to move her to anger. He had thrown her over, as ten years later he had jilted the mother of this girl. She looked down at her hands, seeing, yet not seeing, the taut whiteness of the skin over knuckle. Slowly she unclenched her hands, spreading out her fingers which trembled slightly with the anger that still held her, anger against Henry Erne, and anger, unreasoning and even more bitter, against the other woman whom she had scarcely known save in the gossip and scandal of Galway town five-and-twenty years ago.

"So Violet Martin is dead," she said quietly. She had her voice under control again. "And Henry Erne proposes to relieve himself of the responsibility of her daughter by throwing the girl on our hands."

She dropped the crumpled letter into her work-basket.

"How very like Henry Erne! But it won't do, Charles. You must write and tell him that the arrangement would not be possible."

"We've got to make it possible."

Her son stared down uneasily at his employer's letter. His was a mind that avoided side-issues and clung tenaciously to one problem at a time—and that problem now was his own pressing problem of money.

"Can't you see that this is just the one very time when I can't afford to quarrel with Erne. If I refuse to do this . . ."

"You must refuse. The position would be impossible, intolerable. Do you think it will make it easier for you to find a suitable wife if you have this girl here in the house?"

That terrible, cold, old-woman's anger flared in her again. "A girl who has very likely been banished here to prevent her marrying some of her father's stable-boy associates," she said. "Some racecourse lover whom even Henry Erne cannot stomach."

There was a very real anger now in Captain Boycott's face. The simplicity, the essential decency of the man, was affronted by this spate of vituperation and insinuation.

"I see no point in the malicious and quite unfounded slander of a defenceless girl," he said stiffly, choosing his words with frigid formality. "If you don't choose to help me by making this"—he consulted the letter again—"this Judith Wynne welcome, there seems to be nothing else I can do but make arrangements for someone else to chaperon . . ."

"Oh no, Charles!"

His mother was stooping over her basket, packing away the lengths of coloured stuff. Her voice sounded quite light and friendly.

"Oh no! I have no intention of leaving. No such intention at all." She could not resist the edged sneer. "Who knows but that in my absence your chivalry might plunge you into marriage with Henry Erne's young and charming friend."

She snapped shut the lid of the basket. Her anger was now perfectly under control, but the smile she forced was wintry.

"And when may we expect . . ."

"'Judith,'" Boycott read, but now heavily and with no mimicry of the old and faded gallant in London who had written this disruptive letter. "'Judith has already left for

Ireland. She will advise you from Dublin when you may expect her. . . .' "

On a sudden thought he picked up the letters which he had laid aside and turned them over quickly. He took up a letter boldly inscribed in a feminine hand, a dashing, flowing hand.

But he did not open it. He looked up from the unopened letter, and what he saw woke a dry humour in him: a humour wholly masculine, enjoying the defeat of the old woman's planning. In silence he pointed to the car that was whirling down The Neale road in a cloud of dust and slowing for the turn at the entrance gate.

" We'll not have long to wait," he said softly, amused yet undecided as to what he should now do. " Erne's guest is as soon here as her letter. That's Kirwan's car from Ballinrobe station."

Caroline Boycott said nothing at all. She sat silent in her chair, her hands gripped on the carved arms, watching the girl alight from the car which had now drawn up in the gravelled sweep before the house.

The girl dropped from the high seat of the car in a smooth, lithe movement, a slender tall woman of strong supple curves and flowing line. The western light was behind her, and in that pale light the loveliness of her colouring was most evident. Her hair, that was not merely fair but corn-coloured, rippled back vibrantly from a wide brow over eyes that had a live and stormy colour of their own, the vividly lit grey-blue of broken water under an ardent sun.

That aura of the sun was all about her. Her face was tanned to a deeply golden brown, a mask of bronze for the firm sculpture of bone—the clear upsweep from chin to ear and the high, boldly defined arch of brow—which gave to her face its own unique stamp of eagerness.

For the draw of a breath she hesitated on the verge of the lawn ; and in that moment of hesitation her air of eagerness, of daring, was somehow shadowed. She paused, and Caroline Boycott paused too in the moment of rising from her chair.

A moment only, but a moment that dragged with infinite slowness. It was Charles Boycott who broke the spell of that moment. He let the letters spill from his hand in unheeded confusion and went striding down the steps and across the lawn.

Ever afterwards he was to remember how in that instant he was not touched at all by the slow, fumbling diffidence that so often marred and chilled his first contact with strangers. He strode towards this strange girl on a free and eager stride; and his voice was eager too.

"Let me make you welcome to Lough Mask." Her hand was within his hand's clasp, a strong, warm, vital hand. "You are welcome indeed."

CHAPTER THREE

THEY heard the drumming of hooves in the stony fields before they saw the wild horseman sweep across the sky and go thundering into the shadows beneath the hanging wood. For the brief, wild moment while the horseman went hurtling past on the dim sky-line neither man spoke; and when Watty Connell broke the silence it was to hide under a bluster of venomous humour whatever startling of terror he might have felt.

"A beggar on horseback, and him riding to the devil—riding fast and hard." His mouth thinned and hardened. "Aye! like father like son. And 'twasn't a donkey-butt even ould Peter Carroll had under him the day they carried him out of the back of a ditch to the burying ground at Cong."

He faced to Killower, peering into the twilight that still echoed clamorously with hoof beats; but horse and rider had by now disappeared in the shadows.

"Ah! Well! Young Michael is going far and fast on his father's road."

He strode on, busy with the thought of what he had to do at his journey's end and how he would do it. Hugh Davin, far-striding at his side, wasted no further thought on the business into which he had been drawn, now that he saw his part in it to be inescapable.

Seven years ago, when he had come home after three years' fruitless preparation for the priesthood in the Irish College in Paris, he would most certainly have been aflame with anger, raging at his powerlessness to check this bailiff in his brutal business of process and eviction, storming at the apathy of the people under this brutality. He would, perhaps, as he had done more than once in the early days when he held school-mastering posts in Cork and Tipperary, have betrayed his rage in angry, futile outbursts.

But he had learned wisdom with the years, the only wisdom a man could learn in this crushed and dispirited country. There was a better way than futile outbursts of rage. And if that way sometimes as now tricked him into a false show of friendship with men like Boycott's bailiff, there was no help for it. He would travel his own road in his own way ; for all that in his own moments of doubt, he knew it to be a long, slow road with the end not in sight and few to keep him company in the going.

He began to whistle softly a light melody that wandered idly in tune to his thoughts. Idly at first, and then with firmer purpose his thoughts centred on Connell's casual remark about Captain Boycott's guns.

The gun-room! That he thought would be the room on the right-hand side of the house where the slanting tree—a cedar, wasn't it?—shadowed the narrow window. And that window was barred. The softly whistled tune slid and rippled to a high shake of grace notes. He could see the room clearly in his mind's eye. A small darkened room with no more furnishings than a table littered with fly-books and cartridge cases, it would be, and a scattering of chairs in which dogs lazed and slept undisturbed. But the gun-racks would be orderly and kept in barrack room fashion, stack upon stack of gun-racks with their marshalled load of weapons, the wooden butts glowing with a mellow polish in the light, the grey-blue barrels gleaming coldly in the dusk.

The tune broke and tailed off in a flurry of shaken notes, notes shaken by mirth. Softly he laughed at himself and at his own thoughts ; and in that moment of laughter his dark lean face lost something of the sombre strength that so often shadowed it, as it had shadowed it over those last striding yards of the Killower road. In the lightened moment the line of his face seemed less strongly drawn, the curve of his mouth finer and more sensitive.

A fool he was, he mocked himself, picturing a room he had never seen and guns that he would never see nor handle. He eased the grip of his arm on the fishing pole, his shoulders slipping into their tall man's slouch as his hands dug deeper into the pockets of his shabby tweed jacket. His felt hat was thrust far back on the crisp dark thatch of his hair so that the wide leaf no longer shadowed his eyes. And now a dark eye that was bright with speculation considered the bailiff's face.

"You're a hard man, Watty," he said softly, tauntingly. "Aren't you afraid that some gay lad 'll take a gun out of the thatch for you one dark night?"

"'Tisn't their hearts would stop them. But you needn't be fretting, Master. No one will be taking a shot at me to-night—or at you for walking with me." The hard mouth tightened round the pipe stem. "There isn't gun nor the shape of a gun in any house from Kilmaine to Clonbur to-day, or for any days this ten years past. We're safe enough."

"Safe enough surely," Hugh Davin said, and said no more until they had rounded the bend of the road below Michael Carroll's house.

It was a small house, cowering under its weight of thatch in a shallow dip of stony land under the shadow of the hill. The thatching straw had blackened and rotted and now sprouted a beard of green weed. Rain had dripped from the eaves and streaked the once-white walls. A curtain of sacking bellied listlessly in the wind over an unglazed window; smoke drifted over the half-door. A wretched cabin, less snug than the stable behind it, a small building of unmortared stone, roofed with reed thatch and built in the dry and sheltered angle of the hill.

Between house and stable a man was grooming a horse,

so intent on his task that he neither saw nor heard the approach of the others. He was more than intent, he was absorbed, a lean wiry lad, stripped to ragged shirt and breeches tucked into ungreased gaiters. A wing of yellow-fair hair tumbled over eyes deeply set in a long-jawed, hollow face ; those eyes were light and wildly lit as, aware of the newcomers, he came erect in a whirl of explosive speed and turned to meet them.

"Keep your own side of the wall, Connell," he ordered harshly in a high voice that lacked volume but not strength. "I mightn't be able to keep this lad from injuring you—and I mightn't try too hard."

That hint, or threat, seemed to have reason enough behind it. Startled by the sudden, angry voice, the horse was jerking and straining at the leading rein which had been hitched through a ring set high on the wall of the stable. Fretfully he lunged and jibbed in a narrow, limited arc, a high rangy gelding with mane and tail uncut but well groomed.

It was at the horse and not at his owner that the two men were looking, and that horse was well worth looking at. Long lined he was and beautifully muscled, a big, upstanding gelding with a sleek black hide shading to chestnut at the points. A well-balanced horse he was too, a little narrow of chest, powerful of quarter, his lean, fleshless head well set. Three-quarter bred, maybe, the better blood of his breeding coming from a hunting, jumping strain. Watty Connell said as much—in his own way and for his own purpose.

"A bit light in the shoulders," he said. "A trifle, no more." He began to fill his pipe, making a great show of being at ease. "A pity now the dam wasn't a wee shade better bred. Just a wee shade now. Too much blood isn't good either."

His pipe was drawing freely now, he leaned comfortably across the wall intent on his own set purpose. Hugh Davin remained silent. Michael Carroll's greeting to him had been no more than a curt nod ; but he had expected no more than that. He looked sidelong at the bailiff and noted the tight, ugly smile that puckered a network of tiny lines about the man's mouth corners.

" Rising five he'd be, Michael," the bailiff went on.

" You have a fine memory."

Michael Carroll's hand must not have been as gentle as it might have been on the bridle, for the horse suddenly lunged and reared across the yard. The lean and ugly head whipped up with a violence that lifted the man from the ground for a moment before he mastered the plunging brute. He was breathing heavily as he pulled the horse's head under control.

" A fine memory," he said again in that high, thin voice of his.

" Middling. Middling enough," Watty agreed. " I mind the day Lord Erne's great sire horse, Sir Conn, was staked and killed. 'Twould be the better part of four years ago."

" What's that to do with me? "

" Nothing, Michael. Nothing at all." Blandly the bailiff regarded horse and man. " Barring 'twas by Sir Conn yon beast of yours was bred. You bred him out of Sir Conn, didn't you? And no one a ha'porth the wiser. Heh? "

" Did I so? " Carroll's voice lifted to a shrill note.

" You did faith," Connell answered in a quiet, conversational tone. " And 'twasn't stud fees and groom fees was troubling you. 'Tis how you ran the mare loose when the sire horse was at grass in the lake field. A fence down here, a gap opened there." He tilted his head, half closing an eye to see the horse more clearly. " Sure I'd know the breeding anywhere. A blind man 'ud know it."

In the heavy silence which followed that accusation Hugh Davin leaned forward and laid his rod along a ledge of unmortared stone on the inner side of the wall. He well knew the hatred which old Connell bore against the son of the man who, almost alone amongst the tenants of Kilmaine and Erne, had given as savagely as he had received in the campaign of evictions which, a score of years ago, had ruthlessly cleared a wide spread of country from Cross to Cong. And only too well he knew Michael Carroll's wild temper and the wildness with which that temper could explode. If it exploded now, as well it might, he was determined to take no part that would spoil all his own cautious plans. But he would be glad of a reasonable excuse to return later and alone to Carroll's house. He had work to do this night that would not wait.

He moved the pole securely into place and leaned across the wall, his face dark and heavy with his own unpleasant thoughts.

But the outburst of anger did not come. Firmly, and more gently now, Carroll drew down the horse's head and soothed the beast to a trembling, nervy quietness. His hollowed face was flushed now by exertion—or by triumph.

" So you know? " His face was fleetingly lit by a wild inner excitement. " Much good knowing will do you. You're a day late looking for your fistful of guineas now."

The high note in his voice had made the horse restive again, and its whistling, snorting breathing was loud in the quiet.

" The horse is the one thing me or mine ever won from Lord Erne," he said. " The only thing. And it's mine."

" Aye! Faith! " The bailiff stroked his unshaven jaw reflectively. " You had the best of us there. No denying that. You're a gay lad, Michael. A gay lad, surely. But you've no right to be keeping a horse like that."

There was no anger, no bluster in his voice, and yet to the other men that slack, casual phrase laid bare his mind and uncovered the very core of his resentment at the other's possession of the horse.

" Tell us, Michael," he went on quietly. " When are you going to sell? You could ha' sold the horse last year at Ballinrobe or Headfort, or the year before at Ballinasloe. Or at Clonbur when the colt was rising two." His hard and wary eye ranged over the trim stable and the tumbledown house. " 'Tis my belief, lad, that you have no notion at all of selling."

He said that quietly and without any trace of menace, but Michael Carroll seemed more taken aback than he would be by threat or anger.

" I'll be selling at Ballinasloe in October," he said surlily. " The remount officers 'll be paying big prices for five-year-olds."

"October! That's a long day away. You could sell at Ballinrobe the month coming. Michael. You'd get a grand price. You would so."

"I would—if I was a fool."

"What are we all but fools—every mother's son of us," the bailiff countered.

He put his cold pipe away and began to rummage in his tail pocket.

"Let you have sense now, Michael, and be led by me. Sell at Ballinrobe, and you'll get enough to pay up the year's rent you're behind with and maybe have two or three pound left over in the heel of your fist."

He had found the greasy square of paper in his pocket and he placed it on the wall before him, pressing out the creased and crumpled folds.

"Two or three pounds!" Michael Carroll's voice was high and harsh still, but there was a baffled, hunted look in his eyes. "Much good two or three pounds 'ud be to me. Leave me till October, Watty, and I'll have every penny of what's owing and as much left over . . ."

"As much left over as would take you off to America. 'Tis what I told the Captain. The very last word of it. I told him you had devil a thing in your head but scraping together the passage money so that you'd be off to make your fortune in the green fields of America. Aye! I told him that—and I told him that he was hell's own fool ever to let you put foot back on your father's farm."

With surprising agility the old man stooped forward over the wall and thrust the folded sheet of paper into the breast of Carroll's ragged shirt.

"There's your process served on you in proper legal form and before a witness," he announced. "Let you sell now in the time named or 'tis to distrain we will or evict if must be. But," he added with evident relish, "'tisn't a thing we're going to wait till October and maybe have you skipping off across the high seas on us, and not a penny piece of the rent paid."

He had one more word to say, and he said it viciously:

"Rent or no rent, Carroll," he said, "let you sell that horse. 'Tisn't for you or the likes of you to be owning a beast that's better bred than your own self."

Michael Carroll did not answer him at all. He stood silently in the fading light, a hand groping over the tattered breast of his shirt where the process crackled against his skin. Over his shoulder the horse's head jibbed and fretted, reddish eyes agleam in the deep sockets of its bony skull. In the paling light man and horse seemed fused and blended into a single entity of wild strength. And it was to the horse young Carroll spoke.

"Easy, lad! Easy!" he whispered. "We'll be match for the whole of them in our own day."

CHAPTER FOUR

It was late before Watty Connell took himself off on some other hidden business of his own, and the twilight had deepened to darkness before Hugh Davin was able to set out again on the road he had been travelling when the bailiff had hailed him on the lake shore.

Under cover of the darkness he went quickly and without secrecy through Dringeen and Gortnaclossa to where the ruined tower of Ahalard Castle thrust a broken spear of masonry into the shadowy arch of the sky.

Cheerily, but in a lowered voice, he answered the challenge of the boy who kept sentry post in the shelter of the hedges encircling the ruins, and went quickly across the uneven field towards the group of men in the shadows beneath the curtain wall of the castle.

His eyes had now grown accustomed to the darkness and he could see the men clearly; not more than thirty of them he reckoned with disappointment. Michael Carroll, he noted, was missing to-night. Then he saw the man who stood in front, and a little apart from the group in the shadows, a small, stooped man. He quickened his step.

"I'm late, Colonel; but it couldn't be helped," he said quietly.

Punctiliously he gave the man his full style and title out of the older days, although often in his not infrequent moments of self-distrust and doubt he found himself rebelling against that formality as against an insincerity felt but never acknowledged.

"It was safer for me to take my own time coming."

"Just as well, maybe," James Hannin answered him, not very graciously. There was the faintest nasal touch of American accent in his voice, a curt voice. He set down on the grass, at his feet the leather case holding a pair of heavy cavalry pistols and a short belt of cartridges. "It's no circus trying to make soldiers out of a darned debating society. Only a handful turns out—and they think it an idea to waste their time talking bunkum."

It was odd, Hugh thought inconsequently, how that slight burr of accent held to the man's voice after the thirteen or more years of exile from the country in which he had grown to manhood; stranger still when one remembered that ten of those years had been spent in the silent cells of Millbank Gaol. An affectation, maybe, he thought idly, like the beard in the trim American fashion, and the square-shouldered clothes of American cut which sat with such an air of incongruity on the man who was now a miserably paid clerk in the offices of a miller in Westport town. And then, remembering the ravaged face above the trim beard and the prison-broken frame beneath the clothes of aggressively military cut, he was suddenly ashamed of his idle thought. Ashamed and yet exhilarated. He no longer regretted that punctilious use of the old Fenian's title.

"A small muster," he said, apologetically, sensing the main cause of the other's irritation. "Our full roster is close on fifty. The others . . ."

"The others are better employed," the American interrupted him bitterly. "Over in Clonbur listening to the bands playing for Michael Davitt and his Land Leaguers." There was a fierce intensity in his low voice. "Dear God! Cheaper grazing and bigger potato patches! And 'twas for that men rotted and starved and died raving mad in Millbank and Chatham . . ."

He spoke under-breath, but anger made his voice strong and carrying. The men in the shadows heard him, and one man answered.

"Erra! Small blame to them, Colonel."

Hugh Davin swore softly to himself. He knew that cheery voice and could picture the grin on big Steve Nalty's face as the boy took sides with his absent comrades, partly in loyalty, partly in good-humoured independence of spirit.

"What blame to them to hould fast to the bit of land they have—them that have a bit of land to hould to." Nalty's voice was the soft Mayo lilt that rippled musically along a rising scale to a high clear note. It lifted now to a sudden criticism: "Devil a much we're doing to help them."

A murmur of approval supported that implied criticism. Hugh had picked Nalty out now and could see him clearly outlined in the shadows, a giant, huge-limbed lad, his cap aslant on his thick curls. As clearly, he could picture the boy's quick smile, the white flash of teeth against swarthy skin, the hot spark of laughter in dark eyes. But for once he was not moved to amused appreciation of the lad's ready tongue. He recognized the danger of the criticism—a criticism that marched uncomfortably close in step with his own not infrequent doubts.

"We've our own work to do," he answered sharply. "The Land League men are making their own fight. Every man here to-night has sworn his oath for another kind of fight."

Even as he said that he realized, as he had so often realized of late, that his words lacked the firmness of definite purpose which would give them conviction.

"A bigger fight," he added.

"Maybe so, Captain." It was not Nalty's but a deeper, graver voice that answered him, the voice of Darby Haire. "But the lad's asking a question that's, maybe, troubling many a man to-night." He leaned forward in the darkness, a stocky, powerful man. "Look at the boys you have here to-night: a couple of weavers from Cong; a handful of labouring lads; a carpenter and a hooper; a few fishermen; another smith and myself. . . ."

"Sound men all, Darby."

"No one's denying that, Captain. Sound men enough, and willing to do the job they're pledged to do—if so be they're ever given the chance or the guns. But the others are sound men, too: the farming men and the sons of farmers that are about their own business in Clonbur to-day."

The smith was in no hurry at all to say all he had to say. He spoke as a man who would not speak until he had been driven by the slow, relentless process of thought.

"And maybe they're doing as good a day's work standing behind Davitt and the League as we're doing here—learning to fight without a gun to fight with. . . ."

Hugh Davin interrupted him. In a moment like this that lean, dark face of his could have the stripped, lean hardness of leadership in it.

"That's twice in as many minutes you've talked of guns, Haire," he said. "You had my promise, the night ye made me your Captain here, that I'd find arms for you some day, somehow. That," he said softly, "is a promise I'm keeping."

The blacksmith was unperturbed.

"Who is doubting you?" he asked pleasantly. "Well we know that your promise is safe with you. But it might be," he added with the courteous air of one unwilling to stress an unpleasantness, "it might be a while and a bit yet before you get that job done.

"And while we're waiting," went on Darby Haire, "why should we be idle? Haven't we the word of Devoy and the American men—as good Fenians as the Colonel himself—to stand behind Davitt? So, why wouldn't we lend a hand to the men that are making a good fight for their own, Captain? Why wouldn't we now?"

A reasonable question that, Hugh Davin knew; and a question that had been in many men's minds, demanding an answer, during the past year or more.

Five years ago, down in Cork, when he had been sworn in

as a member of a Centre that was no more than a pitifully small remnant of the Irish Republican Brotherhood, there had been no such question to trouble men's minds. Fenianism was almost dead then. The flame that had been quenched disastrously in '67 had all but guttered out. The small spark had been kept alive by men who had survived the brutality of the jails or who had escaped after the debacle. Up and down the country, scattered and isolated, often having no real cohesion or contact with each other, these lone believers in the creed of physical force had striven to keep the spirit of the movement alive. Generally, they had worked by trying to hold their old comrades steadfast; but often, with no more authority behind them than the oath they themselves had sworn in the old days, they had recruited and sworn in young men, as James Hannin had done here in Mayo.

It had been simple enough, five years ago, to swear the oath and to work hopefully, confident in the coming day when growing membership would make the Brotherhood a force out of which an armed fighting body might be forged. Later, it had been less easy to ignore the want of any immediate purpose, the lack of any pressing plan of action. And now, in recent months more than ever, the new Land movement was drawing and holding the men who had once shown willingness to listen to the fierce whisperings of the old Fenians.

It was the question underlying all these doubts which was now posed and demanded an answer. Davin faced the men in the shadows, not yet certain what his answer should be. But James Hannin answered for him.

"I'm asking no man here to do anything I'm not ready to do myself," he said simply. "And I'm ready to wait. I waited half a lifetime for the chance we missed in '67. I'm ready and willing to wait another lifetime for another chance."

He moved stiffly down past the silent men, small and stooped, a broken shadow of the man who had ridden in Corcoran's Guerillas with Condron, Burke, and McClure during the American Civil War. They listened to him silently, and with respect. No man there but had felt the lash of his tongue; but no man could deny respect to the courage which had brought the ex-convict back to Ireland and danger when he might well have taken the road others had taken, with no loss of honour, to America and a new life.

"Fighting's my trade. The only trade I ever learned or knew. And it's the only trade you'll learn from me this night or any night." He came to a halt. "One man here to-night complained that I have no guns to give you. What your Captain promised to do for you, he must do by himself. That is for him to do. I'm making you no promises. I've no right to make promises of guns or help. All I'm asking you to do is what I'm doing myself, to make yourself ready against the day that's sure to come—in our time or another time—the day when men 'll be trained and ready to use the guns and use the help."

He fell silent for a moment, and when he spoke again there was no faltering in his voice, no hesitation in uttering a decision that might well meet with little approval.

"I have no guns. But if I had guns to put in the hands of every man here to-night, I'd let no man waste bullets on one landlord that could be used another day against six soldiers."

His voice beat down the sudden mutter of protest.

"That's all I have to say to you to-night or any night. All I can try to do is make soldiers of you."

"Aye, faith! And a mighty small army we'll make, Colonel, when all's said and done."

Again it was the soft, lilting voice of big Nalty, ruefully humorous. Very quietly James Hannin answered the boy.

"There's only a few of you," he said with sombre conviction. "There never was more than a few. There never will be more than a few."

He ceased speaking abruptly, and no man questioned him. To Hugh Davin he said briefly: "Hold them together as best you can." And then he went striding stiffly through the shadows, a lonely, broken figure in the dusk.

It was not James Hannin's going but the manner of his going that brought the night's business to an end. For a little longer the men marched and counter-marched and moved with practised smoothness through the figures of elementary foot-drill. But their movements lacked zest ; and it was with relief that Hugh Davin gave them the order to dismiss.

It was then he noticed, lying in the grass where Hannin had set them down a few minutes earlier, the worn leather pistol case and the pistols. He picked them up. Colt's patent revolving pistols of an old-fashioned make they were, the cavalry pistols of Hannin's days in Corcoran's Guerillas. Hugh clipped them into the case, securing them under the short belt of cartridges. He touched the dully gleaming barrels and the ornate handgrips that had Hannin's name lettered on them. Heaven alone knew by what risk of friendship these pistols had been kept safe for the American during all the long years of his imprisonment. Hugh snapped shut the case. He would put them in a safe place until Hannin came again from Westport.

" Darby. And you, Nalty," he called to the two men who had lingered on after the others had drifted away into the darkness. " Wait here for me. I'll not be long."

He went quickly through the shadows to the wall of the tower and climbed on to a loose and crumbling pile of stones. From this height he was able to reach into a shadowy cleft between the stones, a deep, dry hole in the stonework, not visible from ground level. It was as good a place as any to hide the pistols, a place in which certain of the trusted ones amongst the men who drilled nearby had often hidden messages or gear. He dropped the case into the depth of the cleft and raked a scattering of dry leaves over it. He rejoined the others.

" Coming my way ? " he asked them.

" Why wouldn't we ? " It was always hard to know the smith's mind from his voice, and now his voice was no more than pleasant. He fell in at Hugh's left side. " We might have this and that to talk about."

" We might so," young Nalty agreed from the darkness at Hugh's right shoulder. " And sure we might as well hear the worst of ourselves first as last, as the man said in the story. . . ."

"I heard that story, too, Stephen," Hugh cut him short, his voice soft and easy. He was determined not to be side-tracked so readily. "You had a harder story to tell James Hannin to-night—with your fine talk of guns."

They had passed out of the ring of bushes about the castle and were walking between low hedges along a grassy lane that was soft and springy underfoot. The boy paced off a dozen long and silent strides before he replied.

"If I had so, hadn't I good reason ?" he said, and his tone was strong and earnest. "Let the Yank say and think as he likes—he earned good right to that same—but there's one thing I know and you know : you'll never put heart in a man to fight till you put a weapon in his hands to fight with."

He stepped out more quickly when he had said that, as if ashamed of his sudden earnestness. He began to whistle very softly through his teeth, not a melody, but a defiant, tuneless whisper of sound.

Beside him Hugh Davin also lengthened his stride. He was remembering Hannin's last fierce order to hold the men together at all costs ; and he realized fully now, as he had come to know with gathering strength during the months that had passed since he came here to the West, that his best hope of holding the men was to arm them. Well ! That would not be an easy thing to do ; if any other way offered he would have to take it.

"I'll not go back on my word," was all he said, and when he said it the strength of his thoughts sounded in his words. He went on firmly: "But if ever we lay hands on guns, they will be for our own fight when our own day comes, not for work like that in Tourmakeady."

"Is it Hussey ?" Young Nalty's voice was at its old trick of mocking humour again. "Faith, I wonder ! There was one man that'd likely be right thankful to see a lad with a gun in his hand at his latter end. To die like a mad dog in a sack. . . ."

"That was murder ! "

Instinctively they stopped short on Hugh Davin's sharp comment. Almost imperceptibly the night had lightened in the first of the moonrise. The hills bulked more blackly and with sharper outline against a sky that was still dark but no longer vague and shadowy. On the wet grass was a ghostly sheen of light. Light faintly edged each separate twig and leaf of tree and hedge. Nearby was the tireless, soft babble of running water. A wind was whispering through the bushes, the loneliest of all night sounds.

"Murder!" Nalty said deeply. "An ugly word. . . ."

"Wait!" With a gesture Darby Haire silenced the lad. He turned to Davin. "Does that mean that you'll not stand by us? That you'll not help us, Master?"

His tone was quiet and reasonable as ever, but it was noticeable that he no longer used the other's military title.

"You'll not help?"

"To kill a man for revenge, Darby? To settle the scores of a lifetime in one night's wild work? I'll have no hand in that," Hugh said sombrely. "In the end, what is it but mad bad work that'll serve no man but the hangman and the informer?

"Where you have murder you have spies," he went on, and his voice was as sombre as his thoughts. "Leave that work be, Darby. There's bigger work to do than harrying bailiffs."

They moved forward again down the silent path and came out on the last wide tilt of meadow that skirted Killower Hill. Beyond the hill, and hidden from them, Michael Carroll's house lay. On all this nearer side of the hill one house only stood, a single window lighted against the night. That single point of light gave the house shape and warmth in the darkness. Squat and low, its limed walls catching a faint shine of moonlight, the house shouldered the crest of the hill in the shelter of a belt of trees. Hugh Davin lifted his head to look up at it. A figure passed blackly against the light. As he watched that dark figure pass across the light of her father's house, his mind called up again the quick, warm picture of Anne Killian's dark and troubled eyes and live, bright mouth. For a moment the picture held, and then the lighted window was no more than an empty, glowing square of light.

Out of the lessening darkness the smith's voice cut across his thoughts and brought him back to the present, pressing reality.

"I'll not say but you're right, Master," Haire was saying. "There's bigger work surely."

He stopped short on strong, bowed legs, stooping forward a little. Briefly he gestured, taking under that swift, wide sweep of his arm the whole empty stretch of country which lay between the dark woods and the hill. It was now light enough to see clearly the jagged rubble of walls, close on a score of them, which stood up out of the empty fields : the gable walls of houses left standing after the roof-trees had been stripped.

"I mind the smoke of twenty fires down yonder from Killower to Cong," he said soberly. "Twenty warm houses, Hugh Davin, with women about their work and childer on the floor. I mind them well. And where are they now ? "

He expected no answer to that question, nor did he get one. He went on, deeply :

"An' 'twasn't the bailiff that served the process, nor the landlord that signed the notice-to-quit that should take the blame for the empty houses and cold hearths . . ."

Young Nalty spoke angrily, but the smith went on unheedingly.

"In the end, when all was said and done," he said, "the men that stripped the roofs and quenched the hearths were the grabbers that took the evicted land. The land of their own blood and breed."

He turned his back to the empty land, and it was to Hugh Davin he spoke now.

"If we find a way to stop any man doing that again, we'll be doing a day's work that'll be remembered to us." He raised his voice a little. "Are you with us in that work, Hugh Davin ? "

Over the small man's wide shoulder Hugh Davin could see the sweep of tenantless land, bright now in the moonrise, the blackened gables, the crumbled walls. The memory of James Hannin's face lifted against the screen of his mind, the ravaged face under its sweep of whitened hair. But the picture of the empty fields and deserted homes was nearer and clearer still. Here was a cause for which men, for which any man, would fight. It was work that could be fitted within an immediate and definite plan, as his present work could not be fitted. But his present work was his life's pledged work. Even now he hesitated.

"If there was a way of doing this," he said, undecided. "A right way. . . ."

"We'll find a way," the smith told him firmly. "We'll show you the right way this very night, if you'll come with us."

Davin drew breath softly in a deep sigh. Well, so! He might find in this work the content of a definite purpose. At the worst it would help him to hold and keep his grip on these men.

In that lax mood, and without further argument, he fell into step again between the two men and went on down the brightening road.

CHAPTER FIVE

The men he had been brought to meet, elderly men for the most part, were gathered in a voluble group at the other end of the long barn, down where the fiddlers and lesser musicians were mounted on a rough platform and planks laid over upturned barrels.

Hugh Davin made no move to join them yet. In his own time and his own way he would approach them; but he would not be hurried again. He had been hurried, half an hour ago, by Darby Haire and Nalty into making this decision. He would not be hurried now. Besides, the low, deep voice of the girl beside him was urgent, and not untouched with temper. The pressure of her fingers on his wrist was firm and urgent too. That small, dark touch of anger gave fire and warmth to Anne Killian's presence here beside him and made that nearness, as it ever and always would do, stir his blood with quickening excitement.

"You're late, Hugh," she accused him, that small note of earnestness underlying the light words. "Well you know I have to be leaving early. Where were you at all?"

Her voice was lower than the shrill scraping of the violins. The faint dark passion that deepened it was not merely anger. He was aware of it as a force deeper and darker than any passing cloud of jealousy. That awareness of the strong emotion stirring her, as it stirred him, held him, for the moment, silent.

He would not look down into her face yet. He put off that moment, savouring it, anticipating it. Clearly he could picture the fine, clear modelling of her face. He could see it in his mind's eye, as something held and permanent in the mind's core: the pallor of her cheeks, touched and no more with colour; the bright darkness of her eyes under their darker curve of brow; the warmth of her mouth. The pressure of her shoulder, brief and fleeting against his arm, stirred him out of his moment of restraint.

"My own reasons I had; my own strong reasons. Let you not doubt that." His voice was low, too, creating a moment of intimacy in all the throng and clamour of the crowded room. "But what matter now."

He looked down at her then, swiftly, unexpectedly, so that he looked into her uplifted face in that moment when she had turned towards him. Her face was not touched with the fire of anger at all, but had its own smooth pallor still, as of ivory warmed from within with light. But under the dark and curving brows her eyes, that were a deeper and clearer brown than the brown of velvet, were darkly lit, not with anger but with a sudden intensity of emotion. That deep, shared emotion held both of them for the long moment.

But that moment passed. Anne had turned again to watch the dancers, waiting for the moment of their own entry into the dance; and from his greater height he could now see no more than the poise of her dark head and the flowing line of her throat.

The fiddlers swept into the second movement of the dance, and the dancers were crowding into line. Hugh stooped quickly until his lips were level with the sleek, dark wings of her hair.

" There's men here I have to talk to to-night," he whispered. " Don't go away on me if they talk too much and too long. . . ."

A little vein of laughter threaded the upsweep of voices and music as Anne swept away from him in the long line of dancers and that laughter was her only answer. When they came together again at the room's end, her face was bright with the excitement of the dance ; and her shining eyes and the flash of her mouth in laughter were brighter than the faint dark fires of that other and deeper mood. She swung into Hugh Davin's arm.

" Remember that," he warned her, striving after her own newly-found lightness. " Don't go away on me."

He swung her into the last figure of the dance, his arm firm about her. She was close to him for a long moment in that laughing whirl of movement, the light stuff of her dress pulsing above the rise and fall of her young breasts, a vein throbbing with life in the slender white shaft of her throat.

" Don't go on me." His voice was not light now, nor laughing. " Don't ever go on me."

The violins shrilled to a faster tempo, surged upward in a final rhythm and died away. For a moment the dancers stood still, stirred yet by the throb of the music that was done, their minds still touched by the rhythm that had died away. " Don't ever go from me," he said again, and although his tone was lightly attuned to the gaiety of the moment, there was a sudden depth of emotion in it.

All about them the voices of the crowding dancers broke out afresh from the moment's involuntary stillness, and he could not hear Anne's reply. But he could see the soft, swift movement of her mouth as she whispered and the sudden darkling light of her eyes.

The dancers, moving about the floor, pushed them apart, and he watched her go through the crowd, a slender, lithe, swaying woman, her dark head held high.

He made no move to follow her. Too well he knew that the

swift surprised passion of that unguarded moment was lost, not to be recaptured now. But he was well content. The glow of his quickened thoughts was warm in him, and there was a new lightness in his step as he passed down the room to where the older men were grouped.

That warmth was chilled a little as he passed by the knot of men standing inside the door and saw Michael Carroll push his way through. Unaccountably the passing glimpse of the man's hollow, haggard face touched him with unease ; he passed on more quickly.

"Yourself, Master ?" It was Martin Egan's voice greeted him, a ripe, mellow voice with a boom of good humour in it. "It's over in Clonbur you had a right to be to-day. A grand meeting we had there—a hosting you might say. He's an able lad to speak, this Michael Davitt."

"Why wouldn't he be ?" Hugh agreed amicably. He would be cautious yet a while. "He knows the truth of what he's talking about—not like some."

Old Egan smoothed out the folds of the paper on his knees. He pursed his mouth, the full lips soft and red against the white of his beard. His light, quick eyes flickered in appraisal over the newcomer. He, too, was a man who could take his own time and his own way in doing what he had to do.

"There's the true word for you," said he complacently. "The very thing I was saying myself not a minute ago. Eviction and hunger and hardship—he knew them all. The true word surely—if I could get some that's listening to me to believe it. . . ."

"Wait now ! Wait you now, Martin," a reasonable man put in his reasonable objection. "All I said was that Davitt's a fine man and a grand man, but the king of them all is Parnell himself. And what Davitt said to-day in Clonbur was no more nor less than what the Chief himself said before this. . . ."

He sat back when he had said that, a dour and bearded man with tired eyes and a droop of weariness about his shoulders. They were all men of heavy dourness, Hugh thought suddenly, the life and force crushed out of them by the grinding weight of life. But there was a fire in them yet, a spark of living fire that smouldered behind their tired eyes. Some day that fire might flame ; and then. . . .

Beside him Darby Haire had found a seat on the bench. Michael Carroll had crossed the room and was leaning against the wall, his arms folded across his chest, his eyes on the dancers. Old Martin Egan pressed out the last creases from his *Freeman's Journal* and folded the paper.

" Wait now till I explain to them that wasn't there," he said easily. He turned courteously to Hugh and Darby Haire ; Carroll, lost in his own sullen survey of the dancers, paid no heed. " It was this way : Over in Clonbur a lad in the crowd shouts up to Davitt, an' him speaking, ' What'll we do with the grabbers ? ' And what does Davitt do but read them the advice Parnell gave the men of Clare in Ennis a week ago. And, my soul, but that was the very cream of counsel. Wait ye, now ! I have it here word for word, the way it was set down in the *Freeman* itself. Here we are:

He held the paper nearer to him in the smoky light. His eyes narrowed over the small print, and tiny puckerings furrowed the veined, reddish skin of his cheeks. He began to read, and his voice was no longer rounded with humour but was deep and strong and earnest with purpose.

" ' When a man takes a farm from which another has been evicted (said Mr. Parnell), you must show him on the roadside when you meet him, you must show him in the streets of the town, you must show him at the shop counter, in the fair and in the market place, and even in the house of worship, by leaving him severely alone, by putting him into a moral Coventry, by isolating him from his kind as if he was a leper of old ; you must show him your detestation of the crime he has committed ; and you can be sure that there will be no man so full of avarice, so lost to shame, as to dare the public opinion of all right-thinking men and to transgress your unwritten code of laws. . . .' "

Above their heads, on the platform, the keen notes of the fiddles leaped and spilled in lively pattern. The tread of the dancers held to its soft, muffled rhythm. Somewhere at the room's end a girl's voice pealed in laughter, an upsurging of mirth, bright and tremulous, that called up a quick vision of a back-thrown head and a rippling white throat.

Martin Egan's voice, deep and strong as the grim threat he had been reading, died away in a little pool of stillness. No man spoke. Near him Hugh Davin could hear the quick, shallow breathing of men stirred to excitement. Were they too, he wondered, picturing the misery and grey loneliness that Parnell's plan could call down upon its victims, on men shunned and isolated and abhorred ?

The thought chilled him as he watched the dancers. They were dancing *The Waves of Tory* now, a double line of them, the young men released by the music from the stiff clumsiness of the fields, the girls quick and bright with whirling gaiety. And then, beyond the line of dancers, where the low-murmuring groups of older women sat huddled and gossiping under their shawls, he saw Con Morahan and his wife, the man's face dazed and empty, the woman's eyes red with weeping for loneliness and in fear of the unguessable perils of the ocean journey into exile that lay before her and her man. For a long moment he watched them, seeing them through the make-believe gaiety of this American Wake, of this merriment that was speeding their going from the farm and home out of which they had been evicted.

He turned to Martin Egan, and for the first time he realized how taut and stiffly he had been holding himself.

"All right, Martin," he said slowly and roughly. "You can count on me. I'll stand by you in this if you have any need or use of me."

All about them the little pool of stillness was broken now by the quick assenting voices of the other men making their promises. There was a force and an eagerness in their voices now. The spark had leaped to flame.

"Right so! Right so!" Martin Egan was saying, his voice rounded and smooth with satisfaction. "That makes twelve of us. 'Tis enough. When the time comes, and 'twill come soon, the twelve of us will make our own plans to do what Mr. Parnell has bid us to do."

They were all talking now, quickly, eagerly. Hugh came to his feet and moved past Haire to where Michael Carroll was standing.

" You didn't turn out with us to-night, Michael," he said, his voice low.

" What matter if I did or not. What good did you do this night or any night? What good will we ever do—that way ? "

Carroll's answer was low-voiced, too, and harsh. He hunched his shoulders against a cough that racked and tore him. He breathed heavily and shortly.

" Drilling an' marching an' talking. An' while we're drilling an' marching an' talking, Con Morahan and his likes are flung out on the road. Leave me be, Hugh Davin. What good is there in any of it ? "

" We'll find a way, Michael." For all his dislike of the man, and for all his certainty of the man's dislike of him, Hugh held his voice to an even note. " Martin Egan has a way that might do good."

" Is it him, or his likes! The weighty part of that work'll be done in the back of Egan's pub.—making speeches an' passing grand resolutions. The day for that kind of work is past, Davin." The low voice was bitter now and with a wild chord of excitement in it. " Leave me be, Davin. Let me go my own way, and you go yours. 'Twill maybe be better for you in the hinder end."

The dancers were formed into line again ; and now the lines swept forward and swung back, advancing and retreating in rippling waves. Near where the men stood, not a yard away, Anne was poised in the line, her hands raised head-high to link with the upraised hands of the dancers on either side of her. In that moment between retreat and advance she seemed to rest with bodiless lightness on the tips of her toes, her upthrown arms poising her body in slender, flowing lines.

Michael Carroll moved from his slouch against the wall, turning to watch the girl as the line of dancers swept back for the last time and broke up ; the dance ended. He was by her side as quickly as Hugh Davin, but he made no effort to claim her in the next dance.

"Don't fret, Anne," he said roughly. "I'll not trouble you to-night or any night. It's little enough welcome you had for me when I did." His light, wild eyes brightened with sudden malice. "Though, my faith, it could well be more than the welcome your father and mother above will have for your schoolmastering friend."

Before either of the others could reply he was gone from them, his narrow shoulders hunched high, and had pushed his way through the crowd about the door.

"No! We'll not dance again," Hugh said in quick decision.

He slipped his arm under the girl's arm and drew her closer. He could feel the cool softness of her arm against his hand and the sudden pressure that imprisoned his hand between arm and breast. Under breath he cursed Carroll and his drunken humour, but he could not quite cover a wry smile at the shrewdness of the other man's thrust. It was true, and more than true, that Anne's father and mother would seek a husband for their daughter farther afield than the schoolhouse of The Neale. Ah, well! That was a problem he would have to face in his own way—and in his own time—and that time could not now be long delayed.

"Pay no heed to Carroll," he said deeply and sharply. "His own troubles are thick upon him to-night; and it's drink and trouble that are talking in him now. . . ."

But he knew that his voice, for all its depth and strength, lacked conviction. He did not wait for her to speak, but moved with her towards the door. That pressure of rounded arm and firm breast told its own tale of strain; but the tautness went out of her little by little, and by the time they came to the crowd about the door the pressure of her arm was no more than warm and friendly.

The men about the door, young men mostly, with a quick and roving eye for every passing girl, were loosely knit into a wedge that overflowed on to the dancing floor each time the door opened to admit a newcomer. The crowd eddied inward now as Hugh and the girl came to the door, which had been flung open roughly.

Blinded by the sudden glare within, Sergeant Dempsey stood framed in the doorway. On either side of him a constable held a carbine at the ready; and behind them in the outer darkness Captain Boycott waited, much more the soldier than any of the uniformed men.

Somewhere in the darkness a man was walking a horse and gig up and down the roadway. With odd inconsequence Hugh Davin found himself noting the sharp and musical ring of hoof on the roadway and the tiny jingling noise of harness fittings. He stepped out into the darkness as the Sergeant lurched forward and caught at his coat collar. Behind him the door slammed shut, silencing the singing fiddles sharply. He stood very still, making no effort to shake off the policeman's grip. Anne's hand had slipped down along his arm, and her fingers closed on his wrist. He waited through a moment that dragged slowly.

" Just in time, Captain," Dempsey was saying, and he could sense the triumph in the man's voice. " Just in time to stop him slipping away—the last man to see Connell alive. . . ."

" Don't be a fool." Boycott's voice was rough with irritation. " No need to talk of Watty as if he was at the bottom of some confounded bog-hole. Just a moment. . . ."

The gig had turned and was being paced back towards them. It halted at Boycott's gesture, the yellow, wavering light of its carriage lamps softly lighting the road. In the dimness above the faint flood of light Hugh Davin could see the shadowy figure of a woman leaning forward from the high seat, but it was too dark to see more than that she was a slender, tall woman of strong, supple curves and flowing line.

The gig stopped, and she leaned forward and gathered the reins as the man stepped away from the horse's head. Hugh could see now the pale blur that was her ungloved hands as she lifted the reins and stilled the horse. She did that competently, and sat looking down out of the darkness on the group below.

Hugh Davin drew an easier breath. The presence of that woman, whoever she might be, in Boycott's car reassured him. This business could not be so grave if Boycott went about it with a woman at his side.

"You were wanting me, Captain ?" he asked quietly. There was no hint of fear at all in his voice. "Or is it a notion of Sergeant Dempsey here ?"

Before the policeman could speak, and he was more than ready to speak, Boycott answered. He could be courteous enough, this soldierly man, for all his bluff air of authority.

"We're merely looking for information, Davin," he said briskly, but not unpleasantly or with any excitement. "Information about Watty Connell's whereabouts."

It was easy to see, Hugh guessed, why he was speaking so calmly. Whatever fears he might have for Watty Connell's safety, Boycott had no wish that this strange woman in the car should be given cause for fear. Well ! Maybe that was a matter that more than one man could handle to his own advantage.

"You're afraid something happened Connell, Captain ?" he asked softly.

"Nothing to be afraid about." Boycott's voice was curt. "It's just that he failed to turn up when he was expected—a full two hours ago. So I thought it might be a good idea to drive down and find him."

And a good idea, too, to seize the opportunity of taking this strange woman driving through the twilight, Hugh thought in sudden sardonic discovery of the truth.

"I expected to run him to earth in Egan's publichouse," Boycott went on easily, too easily.

"And when you didn't find him there you let the Sergeant persuade you that I had him in the bottom of some bog-hole," Hugh said quietly.

He saw the swift glance that Boycott cast at the woman in the shadows above, and he pressed his opportunity.

"Murder that would be, Captain. And well you know I didn't do that. No, Captain Boycott, I left your bailiff as I found him—on his own two feet."

The Sergeant, so long baulked of his opportunity to speak, would be silent no longer.

"By your leave, Captain, we'll take no chances with this man." His grip tightened on Hugh's arm. "You're a magistrate yourself, sir; say the word and I'll clap him under lock and key and hold him tight on suspicion. He was the last man seen in the company of Watty Connell—and if so be there's anything happened to Connell, we'll have our man here safe and sound, and 'tis hard it will go with him. . . ."

The horse, restless again, moved uneasily, so that shoe and harness made small metallic noises in the stillness. On his wrist Hugh could feel the tightening of the girl's fingers. He could sense her fear; and suddenly he felt anger surge in him at that other woman who sat above them in the darkness looking down coolly and without any great interest.

"Say the word, Captain," the policeman was urging eagerly, "and I'll hold him for questioning."

A chill sense of helplessness that was colder than fear touched him. If anything had happened to Watty Connell in the past two hours it would go hard with him indeed, for he could give no account of his movements during those two hours that would not involve James Hannin and the others. When he spoke his mouth felt dry and stiff.

"This is nothing but foolishness, Captain. I know nothing about Connell. . . ."

"Only this: that you were with him when he was last seen," Boycott persisted. He was a man who would hold firmly to one point, small or large. "You were the last man to see him. . . ."

"That was more than two hours ago. . . ."

"So it was."

Boycott had moved nearer to the gig-lamps and his shadow sprawled darkly in the yellow light. His voice was still easy and quiet. He looked up again at the woman in the driving seat, reassuring her.

"So it was, indeed," he said. "And where has he been since—or you for that matter?"

In the little silence the jingling of harness and soft, pawing noises of the horse's hooves sounded loudly. The music from the barn drummed and lifted faintly through the closed door. Beside him Hugh was suddenly aware of Anne's quickened breathing, a deep in-taking of breath.

"You'll have to take my bail for him, Captain," she said suddenly into the stillness that was fast becoming unbearable.

There was in her voice just a small, false shading of coquetry; but her voice rang true enough. "With me he was the whole evening—ever since he left Connell on the Killower road."

Above them, in the darkness, the strange woman's voice chimed out in a long, light peal of laughter. Her voice came to them, rich and rounded, from the shadows, a voice warm and vital with life—and with amusement.

"Checkmate," she said softly, speaking down to Boycott. "That move is too old for your blundering policeman to mate."

CHAPTER SIX

Now the shadowy street was quiet again. The gig had gone bowling down the Lough Mask road, its lamps tunnelling a yellow passage in the shadows beneath the roadside trees. Somewhere at the street's end the Sergeant and his policemen tramped noisily towards the barracks. A door slammed loudly, and the night fell silent once more.

The quiet of the night lay drowsily on the field path beyond the village, where Hugh and Anne had passed to take breath after their fast walk through the gently-sloping fields.

They did not speak at first but stood silent in the murmurous stillness of the night, remembering with excitement the loud clamour of argument in the street below: the doubt with which Boycott had reluctantly agreed to believe Anne's story; the anger and suspicion of Sergeant Dempsey as he watched his prisoner go free.

Hugh turned to look back on the village, on the street shadowed and barred with moonlight and brightened by the orange pools and bays of light at doors and windows. He drew breath deeply, as much in an odd, chill premonition of trouble to come as in relief. His arm, which had been lightly about her in support during that uphill climb, drew Anne closer to him in an instinctive gesture of protection—against what he did not know.

He looked down into the empty street, thinking not of Boycott and his own escape from the policeman's hands, but of the air of secrecy and precaution which Anne had imposed on all their meetings.

" A nice story this will make in the telling," he said out of that thought. " By to-morrow morning that gossiping policeman will have the whole countryside telling the tale you told Boycott tonight. . . ."

" 'Twas the only tale I could tell."

" A right tale. Can't you see, Anne, how little good there'll be any more in all your plotting and planning, when this story is told back at your father's fireside ? "

Another thought struck him, a thought with a touch of dry humour in it. His tone lightened.

" Ah, well ! There's one good thing done, maybe. 'Twill put an end to all this hidden business of secrets and whispers. By to-morrow night the whole world, and your father and mother with it, will know the one you spent the evening with. 'Twill put an end. . . ."

" Wait, Hugh ! "

The girl turned towards him, leaning back so that the strong, slender column of her back was arched and hollowed over his encircling arm. She was breathing quickly and unevenly, as she had been a moment ago after their swift uphill walk ; her breath, warm as the spring night, touched his cheek lightly and disturbingly. The night wind lifted the dark fall of hair from her low, white brow and the faint scent of her hair was as troubling as the sappy scents of the night.

" Wait you now for one minute, Hugh." She put her hands against his breast, pressing lightly, so that she was held tautly against the curve of his arm. " I had no liking for telling that tale with Boycott and all the other men "—her voice lifted—" and with that woman of Boycott's listening to me. . . ."

" Then why ? . . ."

He could see the long, white ripple of her throat as her head went back in its own characteristic gesture of determination.

" It was the only story. A better story than you could tell, maybe—of the place you were in and the company you were with. . . ."

His arm went a shade more tightly about her—no more than that. He had long schooled himself against the slightest danger of betraying the secret that was not his secret alone, but fifty men's. His voice was light and easy, and edged with laughter as he questioned her :

" Now what do you know of where I was, or what folk I was with ? "

" Nothing, Hugh. I know nothing at all," she said slowly. " I don't know and I don't want to know. And if I could guess itself I don't want anyone else to guess. . . ."

If she could guess ? He repeated these words in the inner silence of his mind. The one thing he had always tried so hard to guard against—anyone stumbling on his secret. In that moment he felt that all the happenings of the evening were shaping themselves into an unguessable danger.

" What guessing are you talking of, Anne ? " he asked that coolly and easily. " Guessing what ? "

" Guessing who your friends are and what they're about. God knows I hear plenty about that very thing in my own house. . . ."

" In your own house ? "

Hugh looked out over her dark head at the misty fields, at the hedges darkly banked with shadow and the wet grass palely shining in the moonrise. Her own house! How little, how very little he knew of that house—or of the people in it ; of the mother whom Anne so seldom spoke about ; of Mark Killian, that dark, silent man, to whom his daughter seemed to give a passionate intensity of affection in which her mother could never share. Not a happy home, Hugh felt with sudden conviction, although Anne had never by word or hint admitted so much ; not a happy home at all, an uneasy, divided home, with some secret of its own.

He looked down at the dark head of Mark Killian's daughter and pondered that dark and silent man. He was remembering now the many times he had met Killian in the silent fields during his own secret comings and goings to and from Ahalard.

" In your own home ? " he queried gently. " Have they one more reason now for not liking me there? "

A little of the strain went out of the girl at the lightness of his tone. Her hands no longer pressed against his breast, but moved in a light caressing touch. He felt the cool softness of her hand against his cheek, and was moved to a passing, baffled anger by the need for that secrecy which must, for the sake of fifty men, lie between them.

" A new reason ? " he asked.

" No reason at all," she answered him slowly, as if not quite certain of the precise word she needed to say just what she had to say. " Look, Hugh ! You think they have a dislike for you—my father and my mother. But it isn't that. It isn't that at all ! "

" Isn't it so ? " His humour was dry. " Why so do you insist on meeting me only in the dark of the night or in hidden places . . . ? "

He could feel the life pulsing in her hands against his face and the warm pulsing of his own blood under her touch.

" Look ! " That uneven pulsing was in her voice too. " 'Tisn't easy to make you understand, Hugh. But my mother . . ." Her eyes narrowed and her warm mouth pursed as she sought for the words of explanation that she wanted. " My mother : she seems like a hard woman, a bitter woman, to people ; but sometimes, Hugh, I think she's a frightened woman. . . ."

" Frightened ? " he said, amazed. " Frightened of me ? "

" In a way, Hugh. In a sort of a way." Her dark head was flung back, her face upturned ; he could see clearly the little puzzled frown between her eyes. " Look! She's one had a world of trouble in her day, a world of trouble and heart-break. And trouble, Hugh, puts a hardness on people and bitterness, but sometimes under all the hardness and all the bitterness there's no more than fear and fright. . . ."

"Fear and fright? But what have I to do with that? What reason . . . ?"

"No reason at all, Hugh. But there's trouble gathering. The world and all knows that." She smiled up at him, the brightening of her dark eyes and the soft, swift movement of her mouth clear in the clear moonlight. "My mother talks of nothing else, all day and every day. . . ."

"Trouble! Of course there's trouble," he interrupted her. "But what has that to do with you or do with me?"

"Just this, Hugh: that my mother thinks you're a man that would be drawn deep into any trouble if trouble came. She's certain and sure of that, Hugh. Certain and sure. My father—deep down, maybe he doesn't believe it; but all day and every day he's listening to her . . . to her tongue . . . to her fear. . . ."

So that was it: Mark Killian's wife, even more than Mark Killian himself, had feared to see her daughter's name linked with the name of a man who might yet come into disfavour with landlords or police. The woman, that bitter, frightened woman in the house on Killower, had feared that, and in her own fashion had set her bitterness to wear down the will of her husband and of her daughter.

It was no more than that. But that alone was enough to cause the darkening shadow in Anne Killian's eyes.

The wind blew in his face and brought a strand of the girl's hair across his mouth. His arm tightened about her so that the vehemence of his hold startled her. He drew her closer and stooped over her upturned face, kissing her.

"Hugh! Hugh!" Her mouth moved under his mouth, saying his name over and over, and her mouth was soft and warm. "Hugh, lad!"

A wave of tenderness swept over him. All the strain and tautness had gone out of her now. She lay quietly in the curve of his arm, her slim shoulders soft and relaxed, the dark fall of her hair fragrant against his cheek. The murmur of her voice ceased, and after a little peaceful sigh her breathing came softly and gently in the quiet night.

The desire to hold and protect her was uppermost now in him. In this quiet moment he wanted no more than to put an end for ever to the secrecy and caution that lay between them and happiness and to put an end, too, to the unhappiness that darkened her life at Killower. There was one way only in which that could be done.

" We'll not go on like this, Anne." His voice was lowered and attuned to the deeper quiet of the night. " We can't go on like this. There is nothing to stop you marrying me—nothing ; no one . . ."

" No one," she said softly. " In a little time, Hugh," she agreed, as she had agreed before. " In a very little time."

" There's nothing to wait for, Anne. Nothing." Softly his hand moved over her dark hair. His fingers gently traced the clear, bold curve of her brow. " Your father—your mother more than him—will not like it, Anne, but they will like it no better for waiting—so we will not wait. And if your father and mother must be told that, let them be told now."

She did not protest now, as she had so often protested before, that in a little time, in a very little time, her father's mind and her mother's fretful mind would change.

A little sigh went from her, and it was as if, after all the stress and danger of the hours past, she was content and willing to fight no more. She put up her hands and drew down his head and kissed him.

" We will not wait so," she said, and the faint, dark fire was in her voice again. " Let them be told now," she said, repeating his words. " As well to-night as any night."

CHAPTER SEVEN

SOMEWHERE in the dim fields beyond Killower a dog was barking on a high and long-drawn note of fear. That shrill clamour splintered the quiet and filled the night with unrest.

At the hill foot, within sight of the squat house under its shelter of trees, Hugh Davin paused to listen.

" There's something troubling that dog," he said idly. " Hark to him."

Anne leaned against his shoulder, easy and relaxed. She had been happy in these fast-flying minutes since they came to decision on the hill path, as she had not been happy for many months. She listened heedlessly for a moment.

" There he goes again," she said casually. " Frightened he is. And the fright making him angry."

" Likely enough," Hugh agreed carelessly. He turned towards the house. " Let us get what we have to do over and done with now."

As lightly and as easily as that, they turned to the hill and to the house which cowered against the hill, secret and still under its shadowing trees.

A window square was warmly lit and a gleaming knife-edge of light showed where the house door stood ajar. But the yard was dark and still as they found their way through the shadows, and it was not until their footsteps rang on the cobbled pathway that the door flung open and the house light gushed out to envelop them in a yellow flood. Blinded by that sudden tide of light, they saw no more for the moment than the tall figure of Ellen Killian, blackly outlined against the glow.

" Is it down meeting that daughter of yours you were ? " Hers was a fretful, edged voice that could slide, as it slid now, to a high, complaining note of anger. " A fine doxy, with no more to do than stravaging to dances and ceilidhes. But 'twould answer yourself better to be about your work and to be in your own house when you're wanted, not to be . . ."

The torrent of complaint weakened and spent itself as the woman saw her mistake. She moved back out of the lighted doorway, and the lamplight fell full on her face. Thin and worn her face looked in that flood of yellow light, so thin that the skin seemed drawn too tightly over the sharp line of cheek and jaw by the greying hair that was strained back in a tight cap from a narrow brow, bony and fleshless as a naked knee.

The anger that had been in her voice was in her eyes too, but her mouth was no more than fretful and peevish now.

"Come away in, for God's sake, girl." She was blustering now, pretending to an anger that would cover up her surprise on seeing Hugh Davin. "Isn't it bad enough having that father of yours away off this three or four hours and no trace or tidings of him, without you taking example from him Come away in out of that now."

She had drawn the door over until no more than a narrow slit of it stood open. It was, Hugh thought, as if she was hiding something or someone. He moved closer to Anne and laid a quiet hand on her arm. They had gone too far now on the road of decision to be turned back by a woman's anger.

"As I'm this far," he said easily, "'twill do no harm if I go as far as the fire for a light for my pipe."

He was certain now that the older woman had some reason of her own for holding the door half-shut against him.

"I'll not turn back now," he said very softly at Anne's shoulder. "That would be a poor ending." He slid his hand over the curve of her arm and took a long step forward at her side. "In with you."

The low kitchen, beyond that door which fell open to them with such reluctant slowness, was a clean, scrubbed room, warm and bright with lamplight and firelight. Yet, somehow, it was not a cheerful room. A piled fire of black turf flamed murmurously in the deep cave of the chimney, but no chairs were drawn up in easy comfort to the warm hearth. The hearth was empty and bare and the chairs were ranged beyond the scrubbed table, against the lime-washed walls. And in a chair at the table's head a man sat with a shoulder alean against the white wall, a hard, derisive eye bright under the tilt of the hat which he wore crammed down over his forehead.

"Yourself again, Master," said Watty Connell, breaking the moment's silence. He put a neat second meaning in what he had to say: "You were a long time getting this far."

Hugh Davin had turned in surprise at the sound of that voice.

"Well, I'll be hanged," he said, "How did *you* get here?"

Little wonder that Ellen Killian had endeavoured to hold the door against him. There were few houses from Cong to Cross in those sullen days where Boycott's bailiff could sit in comfort and at his ease, as he was sitting here in Mark Killian's kitchen. Small wonder, indeed, that Ellen Killian had been slow to open her door.

Anne began to draw off her coat. Her face had gone pale, and into her dark eyes had come again that shadow of trouble. Angrily, and uneasily, too, Hugh met the bailiff's eye. He was remembering not only his near escape from arrest; he was remembering, too, the hatred that was growing in the countryside against Watty Connell and against those who would dare to make the man their friend.

"You'd do well, Connell," he said hotly, "to tell your friends where you're off to before you go visiting."

Watty leaned back against the wall. He tilted the mug that stood before him, rocking it to and fro until the pale, colourless liquor in it splashed over the rim and the air was rancid with the smell of poteen.

"Would I so, now?" he asked. "And why would I do the like of that?"

"To save your friends the trouble of searching for you in every dyke and bog-hole in the country." Hugh's voice was hot with anger. "And to save me the danger of spending my night in the jail in Castlebar."

Watty moved ponderously in his chair. He stooped forward, his eyes alive with interest, and the chair legs crashed to the floor with a dull thud of sound. But before he could speak, Ellen Killian's voice raised on its own high note of fretfulness.

"Oh, dear God!" she cried. "Didn't I know well he was that class of man. And nothing to do him but to come straight here to this house with his troubles thick on him . . ."

"Wait, now! There's no need for all this excitement." The bailiff silenced her. His voice was very calm but his small eyes were alive with curiosity. "Hold your whist, like a good woman. 'Tis joking the man is."

"Joking! Grand joking. With the sergeant's hand on my collar and Captain Boycott as good as saying I was the death of you. If it wasn't for Anne here persuading Boycott that I was never out of her sight all evening . . ."

He stopped short on that word. Too late he saw that his anger had tricked his tongue into too free talk. Ellen Killian was staring at him out of startled eyes; her mouth had gone slack and loose.

"Father in Heaven! Is it to say before the police and the Captain himself that it was with you she was. With you! And you up to God knows what mischief and trouble-making." The woman's voice quavered to its own shrill peak of complaint. "Dear God! That I raised such a fool of a daughter . . ."

"Mother! Will you listen?"

Anne still held the coat she had taken off; it was thrown over her arm so that it hid her hands. As he moved a step closer to her, Hugh could see the creasing and crumbling of the cloth where her hands gripped tight on it, the only sign of perturbation that she gave. Her voice was no more than weary and patient, and that patient note told better than any loud protest how accustomed she had become to her mother's peevish temper and nagging tongue.

"Will you listen, mother?"

"Erra, so! Listen! Much good talking and listening will do, and you doing your best endeavour to draw down trouble on yourself and all of us. You and your . . . your . . ." She had worked herself into a passion of anger, the venomous anger that is bred of fear. "You and your fancy bachelor that has no more use for you than courting you in the dark of a hedge . . . Aye! And doing his best endeavours to make your name a byword in the mouth of every gossip in the parish."

The ugly words went home. As he touched Anne's hand in quick reassurance, Hugh felt the startled tremor that went through her. A smother of anger caught at his throat, and the root of that anger was in the knowledge that he himself was in part to blame for making those words possible. He could end that now, once and for all. He held his temper well in check, but his voice was bleak.

" There's one good way of putting a stop to that kind of talk," he said. " Anne and myself will be giving them a wedding to talk about. They can talk as they like when we're married—in a month from now, or less, if Father O'Malley is willing to be hurried."

Often afterwards, in the days of doubt and heartbreak that were to come, he was to remember this moment. He was to remember the swift, startled movement of the girl at his side and that deep, unsteady intake of breath that sounded so softly in the hush. He was to remember the still intentness of the bailiff, an intentness as of surprise frozen in the moment of exclamation. But, most of all, it was Ellen Killian's face he was to remember. Ever afterwards he would remember her face as he saw it then, with the dull, angry flood of colour slowly staining it, and the mouth that was so often no more than querulous and peevish go thin and hard with angry resolution.

" Marry ! Marry is it ? " The thin voice rode high and shrill. " Is it marry the one, only child we have to a black stranger from God knows where . . . to a man we know no more about than we do about the spalpeen labouring man that passes the road . . ."

" Wait ! One minute." Hugh's voice rose in its own protest. " Just one minute . . ."

" Not one minute, nor one half minute. Is it mad you are ? What manner of husband would the like of you be for a girl that has a father with sixty sound acres of good land on a good lease ? Sixty good acres, and . . ." She checked. " No matter. No matter about that. Sixty good acres . . ."

The thin voice filled the room with its shrill clamour, and off the bitter tongue slipped the real reason for bitterness :

" A one, only child. 'Tisn't as if we had a son, or another daughter itself to bring a proper husband in on the floor. Is it to give the girl to a strolling stranger like you, and leave ourselves alone at the latter end of our days ? " She raised her hand to smooth the thin-scraped strands of her hair, and her hand was trembling. Her anger was spending itself. " We have better plans than that. Better plans surely . . ."

Whatever those plans were, she was not to reveal them now. With a clumsiness that was not like him at all, Watty Connell heaved out of his chair. His coat sleeves caught the mug he had been drinking from and sent it clattering across the table, leaving a wet stain of poteen in its wake. He lumbered to his feet and stood staring down with comical dismay at what he had done. The small noise of the falling mug was loud in the quiet, loud enough to catch Ellen Killian's attention and, for the moment, check the spate of her voice. She stopped in mid-sentence ; and into that moment's silence Watty spoke lightly.

" Let you leave your plans and your planning be, woman," said he easily, a shade too easily perhaps. " And let yourself and the master not be arguing and barging. Won't it be time enough for you to talk when your tempers are cooled and when the girl's father is here to listen to what ye have to say ? " He put out a pawing hand to the girl's shoulder. " Amn't I right, Anne ? "

He stood swaying on widespread legs, on his face the loose, fatuous grin of a man far gone in liquor. But the man was not drunk, Hugh knew ; he was not even touched by liquor. He was playing some game of his own ; and whatever that game was it would be a deep and dangerous game.

But Hugh had no time now to trouble about the bailiff or his plans. Anne had moved back out of reach and stood leaning against the table, a hand on either side of her holding her poised and taut as a runner on tip-toe for the start of the race. All the warmth and happiness seemed drained out of her. In the sudden hush that was no more than a moment's length, but which seemed to stretch out unendingly, she stood there poised and tensed, not yet wholly free of one or other of the loyalties that drew her.

Hugh Davin did not move nearer to her, nor did his voice lift above its own deep, accustomed note. He spoke quietly, very quietly.

" Anne," he said evenly, " we can put an end to this for once and for all. There is no one can stop you marrying me, if marry me you will. No one."

Very firmly he said that, but even as he said it he knew

that it was not the whole truth. Not the whole truth, indeed; for always there would be that pull of sundered loyalties, until one loyalty or the other was for ever broken. Always there would be that pull, and a whole lifetime's habit of obedience to put aside in one moment's decision. He went on, very quietly:

"No one. If you will only say the word now."

It was queerly quiet in the room, which seemed now to hold within itself all the stillness and silence of the night, a silence so deep that the murmuring of the tongues of flame amidst the black turfs on the hearth seemed loud as the whispering of countless hushed voices. But beyond, in the night outside, outside the silence held here in the quiet heart of the house, was an uproar and clamour of sound. Somewhere in that outer darkness the dog was still barking frenziedly and in alarm, as he must have been barking unheard and unheeded, during all those latter minutes. The barking was nearer now, so near that the little moan of pain underlying it could be clearly heard. And another sound could be clearly heard too, a sound oddly and unaccountably frightening: the heavy, uncertain footsteps of a man walking slowly, stumblingly.

"Wait! Wait you, now!" It was the bailiff who spoke, his voice sharp with caution. "Let you be cautious opening that door."

There was no need for caution. The door was pushed open from without, and the man who opened it stood for a moment leaning against the jamb. The dog slipped past him and went limping to the fire, not barking now but whimpering softly. Slowly, lurching a little, Mark Killian followed his dog into the light and crossed to the table. He was a slight man, not tall, with a darkly pale face and a low, broad brow that was his daughter's very own. A livid bruise slanted across his forehead from eye to temple.

"Honour of God!" His wife's voice rose high and shrill, as much in alarm as in anxiety. "What happened to you at all, at all?"

He did not answer her, but leaned across the table groping

for the bottle that had stood at the bailiff's elbow. The bottle neck chattered against his teeth as he drank. His shirt, that had been ripped from neck to waist, fell open and showed his naked chest gashed with long, raking wounds, as if a beast had clawed him. Gulping at the neat spirits, he drew the shirt across his wounds; the torn shirt was streaked with blood.

"They carded you!"

It was the bailiff who spoke, and his words called up in the minds of his listeners a terrifying vision of men stooping over their victim in the dark night and drawing savagely across his stripped body a board studded with sharpened nails, the "carding" board.

"They carded you," he said. "How many of them?"

"For all I know there might have been no more than one of them." Killian's voice was almost steady now. He lifted a hand to his bruised forehead and pressed hard on the throbbing hurt. "Whoever it was, was waiting for me when I crossed the stile under the big bush at the Cill Park field. He struck me when I stooped under the bush. He struck hard. . . ." The strength went out of his voice. "That was all of four hours ago."

At the memory a sudden terror showed in his eyes that were dark as his daughter's own—a terror at the thought of the long hours he had lain helpless and at the mercy of his attackers out in the lonely darkness.

"All of four hours ago. . . ."

"Hush! Hush, you! Hush!"

It was Anne who spoke. She had not stood staring at the injured man as the others had. Already she had filled a bowl from the steaming kettle on the hearth-crane and was tearing linen into strips. She helped her father now into the chair that Connell had pushed back from the table and began to draw away the bloodied shirt from his body. A deep and glowing warmth of affection looked out of her dark eyes. Whatever bitterness she might have felt under the lash of her mother's nagging tongue, there was no doubting the warmth that was now in her eyes and in her voice.

" Pay no heed to them now." Her voice was warm and deep with affection. She leaned over him, as if shielding him from her mother and the bailiff and from their questioning. " What matter, now, who did it. What matter at all."

Over the girl's shoulder the older woman was speaking in her own shrill accents of complaint. There was fear in her voice ; but it was not, Hugh thought, with heightened awareness, fear for her husband or the terror that had come upon him in the darkness. It was a fear that went deeper than that. Fear that went back, Hugh thought, remembering tales he had heard, to the hungry days three and thirty years before, when the woman who was now Ellen Killian had been Ellen Bourke —a frightened, starving child who had watched father and mother and younger sister die slowly and dreadfully in the ditch to which they had crawled out of the unroofed cabin from which they had been evicted. A fear like that would twist the heart in a child and would breed a terror of all that threatened the security of roof and hearth. It would breed that terror as it had bred it here.

" Keep quiet, girl. Little you know or care of the trouble that can come on people." She was stooping over Anne now, gripping her shoulder and pushing her aside. " D'you hear me, Mark? Who was it hurt you? "

" For God's sake, hold your tongue, woman."

Mark Killian drew the torn shirt across his chest and came to his feet. Now that the shadow of pain had gone from his face, his was a pleasant face. Under a tangle of dark brow his eyes were bright as bog water and as luminously clear, but they were not steadfast ; and his live, wide mouth had none of his wife's desperate purpose.

" Will you have sense, woman," he said, " and not be making bad worse."

He crossed slowly to the fire and stooped towards the heat, his outspread hands atremble yet with shock. As he stooped, there fell from his inner pocket a two-foot length of ash sapling bound with brass rings which glinted dully in the light. The stick rolled across the floor, a short, stout stick polished smooth with much handling. The ends of the brass rings had been pulled free ; those ends jutted away from the stick like the teeth of a comb, and each jagged brass point was blackened with blood.

It was Watty Connell who said what was in the mind of every one of them.

" Soul, Master," said he very softly, " you do more nor fishing with that rod of yours." His eyes were bright and hard and alive with speculation. " The butt end of your fishing rod. 'Tisn't more than a few hours ago since I saw you with that very rod under your oxter, and me leaving you on the Killower road . . ."

Silence had the little room in its grip again. The fire whispered and murmured in the deep chimney and the dog whimpered softly. No one spoke. To himself Hugh repeated the bailiff's words: ". . . you had it, and you leaving me on the Killower road." So Connell had not seen him drop the rod at Michael Carroll's wall.

The silence weighed down upon them, and in that silence Hugh came to decision, the only decision he could come to. He would say nothing here that would involve Carroll. In his own way and his own time he would discover Carroll's share in this night's work. But he would not, could not, say anything now that might start questionings that would involve fifty men.

He lifted his head and met Anne's eye. With a shock of dismay he realized how damning his own silence must seem. The girl's eyes held him steadily, not in accusation but in puzzled questioning.

" Anne ! " His voice rode high. He scarcely heard the shrill, railing outburst of Ellen Killian or the bailiff's deeper voice. " Listen to me, Anne. You don't think I had hand or part in this night's work ? "

That look of puzzled questioning was still in her eyes. Her thoughts were in her eyes, all her unwilling uncertainty, all her conflicting loyalties. There was doubt in her eyes, a troubled shadow of doubt.

" You must listen to me," he said urgently, heedless of the others. " You must let me . . ."

It was Mark Killian who cut him short. He stooped stiffly, a hand to his torn chest, and snatched up the stick as the bailiff reached for it. He held the stick balanced for a moment in his hand. And then, with a quick, jerky movement, tossed it into the fire. The flames licked it and leaped high for a moment, murmuring on a louder note. Mark Killian drew breath deeply.

"Let that be an end of it all," he said, and for once his voice was resolute. "You hear me, Connell: an end to it all. Let it end here on this floor. And you, Hugh Davin," he added, "I have no wish to bring trouble on you or on any man. Let you remember that. No wish at all. I'm asking nothing from you or your likes but that you'll leave me and mine alone. You hear: leave me and mine alone."

Hugh Davin did not answer him at all, but looked past him to Anne. She did not speak; she looked back at him steadily under level brows. It was not dismissal or disbelief he read in her eyes, but doubt; a doubt which, he knew, could gather and lower until it darkened all that lay between them. He began to speak, but checked himself with a little gesture of discouragement. Only too well he knew that words and protests now would not clear away that shadow of doubt.

"That's all I ask you." It was Mark Killian who was speaking again. "Leave me and mine alone."

Hugh put out his hand to the door and pulled it open. The night seemed to flow into the room behind him. It was to Mark Killian he spoke, but his gaze never ceased to hold Anne's troubled eyes.

"No harm will come to you or yours through me," was all he said as he turned away to the darkness.

He said that strongly, not knowing and with no way of knowing how soon trouble and heartbreak were to weigh down on all of them.

CHAPTER EIGHT

It had rained earlier in the day, but now the sun was struggling through the low-lying veils of misty cloud. The shabby drawing-room of Boycott's house was softly filled with a pale greenish light that was thrown back from the rain-swept face of the lake and filtered through the drenched trees which darkened the windows.

The room stifled in that dim light and in the heat of the unheeded fire piled high under the chimney-piece of white marble. But it was less the stifling heat and dim light that oppressed Judith Wynne than the need for alert and unceasing caution in every word she spoke to these women.

To one woman in particular, for of the four women here in the dim room one was dangerous to her just now. Not Caroline Boycott, for in the weeks since Judith had come to live in Lough Mask House Charles Boycott's mother had plainly shown her bitter dislike for this unwanted visitor ; and open enmity, Judith thought with a wisdom she had learned too young, lost half its dangers in its openness. And not, surely, small dark Alice French with her velvety soft, sleepy eyes and her pale, plump hands that were always ineffectually busy with the flounces and frills of her too-elaborate dress. Nor the tall, lovely, frigid Burke girl with her lifeless blonde hair and narrow, jealous eyes.

No! It was the other, older woman she had to fear, Alice French's match-making mother. She gave all her attention to that woman, alertly watching the incessant fluttering of the plump hand on which the many rings were lost in little hummocks of flesh. She watched, too, the pursed red mouth, a gossiper's mouth.

" Ah, yes! We all knew your poor, dear mother. Ah, yes! Poor, poor Violet." The little note of commiseration in the soft voice was subtly insulting. " And your dear father! He was English, of course. But one met him. In the old days, the good days, he was here so often, at the Curragh for the racing, in Galway for the hunting. Ah, yes! One remembers him well."

Judith leaned back in her chair. Her dress was of a deeper green than the light which sifted softly through the window at her shoulder, and of a soft clinging stuff that moulded every splendid line of her. She was conscious of the Burke girl's jealous eyes upon her. She smiled back at the older woman, her grey-blue, candid gaze steadily meeting the snapping black, curious eyes.

" You are so much luckier than I am then, ma'am," she said pleasantly and dryly. " I was no more than five years old when my father died. I have little more than a memory of him, a faint, far-off memory."

That was true enough, heavens knows, she thought with a sudden bitterness. Reckless and improvident, her father had left her little more than a vague memory of easy-going good humour ; that, and his own love of horses and his skill with them.

" To be sure ! To be sure ! " The gossipy red mouth pursed itself. " Twenty years ago. That'd make you five and twenty now, wouldn't it ? " The snapping black eyes for a moment contemplated with satisfaction nineteen-year-old Alice French. " Twenty years ago ? Ah, yes ! I remember, we all wondered if your poor, dear mother would come home to live in Galway. But she didn't of course. She stayed in England."

They were all watching her out of sly eyes, Judith told herself in a sudden fury of anger, the match-making oldish woman and the two girls. She moved a little, so that the strong, clear line of her profile showed proudly against the dim light. For the two girls—for dark, childish Alice French who would marry Charles Boycott if ever and whenever her mother could arrange it, and for Olive Burke who would willingly marry any man of her own class and kind—she felt nothing but contempt. But the older women, with their spiteful eyes and mean minds, roused her to anger that set her pride aflame.

" Naturally," she said crisply. " It was so much more pleasant to stay amongst one's friends."

" Ah, yes ! " Caroline Boycott's beautiful greying head was stooped over her work-basket, her lovely white hands, as ever, busy amongst the coloured stuffs. She lifted her head, but it was not towards Judith she looked but to the other older woman. "Ah, yes," she said in that cold, bell-voice. "Amongst one's friends. Of course." She held up a silken scrap that glowed warmly in her pale hands. "At Hatfield, wasn't it? I seem to remember that the Vandeleurs—that'd be the present man's parents of course—visited your mother there in the year of your father's death. Yes! Hatfield!" She smiled at the other old woman over the upheld coloured cloth.

Hatfield! Judith remembered without enthusiasm the little cottage under the sweep of the rolling downs. There were no over-bright colours of happy childhood associations in the memory of that house to which she had gone as a child when, on her father's death, Lord Erne had made himself responsible for the care of Hubert Wynne's widow and daughter.

No! There were few happy memories of Hatfield. What pleasant memories there were—memories of spring and summer mornings when all the vast reaches of the downs rolled away into empty distances and to a misty sky seen over the pricked ears of a galloping horse. Memories of spring mornings! And other memories of autumn evenings and of riding back slowly over the darkening downs through a steel-grey dusk under a wan sky. And memories, too, of hunting days in the tame, park-like country farther north, around Bolstead and Creake . . .

And then, suddenly, hurting as if a hand had pressed upon her breast, came the memory she had schooled herself to forget, the memory of Harry Levinge. For a moment sharp with a pain she had thought banished long ago, she could see him again against the screen of her mind: his lean, sun-roughened face flushed with excitement over the unbuttoned collar of his tunic; the sweep of fair hair marked by the pressing rim of his forage-cap and clinging damply to his narrow brow; his hot, reckless eyes alight with life.

The moment passed, leaving her cold and limp. She turned to listen to Alice French, aware of an unusual animation in the girl's soft, cloying voice.

"Hatfield! Oh, mama! Don't you remember? That nice

Captain Radley man who was staying with the Lestranges when we were there last month ? You remember . . . ? "

" I remember Captain Radley only too well," the girl's mother cut her short. Her coy voice and the coy little gestures of her grossly fat hands held Judith's eyes in disgust. " I fear that Captain Radley was a sad flirt . . . And that someone else wasn't altogether blameless. . . ."

" Oh, mama ! How could you say such a thing ? "

The dark girl's fluting, childish voice struck just the right note of simpering coyness, Judith thought with contempt. There was just the right flutter of dark lashes against faintly flushed cheeks as she said over the name of this Captain . . . what was it ? . . . this Captain Radley. . . .

Captain Radley ! Judith sat very still. Somewhere in the depths of her mind that name touched memory elusively, warningly. She heard Alice French's too-sweet voice.

" But don't you remember, mama ? Hatfield ! That's where Captain Radley's regiment was stationed when he was thrown in the regimental races and, oh ! so badly injured. Don't you remember ? He told us so often."

Judith had remembered now. She could see it all again : the wide and rolling sweep of the downs under a high sky ablow with clouds ; the lift of horses and riders over the fences against the sharp brightness of the March sky ; the sudden clamour and terror of crashing horses and flaying hooves, and the limp, sagging burden borne swiftly away through the silenced crowds.

She remembered it all now. Captain Radley ! The name of the injured man had never been important to her, and, in any event, had lost all importance in the storm of misery and heartbreak that had swept down upon her out of the wild winds of that March day.

How much, she wondered in sudden panic, had Radley told his Irish friends of the doings and scandals of that wild day ? And how much had this gossiping woman remembered ? She was conscious of Caroline Boycott's cool, appraising stare.

" Why, I'm sure I remember that day," Judith said, speaking because she felt that she must somehow break the spell of the calculating stare that seemed now, as all through the weeks past, to hold her in vigilant watchfulness. " Of course ! The regimental races of the 19th Lancers, wasn't it ? The Green Gordons? And I *do* remember that dreadful spill. And the poor man who was taken away." She turned towards Alice French's mother, moving a little so that the light was now behind her. " Yes, I remember. It was terrible. Poor Captain Radley. Radley his name was, wasn't it? Poor, poor man. . . ."

" Oh, he'd quite recovered. He was quite *le beau capitaine* again. Isn't that so, Alice dear ? " Again that coy, simpering smile. " He used quite curdle our blood with dreadful tales of that terrible moment while he lay and watched the dreadful hooves flashing in his face. Too terrible." The little snapping black eyes brightened. " There was some gossip, some regimental scandal, wasn't there ? I seem to have forgotten quite what it was. Hardly very important, I suppose."

" Those things very rarely are, are they ? " Judith said easily.

Relief flooded over her as she heard Olive Burke's thin, jealous voice cut in coldly to turn the current of the conversation :

" Must we talk of horses ? " she demanded petulantly. " Horses, and people who are always thinking and talking of horses so tire one ! " She shot a spiteful, sidelong look at Judith. " Coarse and tiresome, I always think. I'm quite sure all this silly scandal was of no importance at all."

And indeed, and indeed, it had been of no importance, that silly scandal, Judith told herself. What had been of importance was Harry's failing her. For months, for six wildly happy months, he had filled her whole world. Only too clearly she could picture again the new life and excitement in the house on the downs during those days of happiness ; the laughter echoing through the dim, shabby rooms ; the unexpected, yet hoped for thud of hooves on gravel and jingle of curb and stirrup in the evening darkness as he came riding over on lightning visits in odd moments snatched from duty ; the vibrant, reckless voice that had won over even the timid distrust of the prim, faded woman whom Erne had found to live with her ; their plans. . . .

But their plans had gone crashing down on that wild March day in the storm of whispered scandal. It had all been so trivial and unimportant when weighed against the happiness that had been hers for six fast-flying months. It had been no more than some vague racecourse shadiness, some trickery, less even than dishonesty, in which Harry had been deeply involved.

Even then, even when Harry had been forced by the whisperings of scandal to seek transfer to another regiment, there had seemed no need to lose all their hold on happiness. She would have married him then, all the more happily for the cloud that shadowed him. But he had failed her. A little thread of pain was woven into the memory. He had failed her, less because of the scandal that had darkened his name than because of the poverty that threatened to come hard on the heels of his money losses of that day. It hurt, the brutal truth that Harry had not her courage and willingness to face life under that threat of poverty.

The voices of the gossiping, inimical women murmured through the green obscurity of the room. She leaned back, closing her smarting eyes against the dim light, fighting hard against that memory.

He had failed her. Oh, yes ! He had made great show of his own splendid reasons, his own high standards of honour, finding half a score fine reasons for all he did—man's reasons that seemed to her empty and hollow and cold.

A tiny spasm of pain puckered her mouth. She did not want to remember those days of grey loneliness before Lord Erne had come hurrying down to Hatfield, a trembling, saffron-faced husk of the dandy he had once been, primed now with a garbled and fantastically foolish account of her relations with Harry Levinge. That faded, prim companion of hers had been responsible for many of those tales, Judith told herself with cold contempt for all gossiping, jealous women. The woman had been responsible, too, for Erne's silly fears that his own name might in some way be associated with all this whispered gossip and scandal, so that, spluttering his fear and rage, he had packed Judith off here to Ireland, hiding her as if she had been a maid-servant foolish in her love affairs.

She sat very still, her eyes closed as if to shut out the memory of that yellow, scolding face. Then, suddenly, she was conscious that the room had fallen silent. She opened her eyes and looked into Caroline Boycott's cold, vigilant eyes.

" Why, Judith ! " The cold, sweet voice brought her back sharply to the need for caution. " Have we tired you ? Are you ill ? "

In that moment she knew how much Caroline Boycott hated her. She felt suddenly without protection or defence against that cold, inimical stare.

" It's my head," she said, snatching at any excuse. " It aches so. The warm, wet day perhaps." She lifted to her feet in a lovely lithe movement that brought the other girls' eyes in envy on her. " If you'll excuse me, I think I'd better rest for a little."

CHAPTER NINE

THE door closed behind her, cutting off the sudden upsweep of vindictive, gossiping voices. It was quiet here in the hall-way, and there was no need now for alertness or caution. Judith picked up the cloak which she had thrown on a chest in the shadows earlier in the afternoon, and drew it about her so that it swung like a cape of military cut from her shoulders.

She did not go to her room to be alone with the memories that had come so painfully to life in her mind, but slipped past the curve of the stairway into the long, low passage that tunnelled its way past kitchens and larders and pantries to the gardens and yards at the rear.

There was now no need for hurry. She dawdled through the low, whitewashed passage with its faintly oppressive odour of damp lime and its pungent smells of cooking, until she came to the doorway facing the stables and yards.

Sunlight washed the wet roofs of the stables with glittering brilliance, and in the wide space between house and stable-yards the rain-soaked grass flashed back the light in countless points of radiance. A murmur of voices droned in the sleepy stillness, and Judith turned to watch the men who were grouped about the open door of the Estate Office, which stood in the angle between house and yards.

Charles Boycott was standing on the topmost step, outlined against the shadowy frame of the open doorway. She watched him now out of eyes made critically sharp by reawakened memory. There was a stiffness and a stolidity about him, she thought, that compared badly with Harry Levinge's fluent, lively grace. The light fell full on his bullet-round massive head, brightening the vigorous sweep of his reddish, grizzled hair. The high-boned, high-coloured face with its iron mouth and hot eyes, had strength and vigour in it, but not the quick life that was always in Harry's reckless eyes and eager mouth.

And yet, she knew, there were qualities in Charles Boycott that Harry had lacked, qualities of straightforwardness and reliability. And, oddly, there was a queer gentleness under all his ruthless vigour that attracted and drew her. It was not that she loved him or ever would love him as she had loved Harry ; but if she married him, she thought, remembering the unexpectedness and the sincerity of his stumbling proposal of marriage on that still evening three days ago—if she married him, as she well might in spite of all her temporizing and her refusal to give him a definite answer three days ago, and in the face of his mother's unvoiced opposition, she would be winning for herself the safety and security that she had lacked for all of a lifetime.

She stood very still, listening to his voice, to the rough and hectoring tone that was new to her.

"That's my last word," he was saying harshly and angrily. "The rent's a fair rent, as fair as any rent in Mayo. I'll recommend no reduction to Lord Erne. Not ten per cent. . . . No, nor five. . . ."

The violent, angry voice, the emphatic gesture, filled Judith with a vague uneasiness. All these weeks past she had been listening to incessant talk of rents and Land League and violence. She watched now the group in the spring sunshine. Watty Connell slouched against the wall on a step lower than his employer, his blue-shaven chin sunk into the dingy folds of his cravat. Ringed on the grass before the door stood a half score men, old men mostly, in the tail-coat of frieze and half-high hat of the countryside. Out of that group a voice flung back now at Boycott.

" 'Tisn't five or ten, nor yet twenty we're asking." The man who spoke moved forward a little, an old man, his mouth soft and red against the white of his beard, his quick, light eyes bright under a whitened thatch of brow. " 'Tis thirty is the figure fixed. A fair figure. There's not a rood of land within ten miles of here worth a penny more."

" The figure fixed. Fixed by you and your blackguard friends in the Land League, Egan," Boycott answered sharply. " You and the Land Leaguers will fix no rent here, Egan." The violence of temper that could sweep down on him like a spring gale possessed him now. " Better get back to your publichouse and stick to your huxtering in bad whiskey. What right have you, with no more than a two-acre garden, to talk for these men? Isn't that right, boys? "

He threw out that remark with jocose roughness, but he raised no smile, created no breach between Egan and the others. The League had welded them too closely in a common interest to be thus easily set against one another. It was Martin Egan who answered him.

" Right enough, Captain. Right enough, now," said he easily. " The bit of land I have wouldn't give diet to a snipe, but sure that's no fault of mine. Five and forty good acres I rented twenty years ago, before I was evicted after the rent was riz four times running on me." He fingered his white beard, and there was no friendliness now in his light eyes. " Four times running . . . till I was paying fifty shillings the acre rent for land that was no more than a scatter of stones and a lough of water the day I first set foot in it. . . ."

Boycott's hand went out in that impatient, violent gesture of his. His eyes darkened.

" There's no sense in this talk, Egan," he snapped out. " No one here is asked to pay a rent as high as your rent was. No one is asked to pay a rent like that to-day. . . ."

" Maybe not, Captain." Egan's voice was low and unflurried. " But the rent they *are* asked to pay is every penny as bad as the rent that was asked from me in my day ; every penny as bad, for these men are no more able to pay the rents asked from them to-day than I was to pay my rent." A throaty murmur of voices rumbled in the quiet. " Not a man of them can pay what they're asked to-day."

" If they can't there's a cure for them." Boycott was quick, too quick, with his answer. " The same cure that was used for you, yourself, Egan."

It was very quiet here in the shelter of the house. A faint wind rustled through the drenched leaves of the trees ; somewhere in the far shadows of the stable-yard the last of the rain dripped from the wet roof, and the tiny splashing sounded explosively in the stillness. Watty Connell straightened and lifted his shoulder from the wall. His boot-heel rasped loudly on the stone step. That sudden harsh noise stirred Judith with an unease she did not understand. She drew back into the doorway, watching the men at the foot of the steps gather together.

" Come away home out of this, men." It was the white-bearded man, Martin Egan, who spoke. His voice had the ring of authority in it. " If there's a cure for us, there's a cure, too, and a damned good one, for the man that'll put foot on an evicted farm. And there'll be few evictions while there's none to take the evicted land."

There was sudden movement and bustle as the men at the foot of the steps gathered together and moved away in a muttering group, stumping doggedly and noisily down the gravel path under the bright, wet hedge of laurels and evergreen. Charles Boycott moved as if to follow them, but the bailiff seized his arm.

" Hould where you are, sir," Watty said sharply. " Let them go their own way ; we'll find a way to deal with them."

From where she stood, hidden in the house doorway, Judith

looked out at the two men, at the tall, violent man and the small, squat man who had held his own temper in tight control. She eyed the bailiff with distrust and dislike, with that same vague distrust and dislike that she had for this countryside she so little understood.

"Don't say another word to them, Captain." Watty's mouth twisted in a soured grin. "'Tisn't talk that'll settle them lads now, but a sudden blow that'll put the fear o' God into them before they've done boasting and bragging of the way they stood up to you and argued with you and gave answers back to you at your own very door-step to-day."

The violent colour had ebbed out of Boycott's face, but his mouth was thin with anger still, his jaw hard-set.

"I'd be slow to do anything that'd give rise to trouble," he began, but the bailiff cut him short with rough excitement.

"Trouble, is it? 'Tisn't for you to start the trouble that they'll wait now, Captain. The trouble was started the minute Martin Egan knew he had enough men to his back to defy you to your face. The trouble is started this very minute, Captain. And if you don't show them now who's master, Captain, your life an' my life an' the life of wan in this house won't be worth a traneen. . . ."

"You've been listening to Sergeant Dempsey, Watty." Boycott's quick temper was easing in its own quick fashion. "There'll be no trouble—not of that sort. . . ."

"There'll be no trouble of any sort if we hit now, Captain, and hit hard. Look! There's distraint notices out with two score of them. Let us come down on them now, and seize . . ."

"Seize! Seize a few sheep and some old woman's ducks and hens? Have some commonsense, Connell. The notices are out with people who owe three—aye! and four—gales of rent. Seizures now wouldn't pay the charges of the sheriff's men. . . ."

"Maybe, Captain! Maybe so! But 'twould have a powerful effect on them that talk most." The hard bright eye considered the man on the upper step. "An' 'tisn't but there's a chance of a few pounds, one way an' another. There's that horse of Carroll's above, the one I was telling you about, that would sell well. An' I'm toult Andy Moore, over, has a pair of fine heifers he's holding for the fair of Balla. . . ."

"No!" Boycott snapped back. "I say 'No,' Connell. . . ."

Purpose spurted in him like an angry flame, Judith thought, watching him, watching that darkening of his eyes in anger and the sudden whitening of the ridged skin over cheek-bone. There was strength in him, no doubt of that; but it was an explosive, headlong strength that would make life with him a violent and stormy affair.

It would be a life altogether lacking in the easy tolerance of Harry's pliant and accommodating good humour. And yet, she felt suddenly, a life tingling and braced with excitement. She watched him out of eyes deep and stormy with thought and indecision.

"'Tis for you to say, Captain. But if you don't make a seizure," the bailiff said softly, "'tis how you'll have to evict."

"Evict! And have a score of empty farms on my hands. I'm told Major Scott can't get an Emergency Man on any terms to take a farm in Tourmakeady." Boycott came stiffly down the steps, hands thrust deeply in his breeches pockets, his reddish head gleaming in the sunlight. "It's a rotten business, Connell, rotten! While this infernal League is strong enough to have farms left idle all over the country, our hands are tied."

"Aye, so! So they are, Captain. But if it was a thing now that we got a man to take one evicted farm . . . if we got one man with the courage to step in on one farm itself that we were after evicting a tenant out of . . ."

"You're looking for more courage in a man than you'll find nowadays, Connell. . . ."

"'Tisn't a man I have in mind, but a woman, Captain. A woman that has a daughter on her hands to settle. A woman with a mind of her own and plans of her own. An able, cute woman, Captain. A match for the best of us," he said softly. "Let you but say the word now . . ."

The hard bright eye and the hoarse, insistent voice were combining now in their own purpose, but Boycott did not see nor hear. His impatient pacing had brought him within sight of the shadowed doorway, and when his eyes fell on Judith he came striding towards her with that new eagerness of his in voice and eyes.

" My dear lady ! "

That lift of eagerness in his voice, the oddly formal greeting, could stir her queerly to a mood of quiet affection as not even Harry's rakish humour could. It was a gentle mood, such as she had never known in the ardour of her relations with Levinge.

" I feared I'd have to go and search you out in the drawing-room."

" Feared ? " she said, on a little uplifting note of amusement, and went on quickly : " No ! I tired of the talk and gossip. My head ached. And so . . ." She slanted a sidelong glance at him. " And so I escaped."

" Escaped ? " That deep, pleased laughter of his warmed her with a glow of pleasure. " I must help to make the escape complete. No ! Not that way." He stopped her as she turned to join him. " This way. Through the stables, to the boathouse."

Judith slipped a hand under his arm, and together they went walking across the wet grass, two tall, striding people, vigorous and eager with life.

Watty Connell tipped hat to them and slouched back to his old stance against the wall, watching them with shrewd eye and impassive face.

That hard, bright glance stayed disturbingly in Judith's mind, and she scarcely waited for the tall gates to swing shut behind them, before she spoke.

" Charles ! " She spoke to him with frank directness, using his name without any hesitancy. "Must you trust that dreadful man ? Let him urge you to do things that . . . that may mean trouble . . . ? "

" Connell, is it ? Watty's a rough customer, I grant you. But he knows his business. He knows how to handle these fellows. He's one of themselves. He's got his own way of dealing with them."

They were alone here in the great yard, under the stare of the gaping windows of the empty stables. Judith paused, and drew Boycott to a halt beside her. Vaguely, not fully comprehending her own fears, she regretted that she had allowed herself to be brought this way, past these empty, tumbledown stables, through this weed-grown, littered yard. All she had come to dislike in Ireland, all its squalid poverty and lurking danger, seemed to be held here in this silent yard. Here were stables echoing and empty, where the stables she had known had been lively with the jingling music of curb-chain and stirrup-iron and the soft, restless stamp of hoof. And where she had known gates thrown open to friendly roads and empty fields, here were gates barred against a hidden and unguessable danger that lurked and watched and waited its time. Fear and hatred of this country, in which she was trapped and held prisoner, swept over her.

" His way is a way that'll cause trouble," she protested. " I know that I don't understand, but I've heard you all talk—you and your mother, all of you—of the danger. But he—he seems to want to . . . to goad these people to trouble. . . ."

Here, under the streaming sunshine, the vibrant sweep of her hair catching its own golden radiance from the sun, her slender, tall body splendid in the golden light, she turned to Charles Boycott, and the violent blood came whipping into the man's face.

" Don't mind Connell and his ways," he said brusquely. " I tell you he's one of themselves. That's very likely the reason why he's harder on them than I would be. Though heaven knows," he added strongly, " they'll find me hard enough if they push me too far."

He put his hand over her hand and drew her closer to his side as they went on across the yard to the wicket gate in the angle of the wall.

" There's no need for alarm, Judith." It was surprising how gentle his voice could be, a vein of tenderness in its rough strength. " You have no cause for fear."

He unlocked the wicket. As they passed through and went on under the trees towards the flashing bright stillness of the lake, the thought came to Judith that her fear was not fear as she had sometimes known it in the thundering excitement of the hunting field—a moment of dry-mouthed panic that passed with the danger and left behind it a wild surge of exhilaration. This was a sense of danger that oppressed her, that clouded her shining air of eagerness and the gaiety that was in her.

She walked on slowly through the green shadow and leaf-entangled light beneath the trees. If she married Charles Boycott she would be caught for ever under the threatening dangers of this countryside. She turned from the bright waters that seemed to tilt away to the sky at the vista's end. He was looking down at her with a puzzled frown that touched her more than any pleading.

" I'm sorry, Charles. Do I seem silly and stupid ? " Her voice, rich and rounded, and vital with life, rang with a clear bell note in the aisles of the trees. " It's the country . . . the people . . . it all frightens me, makes me wish I could get away from it. . . ."

He had caught her hand within his own hands' clasp, urgent, vital hands. She could feel the strength and vigour flowing out of him.

" Judith ! " He said her name with a warm tenderness. " I asked you before . . . three days ago . . . to try and like the country . . . to give us all a chance of making you like it. . . ."

The very passion of earnestness that was in him brought her nearer to him in mood and in emotion. He swept on :

" I can make you like it, Judith—love it. I know that. There's so much I can do here to make you happy . . . Friends ! . . . Visits ! . . . A horse to ride ! . . . Perhaps a winter's hunting with the Blazers . . . Yes ! You'd like that. . . ."

He was like, she thought with weariness, a young and eager boy pouring out his promises and his gifts, his bribes even, with prodigal lavishness. About him there was nothing subtle or experienced. There was a simplicity, a steadfastness, that touched her to a warm glow of affection that had nothing at all in common with the ardour that had burned in her under Harry's kisses. She drew her hands out of his hands.

" I can promise to try, Charles," she said, as lightly as she could. " Perhaps I'll come to like it better. . . ."

It was not anger that darkened his eyes now, but the quick and forceful gesture of his hand was the very gesture with which he had faced his rebellious tenants such a little time ago.

" If you promise me that much," he gave back, his voice high with determination, " I'll promise you that we'll have nothing to fear, you and I, from any man, tenant or trouble-maker, in all Ireland."

CHAPTER TEN

THE little chapel whispered with sound as the congregation rustled to its feet, the shawled, stooping women and the men ponderously deliberate in every slow movement. Light poured coldly through the high window, brightening the closely-cropped greying hair of the priest as he bent over the altar. That clear cold light fell full on Father John O'Malley when he turned to face his congregation. He was silent for a moment, looking down at them, his hands folded under his vestments, his grizzled, heavy brows drawn together in a frown.

" You've a lot to put up with. You have indeed," he said abruptly. " No one knows that better than myself. You have hunger facing you. Aye ! And famine facing you. And there's few of you that's not living under the fear of the process-server and the bailiff."

He leaned back against the altar, a burly, broad man with a strong face and burning eyes.

" You have trouble and plenty to bear ; but that's no excuse for wild work or bad work, for violence." His voice thundered under the echoing roof. " Look you, now ! That was a bad night's work up yonder in Killower—a man and a neighbour that never did wrong to any one of ye, struck down in the dark of the night and maltreated and mishandled in a way you wouldn't handle a brute beast. I've seen the poor man, and

I've seen his hurts, the flesh torn from his body, his health broken. And I can tell you all now that what I saw gave me little cause to be proud of The Neale or the people of The Neale and Lough Mask."

From where he stood amongst the younger men at the chapel's end, Hugh Davin could see the shadow of pain and of anger in the priest's live eyes as he made direct reference to the attack on Mark Killian. His own mind went dark with anger at the memory of that happening—and of all that had happened since.

"I know well that what was done was the work of a few hotheads," the priest went on. "But it's work that'll do little good to any one of you. It'll do little to keep the process-server from your doors or the roofs over your heads. There's another way . . . a good way."

He paused at that, frowning down at the upturned faces before him, reluctant to speak here of the Land League and his own forceful part in it.

"Well! Maybe this isn't the time or place to talk about that," he said, and ended as abruptly as he had begun. "But let this be the end of the violent work and the bad work in this parish."

He turned again to the altar, and again the little chapel was loud with the rustling of moving bodies and the whisper of voices. In a moment the congregation began to pour through the doorway. Hugh slipped out into the sunlight before the door and stepped to one side, waiting and watching.

He was watching for Anne, and he did not take his eyes from the crowding women when Darby Haire stopped by his side.

"I see Michael Carroll at Mass, Master," the smith said quietly in Hugh's ear. "Wouldn't this morning be as fine a time as any time for us to say what we have to say to him? 'Tis our best chance of finding him sober. This morning's the first time in days that I saw him without the sign of liquor on him. Will I get him?"

Hugh was still watching the shawled women streaming through the church door. Anne had not yet appeared.

" Get him if you can, Darby. But we'll need to be careful," he warned. " There's a score and more strange police at the barracks below. They drove up in a long-car and side-cars just after Mass began."

" I saw them," the smith said easily, dismissing the warning lightly. " On their way back to Castlebar they are, likely. There was a sheriff's seizure over beyond Kilmaine, and them's likely the lads that were out from Castlebar protecting the sheriff."

" Likely enough," Hugh agreed with no great interest.

The chapel must be almost empty now, he thought. An old woman, stooped under the weight of a fawny shawl, had paused on the threshold to talk down to a slender, smart girl. But the girl was not Anne.

" Likely enough," he agreed. " But for all that we'll not trouble them. The peelers are in humour to put handcuffs on anyone they see these days ; we'll not encourage them."

" Little encouragement they'll need," the smith answered with brief bitterness. " We'll keep out of their way." His broad, pale face with its swarthy pocking was heavy with thought for a moment. " Wait now! 'Twould be better, wouldn't it, for you to walk out the lake road to . . . wait now ! . . . to the Lough Field beyont. As soon as I lay hands on Carroll, the pair of us 'll be along that way too . . ."

" That'll do grand, Darby," Hugh agreed quickly.

In the shadows just within the chapel door he had seen Anne, her head back-thrown in characteristic poise as she listened to someone out of sight of the watcher here in the outer brightness.

" That'll do grand," he said, remembering that Anne's way home to Killower would take her, too, by the lake road and the Lough Field. " Let you get hold of Carroll. . . . Make him come with you, willing or not." Hugh began to move towards the door. " It's time and past time we had a word with him. . . ."

Anne was coming now through the shadows beyond the threshold. He went forward quickly to meet her, striding through the crisp sunshine ; but within one long stride of the door he stopped short. Anne had come out into the light, but she was not alone ; Father O'Malley was with her, his head sunk into his bowed shoulders, his heavy, brooding face stooped towards the girl. He looked up at the sound of Hugh's footfall, and his live, bright eyes met the younger man's in sharp regard.

"Well met, surely," said he, his voice strong and reverberating even in the lightness of conversation. "I was telling Anne here that I'd have been away down to the school to talk to you only I guessed you'd be making a holiday of Ascension Day." There was suddenly a little edge of purpose in his voice. "And you're not easily found when you're about your own affairs, Hugh."

"I'm easy enough found, the seldom times I'm wanted, Father John," Hugh answered lightly. Not for the first time he found himself wondering how much the priest knew of these weekly meetings under the shadow of Ahalard. "Easily found."

He turned eagerly to Anne. It was the first time he had met her since that night he had walked out of her father's house. But his eagerness was dimmed by the dark uncertainty in her eyes and a new firmness in the soft line of her mouth.

"Your father, Anne ?" he asked, touched suddenly with unease. "He's no worse ?"

"And no better, Hugh." Anne's voice was quiet and friendly, but there was not in it the leap of life that could set his blood pulsing. "His hurts were worse than we thought, and the hours he was lying in the wet and cold of the ditch did him harm he'll be long enough curing. . . ."

Caught in a moment of painful silence, they moved away from the chapel door and stopped again in the village street. A quiet, as of Sunday, hung over the straggling street, but it was a quiet charged with tension. In the far-away curve of the street, between Egan's publichouse and the barracks, were drawn up a long-car and several side-cars. In the barrack door and at the door of Egan's shop two uniformed policemen kept a watchful eye on the cavalcade. A policeman pushed past the sentinel at Egan's and went striding to the barracks ;

his brisk, military swing seemed suddenly to fill the street with all the bustling alertness of an encampment.

"Long enough curing," Father O'Malley said quietly, repeating the girl's words. "That's true, Hugh. Only too true. And it's not his hurts only that'll take long enough to cure, but the memory of the savage, shameful treatment: that'll take its own long time to cure. It will indeed."

He stared down the long street to where the horses stood in patient waiting and the uniformed men watched with a stillness that was obscurely threatening.

"Long enough, Hugh. And last night's business will do little to make forgetting easy!"

"Last night's . . . Aye! That!" Hugh was suddenly cautious. "Sergeant Dempsey set himself on a fool's errand last night when he arrested Martin Mongey and John Foy for something they had no hand, act, or part in. He'll have no choice but to let them go. They weren't near Killower that night when Anne's father was hurt."

The consciousness that what he was saying was true gave conviction to his tone. Well he knew where the two men had been on that night of the attack on Mark Killian; at Ahalard they had been.

"You know that, Father. Neither of those boys had any part in injuring Anne's father. . . ."

"Maybe not, Hugh. And maybe I know that. And maybe you know it, too," the priest said slowly. "Maybe you know it, indeed." He looked up, and his eye held Hugh's eye. "But neither one nor the other of them could say where they were during the hour when Mark Killian was hurt. And 'tis that, Hugh, has them in the hands of Sergeant Dempsey."

He was watching Hugh steadily now, his head thrust forward, his gnarled, strong hands gripping the lapels of his coat.

"Aye! And that reminds me, Hugh," he said. "It reminds me of something Sergeant Dempsey said to me last night. 'Tisn't for love of me he does it, I fear, but there's times, Hugh, when the Sergeant says things to me in the hope that I'll pass them on; and there's times I don't disappoint him. . . ."

" You'll not disappoint him now ? "

" No ! Nor you either, Hugh," the priest answered with a touch of dryness. " It was a strange thing the Sergeant said—that matters might have gone hard with you if it wasn't that Anne swore for you and that her father destroyed what evidence there was against you. I don't know the ins and outs of the story, Hugh, and I didn't ask ; it sounded like a foolish tale that Watty Connell had to tell the Sergeant over a glass of Martin Egan's whiskey. But foolish or true, 'twas a strange story. A strange thing, surely. But I know that you'll not be lacking in gratitude where gratitude is due."

He put his hand lightly on the girl's shoulder, and in that fleeting moment his face was not strong and harsh but bright with kindliness.

" Away with you both," he said with surprising gentleness. " And let you both remember that there's trouble enough before all of us without making more for ourselves."

. . . .

Now the village, with its strange air of furtive quiet, was behind them and they had come out on the high ground above the lake. Here the wind swept up to them from the great spread of dancing waters, a cool, clear uprush of air in the still heat of the summer morning. The swirling air caught at them, silencing them. It was Anne who broke that silence.

" Well I know you had no part in that business, Hugh," she said, and there was weariness in her voice, as if she was tired and wearied by some inner argument. " And well my father knows it too. No ! It's not that that's keeping me from you. It's not so easy as that, Hugh. . . ."

She hesitated. The wind had whipped faint colour into her cheeks and brought a new brightness to her eyes. She looked past him, out over the dancing, sparkling waters. She was silent for a moment, leaning into the wind, so that the light stuff of her dress swirled about the slender young lines of her body. There was a hard-held nervousness about her, and a tautness that was more than nervousness.

" What is it, then ? " Even as he asked that he remembered her mother's face and her mother's tongue. " You have reason ? "

Her eyes widened and darkened. She touched his cheek gently with the tips of her fingers, and her hands were cold. Then suddenly he knew that she was afraid. He caught her gently by the wrists and drew her hands away.

" You have a reason, Anne. What is it ? "

" I don't know. God knows I don't know, Hugh." There was no doubting now the fear that leaped in her voice. " But there's some . . . some trouble hanging over us. Night after night Watty Connell is up there, whispering and colloguing. . . . And my mother: morning, noon and night her tongue is going, nagging and whispering, trying to persuade my father into something he will not do. . . ."

" It's nothing, Anne," he tried to calm her ; but the chill finger of fear had touched his own mind. " Nothing, I tell you. It's no more than that your mother is frightened. Frightened at what happened. . . ."

" It's more than that, Hugh. Night after night, when Watty goes, I can hear her voice, arguing, whispering, taking no heed of the man's sickness. And he is sick, Hugh—sicker in heart than in body. And she gives him no peace, no peace at all. . . ."

She tilted back her dark head, looking up at him.

" That's why I'll not leave him. Not for a while yet. Till his health and his heart are back in him." She drew her hands free of his hands and placed them lightly against his breast. " It wouldn't be right for me to go now, when he needs me. It wouldn't be right for me to leave him."

She dropped her hands and drew away from him. There was a swift, flashing grace in her movement. She seemed poised against the wind in readiness for flight.

" It wouldn't be right, Hugh." And then, so unexpectedly that it left him without a word of protest, she put into words the fear that was on both of them, the cause of the breach that was already widening between them under all their words. " And well we know, the two of us, Hugh, that it wouldn't be right for us to come together while all this shadow of trouble and doubt is over us. 'Tisn't that way we'd ever be happy, Hugh."

She was gone then, so quickly that he could make no move to stop her. And all the morning was empty.

CHAPTER ELEVEN

FROM the shadow of the hedges skirting the Lough Field Hugh watched the three men round the distant corner and come towards him along the road where it curved down to the lake shore. From this high viewpoint here in the shadows, the white road seemed no more than a band of pale colour drawn firmly against the wet green of the rushy fields on the lake shore. Against the clear light thrown back from the sparkling water the three men moved in black silhouette, young Stephen Nalty striding out darkly against the glare, Michael Carroll and Darby Haire a full long stride behind him. Through the far distance along the lake shore, against all the bright waste of light and water, they came swiftly; and Hugh Davin, anger and impatience in his step and in his eyes, went forward as swiftly to meet them.

They had reached the bend of the road before he came face to face with them; and the anger that was in his mind and in his heart must have showed in his face, for Michael Carroll greeted him with a vehemence that was no more than a bluster of fear.

"You're giving yourself a deal of powers, Davin," Carroll exploded violently. The glitter of anger was in his light, wild eyes, and angry colour stained his staring cheek-bones. "A deal of powers and airs of authority. With your two bully-lads hauling me here like I was a peeler's prisoner. . . ."

"The less talk there is about peeler's prisoners the better, Carroll," Hugh said quietly.

He had mastered his own anger, but the memory of Anne Killian's words was still strong, and that memory gave strength to his purpose. It was a purpose that promised little good to Michael Carroll. Davin's face, lean and dark, had in it now its own stripped hardness, and his voice was hard too.

"Over here," he said curtly. "We'll get out of sight of the road. In the trees here."

He turned off the road and led the way to the clearing beyond a low screen of wind-bent ash. Under the shelter of the trees he turned again to the others.

"There's two lads prisoners in the police barracks down there in The Neale, Carroll," he said. "It's about them we're going to talk."

He said that quietly enough, but his words took Nalty and Haire by surprise, and sudden fear looked out of Michael Carroll's eyes.

"About them? About the two that Sergeant Dempsey took last night?" The high, ugly rasp of fear was in his voice. "What have I to do with them lads?" He struck straight to the core of his own fear. "You're not saying that I'm an informer? You're not . . ."

All the abjectness of terror was in the man's voice. He began to back away, awkwardly, uncertainly. The blacksmith's hand touched him lightly on the shoulder, and he stumbled back again into the clearing amongst the trees as if a goad had stung him.

Hands deep in the pockets of his coat, the leaf of his hat shadowing his eyes, Hugh Davin watched the frightened man in silence. The shadow that hid his eyes did not mask his mouth, and his mouth was wry with pity. It was not anger that was in him now but a shamed pity at the other's fear and a wish to get this ugly business finished and done with.

"No one's leaving that at your door, Carroll. No one's saying that you informed on the lads the Sergeant arrested last night. No one is saying that." He lifted his hand to silence young Stephen Nalty's low-throated growl of anger. "As well for you that no one's saying that."

It was very quiet here in the clearing under the trees. The light sifted through the rustling leaves and patterned the faces of the men with its flickering play of light and shade. Young

Nalty moved restlessly, pushing back his cap in a meaningless, nervous gesture. The blacksmith moved a step closer to Michael Carroll and stood very still and watchful. Far and far away a voice called out loudly; for a moment that distant, bodiless voice echoed in the quiet, and then the day was still and silent again.

" As well for you, Carroll, that there's no one saying that," Hugh went on. " There'd be short shrift for the one that'd inform."

" Well so? "

Life and vitality seemed to flow back into Michael Carroll. All fear had not left him yet, but there was no mistaking the lift of relief in his voice.

" What for do you want to talk to me so? " His voice went shrill. " If 'tis about meetings and drillings and oaths you want to talk, you can save your breath; I'm done and finished with all that foolishness."

The far-off voice that had shattered the silence a moment ago called out again on a long, high-pitched shout of warning too distant to be understood. The shout dwindled to silence.

" And what have I to do with the two that were jailed last night? " Michael Carroll asked, blustering.

" Nothing! Nothing at all," Hugh answered.

He was remembering Anne's face and trying to put from his mind the knowledge that the breach which was now widening between them was of this man's making. In all rightness and fairness he must hold his mind cool and fair and clear from any personal bitterness. He stood, shoulder alean against a tree trunk and with his hat shadowing his eyes, outwardly calm; but the strain that was in him showed in the pinched white pucker of skin at mouth corner and nostril.

" But the two lads below, Carroll, are behind bars because of what happened to Mark Killian—and that was your work." His face darkened. " Your work. And the tool you used, you left there to put the blame of your handiwork on me. . . ."

Michael Carroll was no longer afraid.

" Oro ! " he laughed. " Is that the height of your trouble ? "

He whirled about, lean and lithe and venomous. He faced the other men. " And is that the work the pair of ye are doing now ? Is that the height and the end of all your drilling and swearing—to be acting the bully-lad at Hugheen Davin's beck and call . . . ? "

The smith's hand, grimed and muscled and shaggy, came down on Carroll's shoulder and spun him about with an ease that was frightening.

" Let you mind your own trouble now, Michael," he advised in that deep, grave voice of his. " Stephen and myself will look after ours. And let you not be so free with your wild talk. . . ."

But the sudden rebound from fear had loosened Michael Carroll's tongue to wildness.

" Who ever said I had hand, act or part in the 'carding' of Mark Killian? " he demanded. " And if I had itself, maybe I had cause." The wild, bright glitter was in his eyes again. He laughed into Hugh's face. " Och! Not the cause you're thinking of, man. 'Though I mind the day when Killian and his wife weren't too snug or too warm to think of me for a husband for that daughter of theirs. . . ."

Hugh's hand shot out and caught the other's wrist.

" Leave that be, Carroll," he warned. " You've made trouble enough."

Carroll drew back a step, nursing his wrist. The flame of reckless courage was dying in him.

" All right so," he said sulkily. " And let you leave me and Mark Killian be. What lies between us has nothing to do with you, and less to do with them you're drilling and swearing. And if you're drilling and swearing men to keep trouble from the daughter of a man . . ."

Very quietly Hugh Davin pushed aside the hand that young Nalty had thrust forward to restrain him. He took a long stride forward and, with a sudden hard-held fury, gripped Carroll by the throat of his shirt and swung him viciously from side to side.

" Listen you here to me, Carroll," he said with a controlled violence that drained the last vestige of colour out of the other's haggard face. "Listen well to me! The day for wild talk and wild work is past. There's trouble ahead of us all, and neither you nor anyone else, man or woman, has the right to make that trouble worse. Neither you nor anyone else," he said again, "man or woman . . ."

Far away the voice that had shattered the silence a little time before came echoing again through the stillness. A chorus of voices took up the cry, and the clamour of shouting voices tossed and echoed wildly. Horns were blowing now, and a booming trumpet note bellowed and moaned hideously above the din.

"They're 'driving.' 'Tis a Sheriff's seizure. That's what the peelers were brought in for this morning. They're 'driving' for rent, and the crowd's out to rouse the country and clear the stock out of harm's way before the Sheriff's men come to it."

It was young Nalty who spoke. He caught Michael Carroll's arm and held it in a vice-grip, laughing down excitedly at his prisoner with that white, flashing smile of his.

"Let you wait here a minute, Michaeleen," he said. "If we're to miss the fun, we'll miss it all together. . . ."

They moved, all four of them, through the trees to the low wall from which the high ridge of ground fell away to the distant village. Michael Carroll struggled in an effort to tear his arm free from Nalty's grip.

"Let me go, damn you!" he shouted. His voice rose to a shrill, edged scream. "There's work to do down there. . . ."

Hugh Davin was the first to reach the low wall. He scrambled on to it, shading his eyes from the sun glare as he made out the sudden, wild activity in the far-off fields.

"They're too far away from us to be any help to them," he said curtly over Carroll's protests. "They're moving off beyond The Neale . . . Towards Glasson . . . Away from us. . . ."

In silence, Carroll still held in Stephen Nalty's iron grip, they watched.

The fields and low hills beyond the village were hiving with life. Out of the throat of the village street a body of policemen spewed blackly and spread out into a fan-shaped, thin line across the patchwork of little fields. At a walk, at a trot, at a canter, horse-police swept round a bend of the town road, topped the low fence and drove forward with a jingle of sabre and curb towards the hill-tops where the wild clamour of horn and bugle and shouting voice was carrying warning ahead that the grippers and drivers were on their way.

Over the far hillsides the wave of excitement ebbed and passed. Calling, bugling, the warning outposts surged out of sight beyond the hill. In open formation, their carbines threateningly at the trail, the policemen stumbled heavily and stolidly up the slope. On the rim of the hill, prancing magnificently, the horsemen reformed into line and swept forward in a black, ominous group.

Some trick of the wind, flawing and losing itself in a distant fold of the hills, for a moment cut off from the listeners the far-away clamour, and in that moment the distant, emptied scene had about it a frightening air of devastation.

" They'll not get much," Hugh Davin said, but not easily. There was an unaccountable chill of unease in his mind. " I wonder what brought them that direction at all. There was no more than six notices served out towards Glasson. . . ."

" What matter whether 'twas six or sixty," Darby Haire answered, a deep roll of satisfaction in his voice. " The great thing is that the warnings got out in time. There'll not be a hoof or a horn seized between Glasson and The Neale to-day. . . ."

The wind had died again, and the clamour came to them more faintly from farther and farther away. They listened to it in silence. Hugh Davin listened with but half his mind. The trouble that he had seen ahead, that he knew must lie ahead, had come. In that moment his anger against Michael Carroll seemed of little account; the trouble was there, shadowing them all; shadowing Michael Carroll; shadowing his own self; and most of all, he knew with sudden fear shadowing Anne Killian.

He turned away from the emptied fields and from the far, faint shouting. And as he turned he saw the wide stare of fear in Michael Carroll's eyes.

"Look! Look!" Carroll was pointing not towards the distant fields but to the nearer shoulder of Killower Hill, the ridge of hill that hid his own small house. "Look!" he shouted. "The drive yonder was no more than a blind to draw the people away towards Glasson. Look! 'Tis this way the real business lies. . . ."

Along the brow of the hill a score of horsemen were strung out in a fast swinging gallop. Down to the low wall facing the hill path thudded the riders. Stooping, steadying a little, hands down, booted heels rapping back, the trim, bearded Sheriff's officer lifted his mount over the jump. Ring of metal on stone, thud of hoof on sun-dried turf, and Charles Boycott was beside him, straight-backed, heavy-handed, feet rammed home in long-leathered military stirrups. Behind them, lurching and slewing in the saddle of a brute that scrambled like a cat through the fallen stones of the wall, Watty Connell rode, a desperate length clear of the horse-police. For a long moment the cavalcade showed against the hill, and then, with a drum of racing hooves in the stony path, clattered out of sight towards the lakeward side of Killower, towards Michael Carroll's house.

"Look at them," Carroll rasped. "'Tis for my place they're heading. My place! And you held me here till the harm was done. . . ."

He clawed at his ragged coat, pulling it loose, and with a twist of his shoulders drew himself free, leaving the coat in Nalty's hand. A wild, lithe leap carried him over the wall. He turned towards Killower, running.

"After him." The runner was over the nearer field and was scrambling into the laneway before Hugh Davin found his voice. "Stop him, lads. There's no knowing what harm he'll do himself. No knowing what wild foolishness he'll try. . . ."

But there was no wildness left in Michael Carroll when they came up with him at length in the pathway near his house. He was leaning against the loose-stone wall, silent and savage, his shoulders hunched under his ragged shirt, his burning eyes on the group about the door.

Bailiffs and policemen had been quick about their work. In the pathway, on public ground, lay the miserable poor furnishings of Carroll's house, the stools, the table, the straw sack that had served as a bed. The cabin still stood, and a policeman was busy now hammering fast a padlock on the closed door.

Michael Carroll watched in sullen silence. All his interest and attention seemed centred now on the bright padlock which barred his house against him. He stood very still, listening to the thud of the hammer blows.

He did not speak when Hugh Davin and the others closed in beside him. Nor did he, beyond a low mutter of wordless rage, speak when the Sheriff's officer came stamping round the gable of the cabin, behind him two mounted constables herding between them a high rangy gelding that sidled on rapping hooves over the stones, jibbing and fretting, its reddish eyes agleam in the deep sockets of its bony skull.

He did not speak then, but when the last of the hollow hammer-blows had echoed in the quiet, he spoke. It was not to Boycott, nor to the bailiff who watched him expectantly, that he spoke, but to Hugh Davin.

" They barred that door for their own reason, Davin. They left the roof on that house o' mine for their own reason. They left the roof to put another under it," he said. All the life and colour was drained out of his voice ; nothing was left now save a savage, black bitterness. " But the one that walks in through that door under that roof answers to me. He answers to me, Hugh Davin, in spite of any man."

He threw back his head, brushing out of his wild eyes the ragged glib of yellow hair that had come tumbling down across them.

" In spite of any man—or any woman."

CHAPTER TWELVE

In the shadowy, cool cave of the loose-box the horse that had been Michael Carroll's was moving on dancing, restless feet, snorting and whistling still in remembered fear of all this cruel, unfamiliar business of shears and currycomb. The groom, dodging swiftly past the rapping hooves, slammed shut the half-door between him and the horse. His darting eyes looked sidelong out of his wizened face at Watty Connell.

"He was good enough buying in his way, yon lad, Watty," he said. He had a soft, persuasive voice, this Martin Brannigan, the Captain's groom, and a mind that itched with curiosity. "A good enough horse, once the devil would be worked out of him." The darting eyes slid sidelong in appraisal. "But no horse at all for a lady, Watty. No horse for a lady."

"D'you tell me?"

Watty gave all his attention to the cat that was ranging through the pied light and shadow at the yard's end. He crossed one gaitered leg over the other and set his shoulder comfortably against the wall.

"D'you tell?" he asked blandly. "And you tell me 'tis for a lady the Captain has the horse intended?"

"Who else?" The groom straddled before the dark doorway, hands deep in breeches pockets, his narrow, grizzled head cocked, birdlike. "Wasn't he down here to me yesterday before the Sheriff's men brought the horse up from the Pound at all? And, 'Brannigan,' says he, 'let you look out that old side-saddle and the light curb, for we've a horse coming in that'll suit a lady.' That bate all, Watty. I just looked at the Captain, and says I: 'If it's the big black horse of Michael Carroll's you're talking about, Captain, you're a damned poor judge of a lady's mount.' My very words, Watty."

Watty took his pipe from his mouth and spat far into the sunlight. He did not look at the groom. All his attention seemed concentrated on the cat which had been frozen to watchfulness, tail alash, in the shadows. His mouth tightened again about his pipe stem.

"Tell me, Martin," he asked softly. "Wasn't it powerful smart of you to know that the Captain was after buying-in Carroll's horse?" He knocked out his pipe and peered into the empty bowl. "The Captain himself hadn't a notion of buying till the Sheriff's sale was near-hand over. And still and all, you knew all about it, and you a good two miles away here in the yard. Powerful clever that was, Martin. Powerful clever."

His hat was over his eyes, shadowing them; his wide shoulders slouched against the wall. His face gave no tidings of his thoughts, and his thoughts were sullenly angry.

Boycott's purchase of the horse at the sale had been rank foolishness, he told himself. He was remembering the scene down there in the Pound, under the shadow of the barrack wall: the sheep and cattle, the fretting black horse; the lines of dark-coated policemen; the sullen, silent crowd packed tight about the walls of the Pound, watching silently while beast after beast was auctioned and sold for paltry sums to furtive bidders who had taken their stand under cover of the police carbines.

And the Captain! The hard, thin mouth twisted in its own grin of sour humour and cynical judgment. The Captain had sat watching from the high seat of his dog-cart, his visiting friend beside him, her yellow hair piled high over the sun-tinted bold mask of her face, her stormy eyes alight with interest.

Thoughtfully Watty rapped the stem of his pipe against his teeth. Aye! He could see her in his mind's eye, her eyes following every movement of the great black horse as the Sheriff's officer paraded him before the voiceless crowd. He could see the supple, strong curves of her as she leaned towards Boycott, the eagerness of her live mouth, the flash of light in her eyes as Boycott stooped over the rail of the gig and began to bid.

Foolish! Foolish! Watty told himself sourly. The quiet way was ever and always the best way, once the first bold move of seizing the horse was safely over. After that, the right thing to do was to let one of the strange buyers from Mullingar or Parsonstown or Athlone finish the job that the Sheriff had begun. Boycott's own buying of the horse was foolishness—foolishness that might give the hotheads in the village an excuse for troublemaking. And now here was the groom admitting that he had known of his master's purchase almost as soon as it had been made.

His head bowed on his broad, stooped shoulders, Watty slid a slow, caressing hand over his chin. That was queer now. Queer indeed. Could it be that already plans for making trouble were afoot? He remembered now that he had seen Hugh Davin and one or two others move away early from the watching crowd. All the slow, uncertain dislike of Hugh Davin that had smouldered in him during the weeks past flamed now in his mind—but not openly.

" Would it be your friend Davin that told you, Martin? " he asked easily. " If it was, he was quick with his news."

The groom's wizened face puckered into a network of laughter lines. His darting, quick eyes met the bailiff's squarely. He put aside his shears and currycomb and began to button himself into his coat.

" Have sense, Watty," he jibed. " I'd go long waiting for me news if I was to wait for the like of Davin to bring it. 'Twas old Ned Sears brought me the word, an' me down watering the work-horses. Likely enough 'twas the Captain gave Nedeen the message to bring me."

He fastened the last button of his coat and tucked his shears out of sight. He was a lithe, youngish man for all his wizened face, and he wore Watty Connell's dislike of him lightly.

" Up and out of that with you, Watty." He lowered his voice as he moved away sprucely to the stable door. " And now, maybe, you'll believe me that 'tis for a lady's mount the horse is intended."

And indeed Judith Wynne's riding habit, green as a green leaf, and the riding hat she wore crammed down on her yellow hair, told plainly for whom the horse had been bought.

She came across the yard, a light hand on Boycott's arm, crop rapping on boot in a rat-tat-tat of excited anticipation.

" Ready, Brannigan? " she asked. The tempestuous stormy light lit her eyes. The throb of her excitement was in her voice. " Bring him out and we'll see how he goes."

" Careful! You'll be careful, Judith. This horse has been ridden as often bare-backed as with a saddle, and never with a side-saddle."

Concern, fear, an unashamed tenderness: they softened Charles Boycott's voice and robbed it of its normal rough strength. Watty listened to that weakened voice with concern that was not entirely selfish. Weakness! At this very moment when strength was more than ever needed. He considered Judith Wynne sourly.

" Nothing to be nervous about," she was saying. The quick, breathless air of excitement sat well on her. She moved towards the stable door on a quick, dancing step, as if on tip-toe. " I'll be quite safe. I'll manage him."

The horse had come out now, sidling and rushing against the pull of the groom at its head.

" Here, Watty! " The girl gathered her skirts about her boots and flicked free the thong of her crop. " A hand! A stirrup-hand! This way! "

In a lithe, swift movement she was up on to the black. Plunging, jibbing against the unaccustomed saddle, the horse fought with lashing fore-feet man-high from the ground. The great curve of neck arched like whalebone against bit and rein. The crop slashed down, once and again, savagely, and horse and rider went pounding through the stable arch and down under the long colonnade of trees that led to The Neale road.

The clamour faded, and quiet flowed back slowly into the yard and about the three men. From far away, from outside that core of quiet, came the drum of hooves, fading into the distance. Boycott whirled round on the groom.

" Get a saddle on the mare, Brannigan," he rapped out. " Quickly ! We'd no right to let her up on that horse. She'll kill herself. . . ."

"Devil a kill," Watty Connell said flatly.

He looked back over his shoulder, waiting until the groom had gone hurrying from the harness-room to the stable. Then:

"Devil a kill that lady will kill herself, Captain," he said. "No better seat nor hands on a horse did I see in my life. But if it's for The Neale she's headed now, she's likely to stir up a deal of trouble. . ."

Boycott, all his impatient interest centred on the stable, answered him impatiently.

"What the devil is worrying you now ?" he snapped. "The trouble-makers made little enough trouble yesterday."

"Aye ! And that's one good reason why we'd be better to let yesterday's business end yesterday." To the last strained inch Watty well knew how far he could venture under the threat of Boycott's temper. He went on doggedly : "The sooner yesterday's sale is forgotten, the better. And yon horse stravaging round the country-side 'll not help to make people forget. 'Twill cause a deal of bitterness. Give Carroll and his likes room and cause for complaining. . . ."

The groom had led out the big three-quarter bred mare. Impatiently Charles Boycott caught the reins and stooped to give a testing pull to saddle girths.

"Carroll and those like him will find cause and plenty for complaint." He gripped the pommel and thrust a foot into stirrup-iron. Over the bay's withers he eyed the bailiff. "That empty cabin of Carroll's will be a better reminder of yesterday's affair than any horse. If there isn't a tenant put into it quickly, it might be better policy to let Carroll back there."

With that he swung stiffly into the saddle of the bay and, with a rap of heel on rib, went clattering out of the yard, down the road under the trees.

Martin Brannigan watched him go, his wizened face puckered with laughter.

"Me poor man," said he. "It's a hard life, Watty. Between women and horses and the devil knows what . . ."

Watty Connell had no time to waste on the groom or on the groom's jibing. That remark of Captain Boycott had gone home and was rankling. It rankled because he knew well that it was true ; true that until he made good his promise and put a new tenant into Carroll's evicted farm, only one-half of the plans he and Boycott had made had been carried out.

He put away his wooden pipe and crammed his hat far down over his bright, cold eye. He headed for the yard gate.

"Hell roast them all," was all he said. "But maybe where one woman will harm another woman will mend."

He swung through the gateway, a stick aslant on the crook of his arm, and took the road to Killower on his squat man's wide and rolling stride.

CHAPTER THIRTEEN

THE men had drifted in slowly in twos and threes, pausing in the dingy bar-room of Egan's shop to talk or drink for a little before coming here to the stifling room where light came crookedly in wavering, dust-darkened shafts through windows set low in walls so monstrously bulged and thickened that they seemed to slant in upon the room in a crazy threat of collapse. And now, for an hour and more, they had talked and argued and planned.

The hum of voices, pitched a shade high with excitement and strain, died away to an uneasy muttering as old Martin Egan's voice boomed out in sudden urgency.

"Let that be an end to the argument and waste of time," he urged. "The men here were the men chosen to do the job when the time came." He had lifted to his feet and was facing them, stooping over the back of his chair. "The time is here now and everyone knows what he has to do. What is there then but to do it—and let there be an end to this talking. We'll deal with Boycott now as we said we'd deal with him. Just that."

Just that! But it was not so easy as that, Hugh Davin thought bleakly as he watched the old man's quick, compelling gestures, the live eagerness of the old bright eyes, the quick, mobile mouth in its frame of white beard.

It would not be easy, he thought bitterly. His own bitterness was heavy upon him, darkening and shadowing all his enthusiasm and eagerness. Even now, three full weeks after that bitter moment on Ascension Day, he could not rid his mind of the uncertainty in Anne Killian's eyes. It was that cloud of unhappiness, more even than the breach that was widening between them, that darkened his mind.

It was easy to make plans, easy to arrange this man's punishment or that man's penalty. But behind every man punished and behind every penalty would be those who would suffer without having done anything to deserve punishment or penalty. . . .

He jerked himself upright in the hard wooden seat, so that the sudden slight pain and discomfort broke the softly-flowing, sullen stream of his thoughts. There was work to be done, and it was too late now to question the way of doing it.

" Just that, Martin," he called out in sudden recklessness. " What are we delaying for so ? "

As if his voice had been spark to the tinder of their own suppressed excitement, a flame of talk flickered through the room. Out of that sudden uprush of voices Michael Carroll's voice sounded harshly.

" What manner of good will what ye're set on doing," he demanded, " do me or them that was gripped and seized on by the Sheriff three weeks ago ? "

He hurtled that question into the crowded room, but there was little doubting that it was to Hugh Davin he spoke. Over the heads of the crowd his eyes challenged Hugh, his eyes light and wild under the falling glib of hair.

" Answer me that, Davin," he demanded. " What good will it do me, that had every penn'orth and ha'porth taken from me . . . ? "

Wildness was in his eyes and a film of sweat beaded his face. To-day, as on every day for weeks past, he had been drinking heavily, and the feverish sense of injury that racked him was burning now in him like a flame.

" We're doing the best we can," Hugh answered him evenly. He had no wish to goad the man's crazy temper to madness. "What was done to you is one reason we're here to-day. . . ."

"And a deal of good that'll do me." The yellow hair was swept back angrily from the fevered eyes. "Look! The horse that was seized on me was value, and twice value, and three times over value for the few shillings of rent I owed. Twice and three times. Every man here knows that. In the fair of Balla or Westport that horse would make the rent money three times over. . . ."

The angry voice woke anger in the crowded room. The muttering, low voices were sullen as a gathering storm. The crooked, dusty light fell on faces dark with passion, lighting here the smouldering fire in a sunken eye, shadowing there the strong line of a bearded jaw.

". . . and now they have the horse they stole from me for Boycott's fancy-woman to ride," Carroll went on wildly. "And Connell, the bailiff, boasting from one end of the parish to the other that he'll have a new man in on my floor under my roof before the month's out."

The strident anger went out of his voice. It was suddenly flat and colourless—and infinitely threatening.

"Under my roof! But, by Heaven! the man that stands on my floor answers to no Committee or no League. He answers to me, and to me only. . . ."

"Leave that be, Michael Carroll." It was Egan's voice, with an unaccustomed rasp of authority in it. "The day a man takes your house and farm, or the house and farm any man is evicted out of, we'll deal with him in our way. And now we'll do the work that's before us to-night."

He turned briskly to the men, pointing first to one and then another.

"You, Darby! And you, James! Peter! Yourself, John! Ye know the men ye're to talk to and ye know what ye have to say to them."

The light eyes under the grizzled brow considered Hugh Davin.

"And yourself, Master," he said. "You have the job of talking to the men at Lough Mask House itself." The red lips moved in a smile against the white beard. " 'Tis a tricky, hard part we gave you, but we know you won't fail us this time—or any time. You'll start now? "

All the men were watching him, waiting for his answer. What he had to do now, Hugh knew, was a little thing, but it would be the first blow in the fight that was before them. Any slowness now in striking that blow might quench the fire that had been lit in these men.

In the moment while he was coming to his feet and pushing away his chair, he saw those faces that turned towards him, watching and waiting ; he saw them in the light of their own eagerness. No man could take the blame for helping to quench that light of eagerness and hope ; it was something that mattered more than any one man's happiness. He pushed away his chair, listening to the rasp of the chair leg on the flagged floor.

" I'm ready to start now, Martin. The sooner we start the better," he said. He could sense the sudden easing of strain in the room ; it was a relaxing into relief at a decision made finally and irrevocably. " 'Twon't take me long to do all I have to do."

. . . . . .

It was later than he thought it would be by the time he had finished the duty assigned to him ; but the sense of accomplishment, of work well done, was strongly upon him, and he was happier than he had been for weeks as he made his way homeward from Lough Mask House through the cool evening light.

He came by hidden lanes and field paths, cautiously, until he reached the open road beyond Killower. Where the road forked below the hill, his swinging walk slowed to a saunter, to a dawdle. And where the trees of the demesne arched across the road, he swung himself on to the low wall and set himself to wait, cold pipe clenched between his teeth and shoulder alean against a slanting tree, his hat pulled down over brooding eyes.

The last of the day was no more than a brilliant splash of orange light low down on the horizon of the toneless grey sky when Anne came, as he knew she must come.

She had come out of the light into the dim tunnel of shadows beneath the trees before she saw him, and as he slipped down from his waiting place and came towards her, she stood poised in the dusk, as if on the point of startled fright. He called out, stirred by her alarm.

" It's all right, Anne." He went towards her quickly. " There's nothing to be frightened about. Nothing."

He had not seen her in the three weeks since their last unhappy meeting, and now he was shocked by the change those few days had made in her. There was an edged, strained air about her. Her mouth was hard held, and strain had drawn fine, taut lines from mouth to nostril. Only her eyes were brave.

" You're frightened, Anne? Afraid? " His voice was very gentle. Whatever breach lay between them, now or ever, would not be widened by anger. " What is it? "

She had recognized him even before he spoke, and her air of fright passed. She laughed softly on an outrushing air of relief and drew forward her head shawl until she looked out at him from the shadowy depths of the snood. He could no longer clearly see her face.

" Frightened? " Her voice came with a little rush. " What else would you expect and you lying in wait like that. I thought . . ."

" What did you think? "

" Nothing! It's no matter. It was just seeing you there, not expecting you, not expecting anyone."

He fell into step beside her, and together they moved out of the shadows into the pale light beyond. They walked for a few moments in uneasy silence, fumbling for words. Hugh looked down at her, at her head shawled against him and at the fine, lovely line of shoulder and breast.

" Only that? " he said. " Is that all, Anne? Is there nothing else? "

" Where's the use, Hugh? " Her voice rose on a little note

of pain. " Didn't we say all there was to say that last day? " She drew the shawl closer, her hand white against the black stuff. " Things are no better and little worse than they were then." A passionate note of protest throbbed in her voice. " Ach! Leave it be, Hugh. Leave me and mine be. 'Twill be better for you, better for all of us. If we're afeard up there on Killower, maybe we have people to fear and good reason to fear them."

She was walking more quickly now, and he had to lengthen his stride to match her hurry.

" People to fear? " His mind leaped to the memory of Michael Carroll's face and voice. " What people? You can trust me, Anne."

" I can trust you, Hugh. And can we trust your friends? Or can you trust your friends? "

They had reached the side turning of the road that led to her father's house. Here she paused, the shawl fallen back on her shoulders.

" My friends? "

" One of them, then. The strange American man that comes from Westport." She must have read aright the thought in his eyes, for she went on quickly. " Where's the use of pretending, Hugh. It isn't once or twice, but a score of times I saw the man here. And I'm not the only one. There's few had cause to go next or nigh Ahalard didn't see him—and guess what brought him."

" You have no cause to fear James Hannin," Hugh said with conviction. " He has no business here that need trouble you or yours."

" No? Still he was here the night my father . . . was . . . was hurt . . ."

" He had nothing to do with that work. That night he was with me."

" With you? And a week ago I saw him on the road near Michael Carroll's house. And late, after dark, on Thursday night, he was here. And this very evening, Hugh, not half an hour ago, he came down past Killower to wait for the Mail Car on the lower road. What business takes him to Killower,

Hugh? What reason has he to be there one night or another? "

Hugh Davin's face told nothing of his thoughts, and his thoughts were in a whirl of confusion. There was no reason, no smallest reason, for James Hannin's coming here during recent weeks. There was no shadow of reason for the American's strange secrecy. And if he had come his comings had been secret, for Hugh had heard no word of them. It was one thing to keep his movements secret from the police; but from his own . . .?

" Are you sure of this, Anne? Certain? I know nothing of it."

" Nothing? " The sudden hardness in her voice stopped him. " Nothing? " she asked again. " And it wasn't you parted from the American man up there in the fields half an hour ago? 'Twasn't with you he was all evening, since he came walking in by Cong three hours ago . . .? "

" To be sure it wasn't. I never laid eyes on the man for three weeks past . . . for three weeks or more. I didn't see him this evening. This evening I was . . ." He hesitated, remembering the business that had brought him to the yards of Lough Mask House and uncertain of how much he had a right to tell of his doings. " What matter? It makes little difference where I was."

Anne had pulled off her head-shawl and was folding and re-folding it between restless fingers.

" No," she said very quietly. " It makes no difference."

On the heels of her words, somewhere out of sight on the hill slope, a door creaked loudly and a dog set up a brief barking. A voice came trailing, echoing and wordless, into the quiet evening.

" That's Watty Connell," Anne went on quickly. " I have no mind to meet him now, and I doubt but you have less."

The wall was low and gapped near where they stood. Before Hugh could speak she had climbed quickly across it and was moving swiftly and silently away in the shadow of a hedge that would bring her, unobserved, to the house.

For a moment Hugh stood where she had left him. Then, from beyond the turn, he heard the shuffle and thud of iron-paved boots on the gravel of the lane, and he, too, moved quickly away down the road and stood in the deep shade beneath the hedge until Watty Connell had passed.

CHAPTER FOURTEEN

THE bailiff passed on his squat man's wide and rolling stride, the rap of his stick and the thud of his heavy football loud in the dusk.

He was well pleased with his day's work. All about him, for weeks, for months past, he had sensed the gathering anger of the tenants, their desperate recklessness. An angry mood. And the way to meet that angry mood was face to face, giving back blow for blow. Under the twisted, down-pulled leaf of his hat his mouth twisted in its own grin of cynical humour. Aye! Well he had prepared for the striking of his blow, a blow that would show who was still master at Lough Mask. He paused at the bend of the hill road and stood stooping over his stick, looking up at the dark, empty shell of Michael Carroll's house. In a week, two weeks at most, he would have a tenant under that roof, in spite of Land League, Moonlighter or hillside man. He stood for a moment longer looking at the empty house, remembering Ellen Killian's face and the desire that was stronger than fear.

" A great woman. A grand, clever woman," said Watty Connell. " And twice the man of that crawling husband of hers."

With a last look at the dark house, Watty trudged down the boreen and came to the road that led down to Lough Mask House and the lake which lay darkly shining like a mirror in the dusk.

Ahead of him, in the darker gloom which was already thickening under the beeches over-arching the road, a group of men had gathered, twenty, thirty, more of them. Connell quickened his step and tapped his bulging coat over the brace of pistols. He swung level with the watching men.

" 'Night, boys," he sang out in a voice loud with bravado. " A fine soft night. 'Tis holding up well."

No voice answered him. He went past the man who stood half-hidden in the gloom, silent and inimical. As he passed, the silent watchers fell into step behind him. More quickly the bailiff strode forward, and behind him now was not silence but the shuffle and thud of brogued feet in the June dust. Terror added a long inch to his stride, and behind him the beat of marching feet grew louder in the dusk. The open gate of Lough Mask House loomed before him, and beyond that open gate lay safety. He began to run.

. . . . . .

Breathless, the cold fear of those lonely moments on the lake road still touching him, he poured out his story to his employer ; Captain Boycott listened with gathering anger.

" So they'd threaten me? " he said quietly. " Threaten me here at the very door of my own house? "

" The devil a threaten, Captain." Watty was regaining his own dour humour. " Not a single, solitary word had them lads out there to say, threat or promise. Not a word out of them. Not "—he grinned crookedly—" that I'd say they hadn't a small notion of ducking me in the lake. But 'twas me they had that in mind for, not for you, Captain." He laughed throatily, his eye on the open door that led from the shadowy hallway in which they stood to the lighted drawing-room. " 'Twas me they had in mind."

Boycott paid no heed to him. He paused, with his hand on the heavy locking bolt of the door ; then, with an angry gesture, he shot the bolt back, leaving the door unbarred.

" Damned if I'll bar my door against them," he said harshly. " If they think they can threaten me, they've a lesson yet to learn."

He spoke loudly, and his voice carried clearly to the two women in the lamplit room. From where he stood Watty could see them both in that moment of alarm. Caroline Boycott's shapely greying head was thrown back in startled surprise, her eyes dark with fear. She came to her feet in a swift, frightened flurry of movement. The slender, tall girl who sat where the light fell in waves of golden radiance through the mesh of her yellow hair on the dusky paleness of neck and shoulder, did not move at all, but every slender, strong line of her was strung taut with alarm at the rough threat in Boycott's voice.

"Charles! What is it? What has caused the trouble?" Caroline Boycott's voice was cold and clear as a bell. "All the deplorable business about that horse, I feel sure."

Watty saw the quick flicker of colour to the girl's face, the clouding of her vivid, stormy eyes. He tucked away into the recesses of his mind the memory of that sudden flicker of colour and the memory of the older woman's bitter tone. Some day he might need to remember again both these things.

"A deplorable business," the older woman said again, venomously.

"Too late to think about that now," Boycott answered with a roughness that silenced her. "Too late to waste time talking about it."

He strode heavily across the hallway and threw open the door leading to the servants' quarters. He sent his strong voice volleying down the empty corridor.

"Bridget! Delia! One of you. Tell Brannigan have the dog-cart round within ten minutes. I'm driving to Ballinrobe."

To Watty Connell he added:

"The District Inspector in Ballinrobe 'll give us all the police protection we require, Connell; and when the police get here . . ."

He broke off as a young maid-servant entered the hallway. The girl hesitated for a moment, crumpling her apron in nervous fingers.

"If you please, Captain," she began, "Brannigan isn't here. It's how there came a man into the yard a while back to talk to him, a strange man, a man I never laid eyes on before," she added. She was lying, Watty Connell knew. Well she knew who the man was. "A strange man. And himself and Brannigan did a deal of talking. And after a wee bit, Brannigan up and off with him."

"Get one of the others, girl: Conroy, Mullaney, O'Hara . . ."

"It's how they're gone, too, your honour," the girl blurted

out. "Them and the two young lads and the man from the garden." She plucked nervously at her apron. "And Bridget's away, too, sir, and the wee one from the kitchen with her. And if it's equal to you, Captain," said she, "I'd as soon take my own wages the morrow's morn and be off home to my own people in Cong."

For a long time after the girl had gone, Captain Boycott did not speak. He stood by the hall window looking out over the sweep of lawn and woodland falling away to the lake shore. He looked out into the twilight facing the fact that would not be denied: the tenants had found courage to take the advice that Davitt and Parnell were thundering to them from end to end of the country, day in, day out.

He was recalling those words of Parnell, as he had read them only a few weeks ago:

". . . by leaving him severely alone, by putting him into a moral Coventry, by isolating him from his kind as if he were a leper of old. . . ."

"A leper of old!" Charles Boycott repeated the words. "A leper of old!"

Let them try that! He turned away from the window. Across the darkening hallway he saw, in the room beyond, the girl watching him out of widened, startled eyes. He shivered a little in the gathering chill of the evening, but his iron mouth and hot, intolerant eyes told their own tale of resolution.

"Connell," he promised. "I have close on three hundred pounds' worth of crops standing to-day, and as God's my Judge, I'll save every sheaf and ear of those crops in spite of Parnell, Davitt, or the Devil himself."

CHAPTER FIFTEEN

All through the long days of June the rooms and farms and yards of Lough Mask House had been heavy with idleness. No man would save the Captain's crops, no one would drive his car, the smith would not shoe his horses, the laundress would not wash for him, the grocer would not supply him with goods, the very postman would not deliver his letters.

But to-day, under a lowering morning sky that threatened a day of rain, there was suddenly in the air a new sense of strain, a new tautness. Sound carried far under that purple, bruised sky, and the village street echoed with the trot of hooves long before the dog-cart came bowling down the road from Ballinrobe and swung into the street. Erect and soldierly, his hat crammed down over angry eyes, Charles Boycott sat stiffly beside the girl who held the driving reins. The poised, alert driving position stressed and emphasized every strong and supple line of the girl. She leaned forward a little in her seat, a smooth line of power sweeping from shoulder to wrist and through the slender long lines of the reins to the horse's straining head. More than ever, on this morning of threatening storm, she was touched with her own unique air of eager expectation. An eager excitement brightened her face now as she swung the trotting horse to a halt before the open door of the forge.

" Haire ! Darby Haire ! " Boycott's voice rang out in the leaden quiet. He leaned back against the boxes and bales which were piled high on the rear seat of the gig. " Quickly there."

Darby Haire took his own time coming to the open door. He stood in the doorway against the anvil-hearth light, a small, squat, imperturbable man. His eye lifted and went past Captain Boycott to the street beyond. The street was fuller of life now than it had been a moment ago. A band of shouting, curious children were racing helter-skelter past the chapel gates. Here and there, at open doorways, men and women had found urgent reason to take them abroad. Hugh Davin had left the house in which he lodged and, with books under arm, was coming slowly and unheedingly towards the forge and the school-house beyond it.

" You were looking for me, Captain ? " The smith transferred his regard from the street to the gig. He considered the girl gravely for a moment, and then his eye met Boycott's eye steadily. " Something you wanted ? "

" I'm not so sure that I do want anything now, Haire." In Boycott's voice was a lively lift of excitement that stirred the smith to deeper interest. " I sent for you three times this week. There was work to be done, work urgently needed for the haymaking. You didn't come."

The smith's roving eye went over the boxes and packets piled on the rear seat. Foodstuffs and the like, brought all the way from Ballinrobe, as they had been brought these two weeks past. But to-day there was more, much more than usual. Strange ! And strange, too, the glint of excitement in Boycott's eye and voice and the girl's air of eagerness.

" What's your hurry, Captain ? " he asked easily. His trade and his freedom from a tenant-farmer's inheritance of fear made it easy for him to take on an air of independence. " You'll not be starting your haymaking for a while and a bit yet."

Voices carried far in that still, airless day. All the village seemed to be watching, listening. Hugh Davin drew level, sauntering unhurriedly. Leaning back against the rail of the gig, Boycott looked down at him and at the smith.

" Haymaking," he said. His voice rang. " We'll be at the haymaking soon enough. And with workers "—he looked down at Davin—" with workers who won't be whistled away by the first glib talker that comes along."

The reins rippled and ran in a long, shimmering line under the deft, expert lift of the girl's hands. The horse swung out into mid-street, struck his pace at a trot and a canter and stretched out into a gallop. The gig whirled away in a cloud of dust down the Lake Road. In the still air the jingling of harness was loud as the chiming of little bells.

For a little time the smith stood listening to the dwindling thud of hooves. He turned to Hugh Davin, his eyes narrowed in thought.

" The first glib talker," he said reflectively. " Could it be that he knew you were the man brought the lads out from the yard ? "

Hugh Davin, watching the empty road, smiled. That swift, flashing smile lit his face with sudden quick life. His eyes seemed to leap to life under the dark shadow of his brows.

" If Boycott was anyway sure of that, it'd be a poor lookout for me, Darby." He hitched the books under his arm, tapping out a quick tattoo on the covers. " No ! He doesn't know who was the man brought his men out. And he doesn't care—not to-day." That lean, dark face was masked with thought again. " He has more on his mind than that to-day, Darby. I wonder what ? "

They could still hear the faint, far-off jingle of hoof and harness. The dying sounds whispered faintly and more faintly in the ominous silence.

" Leave him be," said Darby Haire placidly. " He's a stubborn, stiff man ; and he'll take his own time to learn when he's beaten."

He leaned against the door-jamb, between the shadow and the light, the leaping fire within outlining him redly, the sullen storm-light on his face.

" Leave him be," he said again. " We'll likely have our own full fill of trouble before the summer's out. And talking of trouble ! " He turned from the street. " Amby Nolan brought word this morning on the mail car that James Hannin will be over from Westport to-day. He'll be wanting to see you."

For days, since he had last talked to Anne, thoughts of James Hannin and puzzled wonder at the American's covert comings and goings had been uppermost in Hugh's mind.

" Not nearly as much as I'll be wanting to see him, Darby." He shifted the books under his arm and straightened out of his tall man's slouch. " If ever there was a time we needed to keep our heads, this is the time. And James Hannin . . ."

He left those words unfinished, but the smith ended them for him.

" James Hannin is apt to go his own way. Well ! You have your chance to-day to see what that way is."

. . . . . .

It was late in the day before that chance came. The storm that had threatened all through the morning had not yet broken, but the day still brooded under a swollen, empurpled sky. The mountains were not smokily blue now, but lay in black reefs of shadow on a near horizon. What light there was did not seem to pour down out of that angry sky, but seemed to glitter back balefully from lake and river and lough and stream.

Beyond the village, on a quiet stretch of roadway that lifted above all that bright waste of water-fretted land, Hugh came on James Hannin, a silent, brooding man in that brooding, still day.

He was leaning, elbow-propped, on the dry-stone wall, looking out over the fall of country to Lough Mask House and the wide meadows that lay between house and lake. And now the meadows were swarming with life.

" Boycott's hitting back at ye, Davin. The man's giving as good as ye gave." The ravaged face over the trim beard was touched with a faint, grim humour. " Landlord or no, the man'll give ye a fight. Look ! "

A full fifteen acres of the lakeside fields were under meadow, and for weeks past the tall grasses had hung in the sun, over-ripe for the scythe. And now the scythes were at work.

Four, five, a half-dozen of them, Hugh counted in amazement. Already they had cut a wide swathe at the upper headlands and were working down towards the lake in an uneven, straggling line.

Straggling ! That's what it was he had noticed at first. The mowers were working hard, but they were working inexpertly. He could see them clearly now in that purple-hazed light. Youngish men they were for the most part, lithe and active, their impetuous attack on the work before them having nothing in it of the slow, practised skill of the men who had toiled, generation after generation, in these fields. There were older men, too, portly men in unaccustomed shirt sleeves, striving fussily with hay-rake and fork. And in the wake of the mowers, gaily dressed and bonneted, fluttered a bevy of girls. The voices of the mowers and their helpers came drifting up through the still air, clear, insolently loud voices.

" Boycott's friends," Hugh said slowly. That was a possibility that had been overlooked, that Boycott's friends would come to his help. " So that's what was cheering him up this morning. His friends are rallying round him. His own friends."

"Every last man of them—and every last woman, too," the American agreed. "They came in not an hour ago, three long-cars from Ballinrobe and a half-dozen cars of police guarding them. See there!"

He pointed to where the long, red-painted cars had been drawn up before Lough Mask House. On every road from the meadows to the village, and on the road to Cong, armed police were patrolling.

"Boycott's friends," the American went on slowly. "They were in Ballinrobe when I came through this morning, waiting for cars and police to take them here." He fumbled out a short pipe and clenched it between his teeth. "Twenty . . . thirty of them. A rare crowd." He laughed in his throat. "You have young bucks of army officers there, subalterns from Parsonstown and Mullingar and Athlone, gay sparks of lads giving up their leaves to help Boycott. You have men from Galway and Tipperary, lads that never did a day's work harder than hunting a fox or schooling a horse. Aye! And old men that have lived fat and easy this twenty years. And girls, too, from every Big House from Dublin to Galway town; girls that never soiled a hand with work before, Davin—and they'll work now for Captain Boycott."

Those angry, unbeaten eyes of his glowered on the distant haymakers.

"They'll fight for him, breed and kind, Davin," he said, almost with satisfaction. "They'll fight. And in the end they'll beat you."

"They'll not beat us . . . if all who should fight for us do fight."

Hugh turned from the wall, his back to the amateur haymakers in the field below. The clear, calling voices drifted up to him, angering, maddening. He knew then how passionately he wanted the work he had started to succeed; he knew how much he was prepared to risk; how much he had risked, and, maybe, lost. He turned angrily to the American.

"All who should fight with us," he said deeply. "It's a fight you could lend a hand in, Hannin."

"A fight! Whiteboys and Rightboys! Ribbonmen and Land Leaguers. They're all one. All one, Hugh Davin, and the fight they'll fight now the same dirty fight they've always fought." The harsh, prison-broken voice rasped. "We taught them something better to fight for than that. And now you and your like would bring me, and better men than me, back into your dirty squabbling. No! If fight we must, let it be for something worth fighting for."

"Keep clear of it so." Memory of Hannin's secret visits sharpened Hugh's voice. "If you'll not help, don't hinder us. There's others . . ."

"Others! By the Lord! There are others, Davin. Two others, Foy and Mongey. As good lads as ever stepped. And where has your Land League and your Davitt and your Parnell brought them? To Westport Jail to take the blame for a piece of blackguardism they had no hand, act or part in. To Westport Jail." The angry strength went out of the harsh voice, leaving it flat and lifeless. "Twice, three times, I came all this way from Westport to listen to men boasting and prating of the help they'd give the lads. Boasting—and lying."

To listen to men! So that was it. That was the explanation of James Hannin's secret visits.

"What men?" Hugh asked. "Lads of ours?"

"Of course." Hannin was watching the haymakers and the patrolling police. "Michael Carroll, Heneghan, two or three more." He laughed shortly, a jerky, angry bark of laughter. "A grand plan they had, to attack the police car and get the two lads off it the day they were coming back to Castlebar to stand their trial. A grand plan."

He leaned heavily against the wall. There was a weariness about the man, Hugh thought with pity, that forced out his earlier anger, a weariness as if he could no longer fight and would not yet surrender.

"A grand plan," he said, bitterness seeping into his voice. "And I was ready and willing to find the tools they wanted to do the job, a brace of pistols . . ."

"Your own pistols are safe and waiting for you any time

you want them," Hugh cut in brusquely. "They're in the place you know of, in Ahalard. . . ."

"Leave them there." The American looked down at the roads below with their couples and quartettes of patrolling policemen. "Leave them there. They'll be safe there until I find a quiet time to come for them." A grim smile touched his bearded mouth. "I'm a ticket-of-leave man yet, Davin; and there isn't a policeman down there hasn't the right to stop me and search me as if I was a common pick-pocket. The right. Aye! and the will, too.

"Leave them there," he said again, deeply. "To-day I found out that Carroll and his friends have another use for the same pistols. Before they'd use them to help Foy and Mongey, they planned to use them for other work—for shooting this bailiff of Boycott's. . . ."

Into Hugh Davin's mind, startled and amazed by this news, sprang the memory of Michael Carroll's face, of Michael Carroll's threat, his own certainty that Michael Carroll had been the one who attacked Mark Killian. Before he could speak, Hannin went on:

"They'll use no gun of mine for work like that, Davin, for shooting landlords or murdering bailiffs." He said again what he had said before, not once but a score of times: "They'll waste no bullet on bailiff or landlord that could be used another day against peeler or dragoon."

All the bitterness of his crushed and broken life, all the bitterness of his thwarted hopes was in James Hannin's voice. He stooped forward and put his hand over Hugh's hand, the dry, cold hand of an aged man.

"That's all I wanted to tell you, Davin," he said flatly. "This fight"—he gestured—"this fight isn't my fight. I'll take no part in it. Till it's over and done with, I'll have no more dealings with the men that followed your lead. When it's over . . ."

"Yes," Hugh prompted. "When it's over?"

"Leave that be! It'll be a long day, maybe. Longer than my day; longer even than your day." He jerked himself upright. "But there'll always be someone waiting for that day. No matter how short or long it is there'll be someone waiting."

He turned to go, but paused for one moment longer.

"Till that day, I'll not waste your time or my time on the work we both had our hearts set on," he said in a voice that showed its own edge of strain. "I'll be off now; and I'll be back, when it's safer to gather those tools of mine."

Abruptly he turned away. The clear, laughing voices from the hayfield drifted bodilessly in the sultry still air, jangling across Hugh Davin's taut nerves. All his own uncertainties, his own fears for the success of the venture to which he had put his hand, all the darkening of trouble that had come between him and Anne Killian, seemed a very part of this still, threatening day.

He leaned against the wall, watching the American, who had left him without a further word, go striding stiffly down the road; and suddenly he found himself wishing desperately that the storm which lowered above the purple sky would break.

CHAPTER SIXTEEN

THE old lady and himself, they were the only sensible people in the house, Watty told himself. The only sensible people. Honour of God! Look at the way things were in house and yard and gardens and fields.

"Rips out of hell and scallywags of lads without a thought in their heads, barring drinking and courting," he said aloud. The wall of silent hostility and ostracism that had grown up in the weeks past about Lough Mask House had bred in him this habit of speaking his thoughts aloud. "They'll have the house ruined, ruined and destroyed."

He set down the pails of water he had carried all the way from the wells in the upper field, and eased his aching back. It was quiet here in the long, shadowed passage-way. At the passage end the cool, greenish light of the rainy evening flowed through the open door, and from the stables came a confused murmur of voices threaded with a girl's chiming laughter. The nearby kitchen doors were closed on the evening bustle of cooking. And somewhere, far away in the quiet heart of the house, a violin was playing. The clear, far-off melody, rippling in the rhythm of a dance tune, forced itself on the man's hearing, stirring him to a dull and vague resentment.

"Dancing and drinking and making their fine holiday out of another man's misfortune," he said bitterly. "Little they care what's happening us. Little they care how quick we're ruined and destroyed."

His bitterness was not entirely caused by self-interest or by the knowledge that his own welfare, his safety it could even be, were bound up inextricably with Charles Boycott's. In his own queer, twisted fashion he had come to find in himself an affection for the stubborn, strong man he served, a loyalty that would never show itself in words.

"Ruined! Ruined is the word." He turned a bitter, bright eye on the kitchen door and his sour mouth twisted in its own humour. "Ould Mrs. Bodkin and the Burke lady and the wee French girl. The three of them in there, and them making nothing but dirt and disorder between them. God above help the chickens them ones was to take the notion of cooking."

Stiffly, grumbling to himself, he went about his work. Beyond the dim windows the fine rain drizzled out of the evening sky, as it had drizzled day in day out during those past four weeks of amateur haymaking.

Well! The hay was saved. Aye! The hay was saved. He clattered pail against pail in a sudden, small outburst of anger. Saved! If ragged, slovenly hay-cutting and the piling of wet grass into rickety hay-cocks could be called haymaking. And the amateur haymakers were tiring of the work. There was no denying that, Watty told himself now. They were tired of it, men and women, sick and tired of it. That was plain to see.

He heaved on to his shoulder a wicker pannier and stumped down the passage-way to the turf rick that loomed darkly in the convenient angle of walls between house and stable. Sheltered here from the soft, sifting rain, he paused to fill and light his pipe before packing the basket with turf. Nearby the stable gates clanged open, and there was a swish of running feet in the wet grass as the people from the yard hurried through the rain to the house doors. From where he stood, in the shadow of the rick, he could not see them pass, but their voices came clearly, a deep murmur of men's voices, and then, bright and keen, the eager, chiming voice of Judith Wynne. The house door slammed shut.

" Herself ! And a rabble of men around her, now and ever." The man's face was heavy and dull. Only his eyes were hot with life, an angry life. " He's a fool. The world's own prize fool."

He slouched against the wall there in the shadows, thinking dully and purposelessly of Judith Wynne and of Charles Boycott. If it wasn't for that woman, he fretted, the Captain would be easier guided, easier persuaded. He'd be readier to listen to advice. Readier to strike hard and often. Readier to . . .

Ach ! Leave it be ! Watty pushed forward his basket to the rick-foot. There was nothing he could do. Nothing ! He began to fill the basket, throwing sod upon sod of turf with unnecessary violence. The yard gate creaked open in the quiet, but he did not more than glance without interest at the people who now passed, a youngish, weathered man with the spare frame and mincing step of a horseman, and a girl whose dark prettiness sparkled in the rainy light.

" It's been marvellous fun, Gerald," she was saying. " Such a pity it's all over."

" Over ? All over ? " A full-mouthed, spluttering voice this weathered man had. A stupid bosthoon, Watty thought, without heat and without any great interest. " But why ? I mean to say, it's been great fun. Helping old Boycott, y'know . . . And the haymaking . . . and the dancing here in the evenings . . . And, and you . . . And now . . . I mean to say, all over . . ."

" How nice of you to mind, Gerald. But I go to-morrow. I've got to. Alice French is going also ; she's going to her cousins, the Brabazons, in Meath. And Olive Burke's going. And Mrs. Bodkin. . . ."

" That old trout. . . ."

" Of course, Gerald. But when she goes, I've got to go too. It was only on that condition that I was allowed to come here at all. Mrs. Bodkin was to chaperon me, papa said. . . ."

" Hang papa."

" Quite, Gerald. But that won't stop me leaving to-morrow. I quite simply must leave."

" In that case. Be off myself. Matter of fact, I've got a horse to get ready for the Show. Besides, quite a number of the others are going. Perrin and Devereux and the other army chaps—their furlough is up. And Dick Martin and the two Blakes are off to Oughterard for the fishing . . ."

" But poor Captain Boycott, Gerald ? "

" Hang it all ! We've done a good job for him. We've saved his hay. Well ! More or less saved it. Besides, the feller's got some crazy scheme or other of his own. He's got some friends of his up in Ulster, up in County Cavan, engaging labourers for him. And he's got friends in London, in Parliament, making all sorts of pleas for him—y'know, trying to get the Government to do something to help him. Then there's all these people who write letters about him to the *Irish Times*, asking everyone to help him, and that kind of thing : not that I read 'em, of course. Oh ! You don't have to worry about Boycott. Boycott 'll manage. He's got friends. Useful friends. He's away to-day in Ballinrobe on some business or other. . . ."

The door slammed shut. Slowly and stiffly Watty packed and cross-packed the last sods of turf in the basket and straightened his back. He heaved the basket on his shoulder and lurched to the door through which the man and girl had disappeared.

Much yon lad knew of Boycott's plans, he told himself. Much he knew of the letters that had gone pouring out of Boycott's office to Boycott's friends, to his friends in the Orange Lodges of Ulster, to his friends in the Kildare Street Club in Dublin, and in the House of Parliament itself in London. Letters asking, demanding help.

Watty kicked open the door and stumbled up the long, damp-smelling passage. It was strangely quiet here. No muffled sound now came from beyond the closed kitchen door ; but from beyond the doors leading to the main part of the house came a humming of voices.

Watty paid little heed to that hum of excited voices. He paused at the foot of the steps leading to the door which opened into the hallway. He knocked out his pipe and steadied the load on his shoulder.

His mind was still busy with the thought of Captain Boycott and those letters Boycott had written. Maybe some good would come of them ? Maybe ? But, to his own way of thinking, a strong, fearless move here on Lough Mask would be better than a mail-bag of letters. It would so. But the Captain had his own notions. And the Captain was a man to humour his own whims.

Watty crooked a steadying arm against his basket and pushed hard on the door. The door swung back under his hand, and voices poured out of the hallway in an excited flood. Before the open hall-door, framed against the rainy night beyond, Boycott was standing facing the crowd of men and women who surged about him, questioning him, calling to him excitedly.

" Easy ! Steady, everyone ! Please ! " His voice leaped and lifted and soared with life. " It's all right. Everything's all right, I tell you. Everything I've been promised has been done. Everything. . . ."

He had swept off his low-crowned hat and was shrugging his broad shoulders out of his drenched driving coat. Rain glistened on his face, and that sheen of glittering drops heightened his vivid, excited colour and pointed the dancing elation in his eyes.

There was life in him and fire in him now, Watty thought, as he stumbled across the hall under his load. Life and fire and a strength that was needed.

" Everything ! Everything I asked. Every last man and every last gun." Boycott's voice pealed. " They were coming through the village with all flags flying and drums beating when I drove past. That was a sight to see. They'll be here in a minute. Any minute now." His voice beat down the gay clamour of excited voices. " And then we'll see who's master at Lough Mask."

Watty had reached the open door of the drawing-room. He braced himself under the weight of his pannier and waited for the woman who stood in the doorway to make room for him. But Caroline Boycott did not move. She stood in the doorway staring down the long hallway at her son. Her face was still and cold and untouched by the least faint ripple of excitement. But her eyes were dark with an anger that seemed to hold her frozen in the last stillness before explosive action.

Watty turned to look where she was looking and saw that Judith Wynne was now standing close to the Captain and that Charles Boycott's hand rested on her arm in a grip at once gentle and fiercely possessive.

" If you please, ma'am." Watty moved closer to the old woman and raised his voice against that hard, hating silence of hers. " If you please. Could I go apast you to the fire? "

" Connell ! " She looked at him blindly out of eyes that were fully alive to one sight only. " You ! Of course."

She stepped back into the room and did not again return to the door. Not looking at her, but conscious of her silent presence, Watty went about his tasks, building up the dying fire, setting to rights the untidy room. He was drawing the curtains against the evening light when the first crash of music came blaring on the wind. The marching melody, fifes sobbing and drums rattling, crashed into the traditional change of garrison tune :

" Fare-you-well, Enniskillen, fare-you-well for a while,
All round the borders of Erin's green isle,
And when the war is over return I shall soon,
And your arms will be open for your Enniskillen
Dragoon. . . ."

The wail of the fifes throbbed through the dying rain, and drums rolled, echoing and re-echoing across the darkening face of the waters. And then out of the trees, at the turn of the avenue, the first of the soldiers came. On to the wide bay of gravel before the house they came, mounted officers trim and smart on horses that were not yet too wearied to swing forward at a jingling, parade-ground pace ; two full companies of infantrymen, their scarlet coats blackened with rain ; the lumbering gun carriages of two field pieces and their platoons of gunners ; and, squelching heavily in the rain, herded between the files of the rearguard, came the fifty labourers whom Boycott's agents had recruited through the Orange Lodges of Cavan and sent south under military guard and escort to the harvest fields of Lough Mask.

Watty pushed open the window. On the steps before the house Charles Boycott and his haymaking visitors had gathered excitedly to watch the military party swing into place and halt.

Orders crackled in the quiet. The senior military officer, portly and heavy-footed, had swung out of his saddle and come forward to meet Boycott, who had gone quickly down the steps.

" Got your fellows here for you, Boycott. Nice work for soldiers. What ? " The florid face puffed behind its bristle of white moustache and beetling brows. " Nice work, I say. But a job's a job. Huh ? " He laid his hand on Boycott's arm and turned towards the officers who were still sitting stiffly in their saddles. " My fellows," he announced throatily. " My Adjutant, MacKinnon—you'll be seeing a lot of him, what with quartering and billeting and that. What ? Boyd ! Fetherstonhaugh ! Levinge . . ."

But Captain Harry Levinge was not paying full and proper attention to his commanding officer. He was leaning forward a little in his saddle, his lean and sun-roughened face tight and hard. Rain glistened on his fair hair where the rim of his forage cap pressed hard. And his eyes, hot and bright with recklessness, seemed to see none but Judith Wynne.

All this Watty Connell saw in that fleeting moment, too sudden for thought : the soldier's sudden excitement ; the flutter of Judith Wynne's hand to her throat ; the instant leap of mutual recognition. The moment passed as quickly as it had come. The officer was sitting back easily in his saddle again, and the girl had turned to the men who stood nearest to her on the steps.

Watty was suddenly aware of the old woman standing beside him. He stepped back from the window, hurriedly.

"Beg your pardon, ma'am." He went shambling across the room to where his emptied pannier stood. "'Twas the band and the sojers."

Caroline Boycott did not seem to hear his stumbling apologies. She was standing still by the window, looking down intently at the soldier who had now stopped forward in the saddle to greet her son.

She stood watching with wide and thoughtful eyes. The fold of the curtain, which she had caught in her hand, creased and crumpled in her grip.

CHAPTER SEVENTEEN

THERE was no comfort at all in life. Watty told himself; no comfort at all. All through the long days of July the soft, drifting rain had come swirling in from the west over the reef of the mountains. Now, with the early days of August slipping away, the rain still fell in squalls and gusts that slowed the work of the men in the harvest fields.

The bailiff came now, as he had come these many days, to the stile in the laurel hedge of the kitchen garden. Stiffly, swearing and grumbling, he heaved himself on to the topmost step and sighted the harvesters in the far fields.

Still in the ten acre! Honour of God! And they called themselves workmen. Fifty of them! And this their sixth day in a field that had been laboured last year in half the time by less than a score of men. Robbery it was. Deliberate robbery. Aye! Deliberate, he told himself; for it was patent now to see that the strange harvesters from the North were deliberately wasting time to enjoy longer the fantastically high wages Captain Boycott had contracted to pay them.

Gloomily the bailiff continued to stare down on a scene that had lost its strangeness in the weeks that had passed. On the high ground above the lake was the military encampment, line upon ordered line of tents arrayed four-square about a flag that whipped and slapped in the wet wind. Against the white cones of canvas the bailiff saw, unheedingly, the flash and glow of scarlet tunic and the glitter of steel in the evening light as the camp sentries marched and counter-marched.

Down by the ten-acre field light flashed back from the bared steel of scores of bayonets, for here, drawn up in a widely-spaced hollow square, a half company of infantrymen cordoned the field, so that the strange workmen laboured in the alien corn behind a hedge of steel. And on the hillocks at either end of the field; their gaping dark muzzles menacing the empty roads, two field pieces dominated the quiet fields.

A grand sight! A grand sight altogether, Watty thought with bitterness as he watched the new camp guard file off briskly to the hill beyond the horse-lines. A grand sight, but too long on show. For a few days, for a week maybe, there had been hopes that all this show of military strength and armed power would overawe the countryfolk. But it had not. Within a week familiarity had bred a lack of interest, and now the wall of silence and ostracism about Lough Mask House was higher and stronger than ever.

Idly Watty Connell watched the ration party come trotting down the lake road and swing towards the camp, its laden carts lurching and swaying over the rutted ground. Daily those guarded carts came trotting in from Ballinrobe or Castlebar; for every ounce of food eaten by soldiers or harvest men had to come from outside. Even their beer and tobacco were freighted in under armed escort.

Watty hawked in his throat and spat angrily. Even for a pint of porter or a twist of plug tobacco, he reflected angrily, a man was beholden to the fitful generosity of the soldiers or to the close-fisted Cavan men; for not a publican in Cong or The Neale would sell ounce or gill to Boycott's workmen or Boycott's guards.

The ration party had lumbered into the open centre of the camp, and the picket sergeant who had ridden guard was now reporting to an officer who had come forward, leading his horse, reins looped over arm.

Beer they were unloading, Watty told himself thirstily,

firkins and barrels of it. Hogsheads of Persse's ale from Galway town. . . .

He stopped short then, staring down at the officer who had now come away from the picket sergeant and was swinging into the saddle of his mount. Even at this distance Watty knew that lean, nervously quick figure, that long-stirruped easy seat, the recklessly gay air as the horse broke from a trot to a canter down the long line of tents and out into the open country beyond.

" Her fancy-man away off to meet her again." The bailiff's mouth went hard and sour at the very thought of Judith Wynne. " Off riding with her Captain Levinge she'll be this evening again ; this evening and every evening. Stealing off to her love-making and her kissing and her courtin', likely. And the Captain himself inside, driven near mad and distracted with worry."

He waited a little longer, watching the horseman canter away out of sight. All these weeks past, ever since that first day when he had surprised the look of mutual recognition in the faces of Harry Levinge and Judith Wynne, he had been watching that horseman come and go, and had been at no trouble to guess what lay between Levinge and the girl under their pretence of training and schooling Boycott's new horse.

He watched the horseman pass along the rim of the hill and sweep down across the sky to the distant fields of Derraglin. Slowly he climbed down from his vantage point and turned back to the house.

" She brought bad luck with her," he told himself morosely. " Bad luck. Not a day's luck had we since the day she darkened the door. Destruction and depredation ; that's what she brought. She'll be the ruin of the Captain. . . ."

If only Captain Boycott knew, he thought, if he was made to see all this trickery that was going on behind his back ? Watty stopped short, fingering his blunt, ill-shaven chin. He pondered that thought, and then stumped on slowly towards the house. What would be the use? Where would be the good ? Finding out the woman in her trickery would not draw Boycott away from his desk and from the account books that now for ever lay open before him. It would not stir the man to strike out, hard and strong, against the forces that were gathering round Lough Mask.

No! Let it be! Watty stumped on in the shelter of the dripping laurels, making no further effort to grapple with the uneasy thoughts that held him.

The rent office door stood ajar, and he stood there waiting until the man within looked up from the books and papers littered before him, narrowing his tired eyes against the light.

" You, Connell ? " Boycott's voice was weary too. " Nothing wrong, I hope ? Those infernal soldiers haven't been up to their tricks again ? They haven't been stealing . . . ? "

" The devil a much, Captain." Watty sidled inside the door. " There's maybe a few chickens less than there was yesterday, and there's more snares and traps in the woods than ever were there when the poachers from The Neale were busy. 'Tisn't the soldiers I mind. 'Tis in their nature to steal and lift a bit by way of food when their own rations run short. 'Tisn't them I mind at all, at all. . . ."

Boycott pushed aside his papers. He ran his fingers back through his grizzled cap of hair, ruffling it on end.

" Those thieving harvesters," he said wearily. " What is it now ? "

" Turf, Captain. Turf and firing. They've the best part of a rick of turf stolen on us, not to talk of the timber that was in the outer yard. 'Tis hard to blame them, I know, for they have little comfort or heat in the wet, draughty oul' shed they're sleeping in above in the Park Field." Watty looked out gloomily towards the corner where the raided turf stack stood. " Little enough comfort they have, Captain ; but sure we'll have less ourselves if this thieving goes on, for devil a sod of turf will be cut or saved for Lough Mask House in Gortnacarrig bog this year. Not a sod."

Impatiently the Captain began to gather and sort his papers. Lines of strain and temper were gathering these days about his eyes and mouth, Watty noted. And his mouth too often now twisted in lines of petulant temper.

"There's little to be done about it," he burst out testily. "I've complained time and again to Major Strickland about the pilfering and thieving of his men and those damned raga-muffins ; but it doesn't seem to do any good. . . ."

"Erra ! Take it easy, Captain. We'll manage. We'll manage fine. Maybe I'll get a few soldiers, an' them off duty, to help me cut firing and timber in the woods. They'll be glad enough to do it if they're paid."

"Paid ! Paid ! Nothing but money. Money flowing out from here ! Boycott smashed down his fist on the litter of papers. "Money to freight in almost every ounce of food we eat. Money to pay outrageous wages to those idlers. And all the time I'm being bled white. Pillaged and robbed by the very men that are here to guard the house. . . ."

Money ! Nothing but money troubling him these days, Watty thought, his eyes on the account books and papers and the long, orderly columns of figures. Nothing but money. And sure there was no sense in that. No sense at all. The old lady, old Mrs. Boycott : wasn't it well known that she had the money of the world, lashings and leavings of money. Hadn't she her own fine payments off the Blake rent-roll over yonder in Tullybrin ; and hadn't she her grand street of houses in Dublin town ; and her share in the Galway brewery ? Money, how are you ! Watty thought with disgust. Hadn't the mother the money for the asking, and who had the better right to ask than her one only child, the Captain himself ?

"Now, now, Captain ! Don't be flurrying and worrying yourself. What's wrong with you is just that you're too long shut up in the house with your books and your papers and your devil knows what else. Look ! Let you have a bit of sense now and saddle a horse and off out with you. When you're away off out in the air with a horse under you and the rain in your face . . ."

"Too much to do, Connell. Too damned much to do," Boycott said, more calmly now. He drew his papers towards him. "That reminds me : Miss Wynne will want you to saddle the *Sir Conn* horse for her. She and Captain Levinge have some idea of trying him in a match that Captain

Levinge's arranged with one or two of the other officers and with Mr. Toby Blake and Kirwan and Lynch and some of those hunting fellows from Tuam. . . ."

"A match, is it? And where will they be riding a match with the whole countryside up and looking for trouble?"

"At Corran. On the fifteenth of the month. Where else?" Boycott threw aside a spluttering pen and picked up a new quill. "Where else? The country races at Corran have never been much more than an excuse for at least one or two matches like this."

It was not perverseness drove the bailiff to protest now. His trade had bred in him a sharp nose for the scent of danger, and he scented danger here in this casual, thoughtless plan to bring horses and riders from the military camp to Corran. At Corran, for more years than anyone remembered, the country folk had gathered at mid-August on the lake shore for horse racing and boat racing, and here, as Boycott had said, the local bucks and squireens had been used to run off their matches. But this year the temper of the crowd would be little in favour of watching the horsemanship of Boycott's protectors or . . .

It was then that Watty remembered the horse, the horse that had been seized from Michael Carroll.

"At Corran, Captain," he protested. "Is it bring that horse we took on Carroll down there in the very teeth of the people that's saying we were no better nor thieves to buy in yon beast at the Sheriff's sale. 'Twould be madness. . . ."

"Even madness might be a change from the kind of life we're living in this house." Boycott jammed pen in ink-pot. His voice snapped. "Better hurry, Connell. Miss Wynne may be waiting for you."

But Judith Wynne was not waiting. Unaided, she had managed to saddle the black, and now she was leading the horse out of the dark stable, her slender, strong body arched against the pull and drag of the brute's head, a pull that threatened to lift her from her feet.

"Just in time, Connell."

Her voice, with its clear bell tone, rang in the quiet on a

high note of elation. Joy in her mastery over the horse, maybe ? Watty's eyes were hard. Or joy of another kind ?

" Quickly ! A hand ! "

She seemed to soar into the air from the lift of his linked hands and to settle in the clumsy side-saddle with a bird-like grace that lacked nothing of firmness. With a flick to her riding habit, she pulled a whip out of her boot and smiled down at Connell where he stood with a soothing hand on the horse's bridle.

" I'll manage him now, Connell." The throbbing, eager life in her voice angered the man. " Let his head go. And if Captain Levinge rides this way, tell him I've ridden on to Derraglin."

" He's likely gone there himself, miss. He started that way a while back." Watty still held the bridle. He drew a deep breath. " Look, miss ! There's talk of the strange Captain riding the black lad here at Corran. Don't let him."

" Why ever not ? "

" 'Twill be dangerous there. Terrible dangerous." No need to give her the real reason of the danger. " 'Tis a most dangerous spot. There's a stone wall there is a death-trap. 'Twas there Mr. Lory Kirwan was killed the year before last. . . ."

" Don't be silly, Connell. Your stone wall 'll mean nothing to a horseman like Captain Levinge." She gave the horse his head a little, jerking the head-stall out of Watty's hand. For a moment she held the black dancing and sidling on the cobbles. " Why, if you had seen some of the race-courses and some of the jumps Captain Levinge's ridden . . ."

The black, fighting hard for his head, brought her out of earshot, and she went clattering through the gate into the wan sunlight that had pierced the swollen clouds to light up with brief loveliness the green waters of the lake.

Watty watched her go, his brows drawn down in a dark bar of thought. What was it she had said? Slowly he repeated her words:

" If *you* had seen some of the races and the jumps Captain Levinge has ridden . . . if *you* had seen . . ."

That could mean one thing, and one thing only, Watty thought. It could only mean that he had been right in his guess on that day the soldiers came. He had been right in guessing that she had known Captain Levinge before that day. She had known Levinge ; yet both of them had made a pretence of meeting as strangers.

He stood staring out through the arched gateway into the faint, whin-gold light beyond, pondering that guess of his. He was still pondering when he came on Caroline Boycott in the empty house which seemed so much more empty now since the loud-voiced, laughing haymakers had left it.

" Is it the Captain, ma'am? " he answered her question with another. " Out in the office he is, writing and figuring and working away at his books and accounts, the same as he is day and night this month past."

He hunkered down on the hearth, building up the fire under the slender white mantel that was now faintly grimy with weeks of partial neglect and unskilled care. Caroline Boycott sat stiffly in her winged chair, her work-basket on her knees. But her hands were idle.

" It would be so much more convenient if he were to bring his books here. Much more comfortable and convenient," she said, the fretfulness that was in all their voices of late edging her tone. " That would be a splendid idea. You could make time to carry in whatever books were wanted. Couldn't you, Connell? "

" Surely, ma'am. No trouble at all."

Watty sat back on his heels and built sod on sod with delicate skill so that the red tongues of flame licked, whispering, about the black turfs. So that was it, he thought sourly. The old lady, for all her unbeaten looks, had come to hate and fear the echoing, empty house. She, too, missed the bustle of morning activity as maids scurried with banging pail and broom through the upper rooms ; the burst of chatter and the sharp volleying of scolding voices from beyond closed kitchen doors ; the lilt of a girl's voice in song as she worked. She missed it all since the house had emptied itself of servants, and later of guests.

Well! Hell mend her, Watty told himself. She had part of the remedy in her own hands. Let her but loosen her money-bags, shake out some of the gold from the Blake rent-roll or the Dublin houses, and one-half the Captain's troubles would be over and done with. For money, Watty reasoned without the slightest shadow of doubt in his own rightness, money would bring the fight between Boycott and his tenants to a quick end.

He added the last sods to the piled pyramid of turf and stared blindly into the heart of the fire. Why, he wondered, had she been so slow with the money help that would turn the tide?

" 'Twould be grand to have him in here. To have someone about the house the live long day," he said aloud. " Times, ma'am, you must find the house desperate empty and lonely? No one but your own self in it." He caught a smouldering sod as it fell from the fire and slowly put it back into place. " Yourself and Miss Judith. . . ."

He did not expect a comment on that remark, nor did he get one. But he could have sworn that he heard a small, angry intake of breath at his shoulder. He waited for one moment longer, making pretence of mending the fire. The tongues of flame leaped and whispered and ran together in an orange flame. The light leaped and brightened.

Strange how bright a light could be, Watty thought with sudden grim humour. He could see now plainly, in a quick light of understanding, why the old lady would not come to her son's aid. It was the girl who stood between Charles Boycott and his mother's money. If the old lady could find a way of putting an end to her son's friendship with Judith Wynne, nothing would stand between him and the money. A way? Any way?

He rested a hand on either side of him and pretended to pause before coming to his feet.

" An empty house these days. And Miss Judith so much out with the horses and what not else." He lifted, groaning a little under breath, to his feet. " Over by Derraglin she is now, herself and Captain Levinge, getting the new horse ready for Captain Levinge to ride at Corran Strand. . . ."

"To ride at Corran? At Corran? Whatever are you talking about? Where all those murderers and ruffians will be. In the old days it was quite all right for people to go there, but not now. Why, it's simply madness, Connell. . . ."

"Erra! Devil a madness, ma'am." Wilfully Watty pretended to misunderstand her. "Devil a harm he'll come to. Wasn't Miss Judith herself telling me that when she used to know Captain Levinge over beyont in England, he had the name of being the best rider in four baronies. Her very words, ma'am. Four baronies."

He took his own time leaving the room. The woman did not speak at all. But he was well pleased. She was a woman who would choose her own time to speak, and her own good time to act.

CHAPTER EIGHTEEN

SHE reined in the big bay cavalry charger and watched the rider on the black take the fence. There was a thunder of hooves rolling like drums, a flash of red coat stooping over black hide, a sudden lift of power and colour, and there, swinging back in a half-circle to range alongside her, was the black and its rider.

"Marvellous, Judith!" Harry Levinge's voice had in it a hard, bright quality, a lightness as if laughter was never far beneath the surface tones. "This black lad's got everything a horse should have. Everything! Speed and power and heart." The light, reckless eyes sparkled a challenge to her. "Heart, Judith! An estimable quality."

She pressed her hand hard down on the pommel of the old-fashioned side-saddle. No! She must not, she dared not respond to the light challenge in that reckless voice. She must never respond again to that half-mocking, wholly reckless voice.

"You must be careful, Harry." Once again her voice betrayed her. "The horse is badly trained, badly broken.

It's dangerous riding him in a match, in a race . . . It's a terrible risk."

The black was edged closer to her, swinging along beside her own mount on its long, free, nervous stride.

"Risks! What a flat, dull business life would be without risks, Judith." Even yet the light voice mocked her, but there was a chord of purpose now in the lightness, reckless purpose. "Or have you become utterly reconciled to dullness here, m'dear? Here, where there's nothing else but dullness?"

She would not look at him. But she did not need to look at him. Always against the screen of her mind stirred emotion could conjure up that sharp, abiding picture of him: his lean, sun-roughened face flushed with excitement over the unbuttoned collar of his tunic; the sweep of fair hair marked by the pressing rim of his forage-cap and clinging damply to his narrow brow; his cool, hard mouth. She could see the picture now as she had seen it a moment ago in the peril of the jump; as she had so often seen it against the darkness of her closed eyes when her mouth was warm with kissing.

She shivered a little in the rising wind. She would have to blot out that picture for ever from her mind.

"Dullness?" She matched his lightness with a forced lightness of her own. "There are worse things than dullness, Harry."

"Wise Judith!" The mocking voice teased her. "Once you didn't think so. Worse things, you say? I wonder."

"There's loneliness, Harry. And fear when you find yourself all alone." All her lifetime's lack of security, all her present need of security, gave strength to her words. "Loneliness and fear."

To that Harry Levinge made no reply at all. He rode forward in silence to the roadway where he twisted out of the saddle and dropped to the ground.

"Better get these saddles shifted back again," he said in a matter-of-fact tone. "That's if you're riding the black back to Lough Mask."

He held out his hand to her, and when she dropped to the

ground he caught and held both her hands in his own hot, tight grip.

"So that's the choice, Judith? Dullness. And safety. And this Boycott fellow to keep you from loneliness. And the last few weeks? Do they mean nothing?"

The last few weeks? Those secret, breathless meetings! That frantic effort to find again the happiness of their days at Hatfield. But all those days were over. She faced that steadily now.

"They meant madness, Harry. Worse than madness—deceit." She rallied all her strength against him. "They're over now." She tried to draw her hands away. "What choice have I?"

She fought against the spell of his stooping, reckless face.

"You must see that, Harry. I have no choice."

"Choice! To choose to bury yourself here amongst savages, with an ill-tempered boor who can't even keep his own dogs at heel. Judith! What a life for you."

"What other life have I?"

"I'll find a way, Judith. Leave it to me. I'll make plans."

"We made plans at Hatfield, Harry. Fine plans . . ."

"I know, Judith. Don't throw that in my teeth. I had bad luck. The very worst kind of luck. It'll be different now. . . ."

"Different?"

"Well I . . . I didn't intend to tell you. Bad luck to make plans in advance an' all that, y'know. Bad luck to cash in on a bet before it's won, if you see what I mean. But the fact of the matter is, I stand to win a hatful of money over this match on Thursday . . ."

"Oh, Harry! Harry!" In spite of herself she laughed. "Plans! Plans! You call that a plan? A silly, wild gambling. . . ."

"Damn it, Judith! Don't try to throw cold water. If this . . . this plan of mine goes all right, I'll be back on my feet again. Able to take you away from this dull, stupid country. Away from that frightful old hag who hates you because her oaf of a son wants to marry you. . . ."

"Harry! Please!" Judith drew her hands free. "And I do wish you wouldn't do anything so silly and wild as this awful bet. If you lose. . . ."

"If I lose! What a thing to say. If I lose, I'm in Queer Street and no mistake. Jews and sharks and sweats and what not, all waiting to pounce on me. But I shan't lose. Not this time. I just can't lose. . . ."

Judith was laughing now on a little shaken note, moved less to anger than to an odd tenderness by this preposterous irresponsibility.

"Darling!" She caught his face between her hands and kissed him lightly on the mouth. She felt suddenly very near to tears. "Sometimes I think that nothing will ever make any difference between us; but this time one of us must show sense."

. . . . . .

They had gone, cantering back against the evening light, before Watty Connell moved out of the cover of the trees from which he had watched them—as he had watched them evening after evening during the weeks past.

He watched them now, his cold and empty pipe clenched between his teeth, his hands fumbling through his pockets in useless search for the shreds and grains of tobacco which he well knew were not there.

All the misery of the day and all the long days before it seemed savagely to concentrate now in his gnawing, aching throat. He watched the riders wheel blackly along the curve of the hill and drop away out of sight.

"With your trapesing and your coortin', me doxy. If the old lady has the wit to see the weight of the hint I gave her this evening, she's the one that'll put a halt to your gallop." He spat out of a thirsty, tormented throat. "But likely enough she put no pass or heed on what I had to say to her. What is she, when all's said and done, but a woman herself; and where was there ever a woman had wit or wisdom? Women! Women!"

In that soured, savage humour he wandered aimlessly down through the dusk, fretful and restless for want of purpose or objective. Where the road skirted Killower Hill he paused, stooping over his stick and staring up morosely at Mark Killian's house. But he did not follow his first intention of climbing the hill, as he had so often climbed it of recent months, to talk to Ellen Killian.

" Women again ! " He hunched over his stick. " The one up there promising me the daylight. The fine, courageous woman, afraid of no man, Land League, Whiteboy or Ribbon-man. Afraid of no man ! But if she's not pushed to it now, she'll be little better than yon water-hearted, shivering fool of a husband of hers."

The far, thin braying of a bugle came drifting over the water from the camp and stirred him out of the thoughts that had come so darkly upon him. He turned his back on that faint, brazen note and on all that it stood for, and went on aimlessly down the road that led to the village.

" A fool, if ever there was one. A weak, cowardly fool, that husband of Ellen Killian's," he told himself. " If the woman was left to herself, she'd have done what she promised weeks ago. But the husband has her talked and persuaded till she doesn't know what to do. Talked and persuaded. Grand, high talk it would be too ; talk full of grand notions and noble reasons," Watty thought with sour disgust. " But the reason that was behind all that same fine talk and all the grand notions was no more than fear. That was all it was: fear! Fear ! The fear that had been bred in him that night the nails of the ' carders ' had ripped across his chest."

He stumped on through the fading day, through a quiet undertoned with bird-song and murmurous with the whisper-ing babble of water in stream and rill and all the hidden water-veins that threaded the riddled rock beneath his feet.

" Fear ! Fear ! " he told himself. " What man with sense would credit all the other high-sounding excuses Mark Killian made for himself ? " The bailiff's massive head sank into the hollow of his bowed shoulders. His blunt chin jutted stub-bornly. " Fear ! A poor day the world was coming to, when one of Captain Boycott's tenants had less fear of the Captain's bailiff than he had of Martin Egan and the handful of trouble-makers that stood behind Egan and the League."

A man passed, not speaking, striding quickly through the shadows under the high, rain-drizzled hedges. His passing drew Watty back from his thoughts to realization that he had reached the end of the village street.

It was the first time in four weeks that he had been in the village, except on those trips when, under heavy escort of police and soldiers, he had come to collect the letters which would not otherwise reach Lough Mask House.

Now he hesitated for a moment, considering the empty street; but his fear of showing fear drove him, and with stick thumping loudly in the dusk, he went down the street on his squat man's wide and rolling stride and shouldered open the door of Martin Egan's publichouse.

Always afterwards, remembering that moment, he would remember how the voices died away to silence on his entry. The low, smoky room had been loud and echoing with talk; then, suddenly, the upsurging volume of voices thinned and dropped and faded as if a great hand had pressed down, stifling and gagging all those loud, laughing voices.

Watty stood framed against the outer twilight, his ears drumming with his own angry blood in that moment of inimical silence. He lurched into the room. He could make out faces now in the smoky light: Hugh Davin and Haire, the smith, with one or two others, at the upper end of the long counter; a scattering of men from the Lough Mask farms gathered in groups of twos and threes in the dimness; and nearer, under the hanging light, Michael Carroll and young Heneghan and three others. For a long moment the bailiff's eye narrowly held Carroll's over-bright stare and considered the hectic, drunken flush on Carroll's face. Then he turned to Martin Egan.

"Fill out a glass of Special for me there, Martin. 'Tis poor whiskey and bad whiskey at best, but 'tis likely the best you've got. A glass of Special," he said again, "and a pint of porter to 'chase' it with." He ran his tongue over his dry lips. "And when you're at it, cut me off a two-ounce bar of Nigger Head twist tobacco. . ."

Through the mist of tobacco smoke he saw the faces in the room loom palely towards him, watchful and hostile faces. Over the heads of the men at the counter Martin Egan was stooping forward.

"Isn't that a strange thing, Watty—a terrible strange thing now! Not a thimbleful of whiskey or a gill of porter left in the house." He fingered his white beard. "And this last quarter-ounce of tobacco sold an hour back. Not a crumb left, Watty. Not a drop or a crumb left—for you."

The reek of spilled porter and the drifting clouds of tobacco smoke caught at the bailiff's throat, smothering him, choking down his rage. Somewhere in the shadows a man guffawed laughter; and Michael Carroll's voice rose in a sudden snarl of rage.

"What are we waiting for, lads?" he shouted. "Isn't the lake beyond as deep as the lough in Partry that put an end to George Hussey's trouble-making? It's deep enough to hold a bailiff with a bag of stones to his heels."

It was too late to run; and, late or early, he would not run. Connell braced himself against the door, waiting for the rush of feet across the floor and the wild clutching of maddened hands. But there was no angered rush. A heavy, ungainly man, moving with surprising speed, had caught Carroll by the shoulder and hurled him back into the arms of his companions. Martin Egan was calling out loudly, and Hugh Davin and the smith had pushed their way out into centre floor.

"Carroll! You and the others! Steady there!" Davin's voice was loud with an authority that the bailiff did not miss. "And you, Connell! Get to hell out of here while you're safe. You hear me! Get out!"

Get out! Ordered like a dog in the very place where he had given all the orders until a few short weeks ago. Watty Connell delayed for one short moment more, deafened by the blood that thundered in his ears. Ordered! By Davin and Egan and Carroll and their likes They wouldn't order him. Let Mark Killian and his kind go in dread and fear of them. . . .

He leaned back against the door, his fingers crooked about the jamb. A joke so grim that it shook him with silent mirth crawled to life in his mind. If they wanted someone to frighten and to give their orders to, he'd find a man for them—a man that deserved the worst they could do to him. He'd find that man for them—and set them all at one another's throats into the bargain. He'd do just that, and devil mend them all.

" Leave Carroll be." His mouth twisted in sour humour. " Hasn't he cause enough to be mad, and fighting mad." He was gripping the door jamb so hard that the edge of wood bit into his fingers. " And he'll have more cause before the month's out, when he sees another man's cattle grazing his land and another man walking in on the floor under the roof that was his own before we took it from over Carroll's head."

The room was very still. A glass had been overset and the liquor ran from it in a thin stream to the counter's edge, dripping to the floor. The faint, dripping sound was uncannily loud in the quiet.

Watty loosed his hand. It hurt now, where the edge of wood had bitten so deeply His throat was raw and dry. He knew what they were thinking. They were saying over to themselves the words he had used : " Another man." And he knew what they were guessing : " Who would this man be ? "

" So let ye leave Carroll be," he said again. " He has enough on his beads."

He paused, enjoying a sudden sense of power. His eye met Hugh Davin's eye in a hard, derisive stare, as he remembered that note of authority in Davin's voice. He would give Davin a deal to think about ; he would give others of them something to guess at ; and he would, maybe, force Ellen Killian out of her shilly-shallying and delaying.

" Leave him be. And if Carroll and the rest of ye want to know more about the man that'll soon be under Carroll's roof, let ye go to Mark Killian for your news."

CHAPTER NINETEEN

HUGH DAVIN came on leisurely foot through the unexpected sunshine of the mid-August day along the mossy lane that led to where the sun-drenched stones of Ahalard lifted against the burning sky.

There was no hurry at all in his tall man's long and swinging stride. Less than an hour ago, while he had been making ready to follow the crowd that was already streaming out to the lake shore at Corran, young Stephen Nalty had brought him word that he had seen James Hannin in the company of some men from Westport.

Hugh had guessed that the American would not be anxious to show himself so early in the day in the village street where the swarming soldiers and policemen were watching with suspicious eyes every stranger from outside. In the hope that Hannin might have come to their usual meeting-place, he had decided to go to Corran by way of Ahalard.

It was not of the American he was thinking as he crossed the uneven field and scrambled over a cairn of stones into the inner square where blue shadows banked under the ancient walls. He was thinking, as he had been thinking every day since that evening in Egan's bar-room, of Watty Connell's threat to put a new tenant into Carroll's farm, and of Connell's boast that Mark Killian was involved in the plan.

It was past all belief that Killian, or any man within sight and hearing of Captain Boycott's guarded house and yards, would be fool enough to risk the anger of the countryside and to risk sharing the punishment that had been imposed on Boycott.

It was past belief, and yet there were many who believed it, Hugh told himself uneasily now, as he had told himself with growing disquietude during the days past. Many, like Michael Carroll and Ned Heneghan and the three or four who were drinking with them night after night in the shebeens beyond Kilmaine, believed the bailiff because his hint gave them further excuse for wild threats and grim promises. But there were others, older and steadier men like Martin Egan, who inclined towards belief in the story reluctantly and regretfully —and all the more threateningly for that regret and reluctance.

It was cool here in the shadows, and he was glad enough to wait a while for Hannin, sitting on the fallen stones and letting the coolness of the shadowed place flow over him, easing a little the taut sense of strain that was upon him.

Under that strong and surely drawn arch of brow of his, his eyes were shadowed by the strain and divided purpose that had been his for weeks. His slender, high-boned face was drawn too fine ; and now and always, when he thought of Anne Killian, his mouth was bleak.

" There's not a thing I can do," he told himself again, wearying of the dreary repetition. " Dear God ! 'Twould be a poor matter to go to the girl with a story like that or to question her about Connell's hinting. Things are bad enough. . . ."

He sat there a little longer in the dim coolness thinking of the events of the weeks past : the fight against Boycott and its promise of success ; the power that had been thrust into his unwilling hands ; the shadow that lay between him and Anne Killian.

His eyes darkened. If Watty Connell's hints meant what they seemed to mean, he himself would be the one who would use that new power of his in bringing the punishment of the League to Mark Killian. He would have no choice. No choice that a man could take when his word was pledged. He came to his feet. It didn't bear thinking about. . . .

There was still no sign of the American, and when he pulled himself up to look out over the fall of land before the castle, field and path were empty. He waited a moment longer, but before he turned to leave a thought struck him.

" There's just the chance," he reflected, " that he was here early and left a message."

He swung himself on to the tottering pile of stones that buttressed the wall and reached into the shadowy cleft between the stones, a deep, dry hole in the stonework, not visible even to the sharpest eye from ground level. Here it was he had hidden James Hannin's case of pistols on that long ago night in May, and here it was that certain trusted ones of the men who drilled by night under the shadow of the walls had often hidden messages or gear. But the deep cleft was empty now. For a moment he groped and searched, rustling the dry leaves and twigs that had drifted, autumn after autumn, through the wide crevices of the wall. He dropped to the ground. The cleft was empty. Most likely it had not been used since whatever day James Hannin had come this way to take away his property.

Within the past week that must have been, Hugh thought, remembering that he had looked at the weapons, examining them for rust and damp not ten days earlier.

His dark, strong brows drew down in a frown as he stood to brush leaves and twigs from his clothes. Within the past week! That meant that Hannin had made yet another of his secret trips to the district.

"Damnation! What tricky game is the man up to? I'll find him at the strand and have this thing out for good and all, one way or the other."

. . . . . .

A long wide tent, snowy canvas bellying in the wind under crackling bannerets, had been rigged up by a squad of soldiers from the encampment. It stood four-square on the brow of the first lift of land sweeping back from the lake and from the wide half-moon of grass and trampled reed and sand upon which the military party was now setting up an array of brushwood jumps to supplement the loose stone-wall fences on the landward side.

All about that central tent was an ebbing and flowing of life and colour. The red tunics of the infantrymen jostled the greenish black coats of the policemen and the blue jackets of the gunners. Here was a rustling of elegant frocks and a prinking of fashionable bonnets; there the pink hunting coat and scrugged-down riding hat of a fox-hunting squireen,

All the sound and merriment of the race-day gathering seemed to have been drawn to this group about the white tent. Further away on the shore, drawn back from the shifting colour pattern of dress and uniform, the countryfolk had gathered in a dark, restless, uneasy throng, low-voiced and sullen. Here were smaller tents, the tented booths of sweet 'standings' and shooting booths and long, low barrows heaped with dilisk. And here in the heart of the crowd a ballad-singer put his heart hopefully into a raucous song:

"And where will they have their camp?
  Says the Shan Van Vocht.
And where will they have their camp?
  Says the Shan Van Vocht.
On the Curragh of Kildare,
And the boys will all be there . . ."

The ballad tailed off into silence, smothered by the sullen muttering of the crowd. There was a restlessness now in the crowd: sudden and purposeless surges of movement ran through it, as if from a seething point of activity at its core. The boats, the light two-oared skiffs and the heavy eight-oared fishing boats, their racing over for the day, had been drawn up on the spit of gravel at Duncairne Point, and their crews were hurrying back to join the crowd, hurrying as if they, too, had been touched by the gathering air of excitement and expectation.

"Give a man room there!"

A youngster on a raw-boned filly came riding across the skirts of the crowd, some lad flushed with a triumph of race-riding earlier in the day. He slammed heel hard home in the filly's ribs and slapped his cap across her withers.

"Up, girl! Up!"

The filly came over the rise, fiddle-head straining at the drag of the reins, and shouldered into the fringes of the crowd in a scrambling rush, her lean haunches gathered under her like a leaping cat's. The crowd scattered on the slope, the sudden movement rippling over it like a wave. A deep-throated, rasping growl of anger followed the boy and his mount as they pulled about and went pounding across the field.

" There's trouble brewing, Darby," Hugh Davin said to the smith who had joined him on the grassy rise above the lake. " I never saw a crowd in more humour for trouble."

" Small blame to them." The smith's deep voice could boom with anger, and it boomed now, deep as a bell and harsh as the clang of iron on his own anvil. " What call or right had the soldiers or the like to come here to-day, making their own of other men's sport ? What call had yon soldier fellow and Browne of Kilmaine to enter a boat in a race that was never, in the memory of man, raced by anyone barring lads that made their living fishing the lake ? And what right or call had that other soldier to try racing his horse against the boys from Moytura ? Ach, well ! " The broad shoulders lifted. " 'Tis all near hand over. This'll be the last race, barring whatever race of their own the crowd above is set on running."

Down on the strand, within the outer circuit where the soldiers had finished building their jumps, the last of the day's races was being run. Strung out against the glittering shine of the lake, the horses swung into the last labouring furlong of the three miles' race. A lurching, lumbering bay, rolling in his stride in this last effort, forged into the lead. Perched like a crabbed monkey on the withers of his galloping mount, his face caked with wet mud and sand thrown up by the galloping hooves of the leaders, the jockey on the bay thundered past the upturned farm cart on which the Judges were mounted.

For the first time the sullen silence of the crowd broke. Cheers and counter cheers rippled along the shore. The cheering deepened to a deep-chested roar.

" My sound man, Maurteen." A man's voice crashed across the uproar. " Would I doubt your father's son."

And then, from the hill, from the crowd that spread out in its own shifting maze of colour about the white tent, came a rattling, crisp volley of hand-clapping and a ripple of applause.

It was as if the laughter and the cheering from the lake

shore had been suddenly strangled in a thousand throats. The shouting and cheering died away to that low, voiceless mutter of sound that did not so much break the sudden silence as edge that silence with threat.

The military working party had reformed and gone swaggering back to the hill with deliberate slowness. A party of police had detached itself from the uniformed throng and was fanning out along the shore.

Over the heads of the crowd about the white tent, pink hunting coats and gaudy silk riding shirts tossed and bobbed, seemingly in mid-air, as six horses threaded through the watchers and cantered towards the strand to where the Starter waited with his flag, a corpulent, stiff-backed military man in the frogged coat and flat forage cap of the artillery. He was mounted on a bob-tailed cob.

Past the quiet, inimical watchers the riders came, a gunnery officer trim and slim in his field accoutrements; Kirwan of Tuam, a squat, pocked dwarf of a man in soiled hunting pinks and leathers blackened with sweat and grime; young Lynch and Browne in crackling silk jackets, mounted on horses that had not yet reached the hard, lean fitness of the hunting season. Down past the crowd, standing in his stirrups, his body alean over his mount's withers, cantered an officer from the encampment, a lean, lithe man with sun-roughened face flushed in excitement over the unhooked collar of his tunic. The horse he rode was the black gelding that had been Michael Carroll's.

The crowd had found its voice now. As the rider on the black swept past, that voice rose and rolled in a deep, threatening groan, a muttering thunder of threat. Harry Levinge canted forward a little in his stirrups and brought down his hands firmly on the black. Under the peak of his cap his reckless, light eyes looked down for a fleeting moment of interest or of contempt on the crowd. Then he, too, swept away across the stand to the starter.

"Boycott and his friends took their own good way of making trouble," the blacksmith said deeply at Hugh Davin's shoulder. "Parading that horse of Carroll's . . . Madness!

Let's away out of this. It's no place for anyone with a grain of sense. . . ."

"No! Hannin is to meet me here," Hugh answered. "I'll wait for him. And maybe you'll find use for that grain of sense of yours if you wait too. There's little enough of it at Corran to-day."

He, too, turned to watch the riders swinging into line on the far loop of the course. They had reached the farthest point of that wide oval of strand and shore. Beyond them the last long wavelet at the lake's edge was no more than a line of cold, clear colour drawn firmly and strongly against the wet sand, the lake a blinding sheet of light beyond it. Against that clear background of light the horses moved in black silhouette at a walk, at a trot, at a canter. The starter's cob pranced magnificently before them, its legs like black knitting-needles against the glare. The silhouetted starting flag dropped sharply. They were off!

For all his faint, uneasy premonition of trouble to come, Hugh found himself leaning forward, watching with quickened interest. Down to the first jump thudded the riders, red coat and hunting coat, silk jacket and gunner's tunic, stooped over the withers of the galloping horses. Steadying a little, hands firmly down, booted heels rapping back, and then over, smoothly, safely.

A thin cheer whimpered along the lines of the throng about the white tent. Down on the lower ground the silently watching crowd was caught again in an eddying restlessness and went flowing out in a dark, slow-moving flood that threatened to engulf the flagged line of the race-course. Slowly the black-coated policemen began to move into position.

The riders were racing now, galloping shoulder to shoulder to their jumps, hunting coat and riding shirt bearing hard on the scarlet tunic of the black's rider as the first three rounded the bend. Behind them, stringing out against all that wild waste of light and water, the gunnery officer and the younger hunting men swung wide on the bend, splashing water at the lake's rim where the light flashed coldly on wind-raised flurries.

Down past the first jumps and the corner flags that the military party had set up came the racing horses. The squat, pock-marked huntsman was leading them, his soiled and muddied hunting pink a huddle of colour against the bay hide of his mount. Young Lynch was riding desperately now, riding with whip and spur, thrusting his hunter over fence and ditch at galloping pace. On the outside, on the wide outer circle, farthest from the lake, Captain Levinge was sending the black along in an effortless, striding gallop.

Up on the hill the thin whimper of cheering was louder now and the crackle of hand-clapping sharp and clear. On the lower lake level the crowd was spreading out slowly and purposefully, pressing down on the narrow lane of the course in an ominous dark line.

The horses were over the last of the stonewall jumps now and were thundering down to the brushwood fence that lay between them and the mounted judge. The squat huntsman was riding now with whip and spur, and beside him young Lynch was driving his Galway hunter with brutal recklessness. On the black, Captain Levinge eased forward a little in his saddle. His hands moved now in a beautifully rhythmic movement. The black forged forward, lifted to the brushwood a full clear length in the lead, swept on with gathering power in a tremendous burst of timed speed.

Up on the hill the cheer deepened. A police officer cantered along the line of the course, standing in his stirrups. He eyed the dark, silent crowd. He brought his mount about on gathered haunches.

" Keep to the field ! " he ordered. His voice went shrill. He paused, uncertain. " Get them back ! All back ! "

All along the last stretch of the race-track policemen began to move into line. Here and there a soldier lent a wide, red-coated shoulder to strengthen the pressing cordon. A burly, broad man in the distinctive riding coat of the Blazers came at the run, his riding crop swinging by the lash in his hand in a wide, threatening arc. Over the heads of the policemen and the soldiers flashed the colours of the race-riders. The black horse that had been Michael Carroll's was now three clear lengths in the lead. Down towards the judge galloped the horses.

"Back! Back!" The police officer's voice had no strong ring of authority in it. "Get them back!"

Somewhere a soldier swung a scabbarded bayonet in a vicious, experienced back-hand blow. A policeman clubbed his carbine and screamed out an oath as he found hands clawing at his throat. A voice ripped through the sudden uproar.

"Pull them down, boys! Pull them down!"

Ever afterwards Hugh Davin found that his single, clear memory of that crowded mad moment was the memory of the swarthy, pocked huntsman's face, wholly absorbed and utterly unfrightened, as he swung his mount clear of the surging mass of bodies that had engulfed the other riders and went thundering on past the judge, the only one of the six riders to complete the course.

Thereafter, for moments that seemed to expand into crazy timelessness, field and strand seethed with fighting, struggling men. The black horse that Levinge had ridden went lurching, riderless, out of the crowd, limping and staggering on a foreleg that buckled grotesquely beneath its weight.

The wild moment passed. Police and soldiers were reforming into line and squad, and the crowd had drawn back in a dark, slow-moving tide. Riders were gentling their frightened mounts and leading them away. But Captain Levinge made no effort to take charge of the black, which had now been led back, limping and lurching, by a mounted policeman.

He turned away and went slowly and silently up the hill to where his coming was as silently watched by the girl who had watched race and riot from the high seat of Captain Boycott's gig.

CHAPTER TWENTY

DUSK was deepening outside the little windows of the school-house and shadow flowed softly into the room, so that the homely, familiar things, the benches and the table on its high trestles, and the tall easel, loomed grotesquely out of an unfamiliar gloom.

The street beyond the window was quiet now and emptied of the dark masses of men surging in wild rushes from the batons of the charging policemen and forming to surge back again after each baton charge.

They were gone now, the men who had been driven to sudden wildness hours earlier on the race-field of Corran; and now the street was empty, save for the policemen patrolling in armed groups and the squad of infantrymen standing-to under full kit at the street's end. Here and there light sprang up in windows, and that familiar nightly blossoming of orange radiance in the blue twilight seemed almost to drain the day of all its alarms.

Hugh Davin leaned against the window, bringing the shadowy scene into focus under a curved hand.

"Quieter now, Darby," he said back over his shoulder. "It's all over, likely enough."

"Sure it was never much to start with," the smith answered equably. "A power of bad temper and a deal of shouting, and little enough blood spilt at the hinder end."

He moved softly through the shadows, a burly, sure-footed man, most amazingly deft in movement for all his bulk. He passed by the central table, touching the wide, ink-stained board gently so that it rocked and creaked on its trestles. He stepped nimbly over a bench and stood peering through the gloom at the figures chalked on the blackboard.

"Well-oh-well," he said softly, head tilted a little to read the figures. "There's a fair lot I picked up at school that I forgot to bring with me when I was leaving; but there's one thing I learned since: that a broken head and a drop of spilled blood often saved a man from worse harm."

"If it ended at that," Hugh gave him back. "But it won't, Darby. I've a feeling that to-day's work was no more than a beginning."

"Ah! God give you wit, man. Brooding and thinking too much you are. Leave the thinking be, and be ready to do what you have to do when the time comes."

The smith brought the flat of his hand down sharply on the table top, so that the cup-shaped ink-pots danced and jingled in their wells, giving off a faint echoing tinkle of sound.

"Leave it be! Come away down to Martin Egan's with me. There was never a cause for brooding yet that a pipe and a glass in good company under a bright light wouldn't cure. Come away, man. Thinking's only for the shadowy places."

"No! I'll wait where I am, Darby. Hannin is likely lying low until all this fuss and trouble are over. If he's about, he'll not head for home without seeing me. I sent Steve to search for him with word that he'd find me here. I'll wait."

"You'll have your own way." The smith moved away through the shadows to the door. He paused. "And let you not be taking it all too hard. What can any of us do but our best?"

He slipped away silently on that word and drifted quietly down the shadowy street. Hugh Davin did not move at all. He leaned against the window frame and let the shadows and the silence flow about him.

The musty, chalky scent of the school-house, the smell of the damp boards and the sour airlessness of a room shuttered against the outer heat, oppressed him. But he did not move. He stared out unseeingly into the dusk, facing a fact that could no longer be evaded. Soon, within days, his connection with the Land League activities would be so clearly established that Lord Kilmaine's agent, Browne, who was also manager of the schools, would have reason for action against him. And he had no doubt what Browne's action would be—instant dismissal.

He searched through his pockets for pipe and pouch. A twist of self-mocking humour touched his mouth.

Small blame to Robert Browne, he admitted wryly. Small blame to the man to use this weapon of dismissal against one who took the other side in a fight that concerned every landlord and agent in the country. Small blame to him indeed.

He began to fill his pipe, ramming the tobacco hard home with nervous fingers.

Dismissal itself had no great terrors for him. There were many places where work and livelihood would be his for the taking: Liverpool, with its swarming Irish families and its toughened, loyal Fenian old guard. Or America, limitless in opportunity. Aye! Dismissal and the closing of every school in Ireland against him would mean little enough.

He turned from the window and rested against the sill, elbows propping him.

Dismissal meant little. But it would mean parting with Anne Killian. Parting with her now when she most needed friends and help. When she had set her face against friends and help. . . .

Down in the shadows a door creaked open. A voice spoke quietly.

" Yourself, Davin? "

" At last, Colonel." He would give the man his title yet, Hugh thought, moved by a humour too swift and deep for understanding. " A minute now and I'll get a light."

" There's light enough. Light enough to suit a ticket-of-leave man in a town like this. Hssh! Quiet! "

Outside in the dusk, a bare yard away, the police patrol went thumping past. In silence the men listened to the heavy footfalls fading away into the distance. When it was quiet again the American spoke out of the shadows.

" Fighting guns with their bare hands, Davin." The man's voice was edged with bitterness. " Will they ever learn that fighting's a trade a man must learn . . .? "

" They're learning a way of their own to fight—without any help from you or much from me," Hugh answered shortly. In some obscure fashion he resented this criticism by the American, for all that he well knew what truth there was in it. " Leave them to it. Leave *us* to it," he said, the memory of the other's unaccountable and unexplained activities stirring him. " If you'll not help, don't hinder us."

" I'll do nothing to hinder you, Davin."

The American was moving restlessy through the gloom, pausing now to peer out into the darkened street. The far-away sounds from outside, the thump of heavily-booted feet, the thud of grounded musket, the faint, fragmentary echo of a voice, all seemed to heighten the uneasy strain within the room.

"Nothing, Davin," Hannin said again. His voice was an old man's voice, leaden and lifeless. "I'll do nothing to hinder you."

"I'm not sorry to hear that. You seem to have a deal of business of your own round here latterly."

"So I have, Davin. Business of my own surely."

Against the brighter square of the window the trim beard and staring bones stood out sharply as the man half-turned to speak to Hugh.

"I had business of my own, surely. The business you and your friends put your hands to, Davin, sent old Martin Foy's son behind bars. My business was to see what I could do for old Martin. Old Martin that shared hardship and torment with me in Millbank and Chatham."

His voice was no longer bitter. It was no more than tired now.

"Myself and old Martin," he said, and laughed softly. "A pair of old fools, maybe, fighting all our old battles again, and winning every last one of them. Aye! That was my business here the night.

"Ah, well!" He came down through the shadows. "I'll not be troubling you again, Hugh Davin. You'll find your own way. And maybe I'll find work to do yet, in towns and places where men haven't the hankering after a few perch of land to turn them aside."

Thereafter he refused resolutely to speak of the things that were uppermost in both their minds. He refused, too, Hugh's offer of hospitality and set off, when night had fallen, to make his own way back to Westport town.

For an hour and more after Hannin had left, Hugh worked by candlelight, urged by that uneasy premonition of trouble to make sure that no incriminating papers of any kind lay in the press in which he stored his school registers and books. The street was silent and empty, the last of the patrolling policemen withdrawn to the barracks, when he left the school-house and started home to his lodgings at the end of the village street.

He had reached the chapel gates when the beat of

running feet in the silent night brought him to a halt. Out of the darkness of the Killower road a man came running, lurching and swaying in great shambling strides. He staggered to a halt, clawing for support at the gate. His breath came in great, gasping sobs.

"Get Father O'Malley! Quick! You hear me! There's murder done!" His voice rose to a scream. "You hear me, man? Murder! Not ten minutes ago. On his own doorstep, within sight and hearing of his wife and daughter. Who? Who, did you say?" The man drew breath in a deep, shuddering sob. "Oh! Dear God! My own neighbour, Mark Killian. Shot down! Shot dead not ten minutes ago on his own doorstep."

CHAPTER TWENTY-ONE

THEY buried Mark Killian in the blazing sunshine of a mid-August evening, in a quiet that seemed to press down out of the brazen bowl of the sky. The shawled women and the heavy, slow-moving men had gathered, ring outside ring, in a wide circle about the open grave. They had fallen still now, and the last faint shuffle of feet in the long grasses had died away. The cordon of armed police had moved into position along the churchyard walls; they, too, were still. Somewhere a gun-butt clinked against stone, and earth thudded, echoing, into the open grave. The voice of the priest lifted a little in the stillness.

The men in the group nearest the grave, Hugh Davin noticed dully, were not neighbours. They were strangers, relatives of Ellen Killian, from Tullycarne, who had travelled all this distance to show not only their sympathy with the widow of the murdered man, but also their support of her against the countryside in which her husband had been killed.

Hostile and defiant, they shouldered forward now, pushing aside the grave-diggers and seizing for themselves the shovels and spades which lay on a mound of newly-dug clay. The priest's voice rose higher, undertoned now by the dull fall of clay on coffin boards.

Anne Killian had not moved or stirred out of that withdrawn, guarded stillness that had been about her in the days since her father's death. Again and again in the days past, Hugh Davin had tried to move her from that hard-held stillness, but always his efforts had failed to stir her out of that mood or to lighten the shadow of guarded watchfulness in her eyes. Alone of the women who crowded round Ellen Killian, she did not crane forward now, wailing and caioning over the red earth that was fast filling the grave-mouth. She stood back a little, her head lifted against the blinding sunlight. In that pitiless light her face seemed pale and shadowed, but it had a new strength and purpose, and a sad gravity that was almost serenity. It was as if she had come to some decision to which she would now for ever hold. Over the stooping shoulders of the grave-diggers her eyes met Hugh Davin's eyes, and her eyes were blinded with tears.

The voice of the priest deepened and beat down the dry, hard sobbing of the women:

"*Requiem aeternam dona eis, Domine*: *et lux perpetua luceat eis. . . .*"

The last words of the burial service were read. For a moment there was no sound save the thud of spades thumping down on the mounded clay; and then there was a rustle and whisper of movement as if a low wind had come whimpering down the burial ground, blowing the watchers to movement and slow activity.

The priest had turned to the dark group of women and was stooping towards them, speaking quickly and decisively. The last thing Hugh Davin noticed as he turned to join the crowd that was now pouring in a slow, murmuring stream through the gate was the quick, deft movement of Father O'Malley's hands as he folded away his stole. Anne Killian had not moved at all; she was still standing a little apart from the others, staring down at the raw billow of clay. The crowd surged forward through the gate, down through the double lines of policemen, and Hugh saw her no more.

"Are you for Egan's, master?" It was young Nalty's voice at his shoulder; the boy's voice, like the voice of many men these days, was harsh with strain. "Old Martin has passed word that there's something must be talked about to-day."

"There's a lot must be talked about to-day. And little good talking about it will do," Hugh answered savagely. "Tell Egan I'll be down in a while."

He hurried on a long and swinging stride through the crowd that was now slowing down and gathering in small, whispering groups. He turned towards the school-house, which he had left untended an hour since, to join the funeral procession.

He strode on, deep in thought. Of Mark Killian's death he did not think at all. He gave no thought now to the certainty that the police would spare no effort to fix the guilt of that crime on the League, nor did he let his mind dwell at all on the whispered suspicions and low-voiced accusations that were the heart and core of every conversation these three days past. He was thinking only of Anne's still face and of the desperate strength that held her so resolutely on the very brink of tears. Unease touched him more coldly and urgently than all his perplexities.

He had passed the closed doors of the forge and was turning to the school before he became aware of footsteps pattering through the dust at his side and of a small, aggrieved voice.

"What is it, Tommy?" He slowed his long stride and spoke down to the tousled, lint-coloured head. "I didn't hear you the last time."

"You didn't hear me the time before that again," the small voice, less aggrieved now, pointed out with great fairness. "That was twice I told you about the man . . ."

"About what man?"

"The man within in the school. You weren't no more than gone to the funeral when he came. An' 'twas me," the child boasted, "he sent down to keep watch for you."

Hugh slowed his step.

"The man within in the school," he repeated blankly. He

tousled the fair head and sent the child scampering across the yard to where his companions played. " Away with you." He repeated the boy's words again: " The man within in the school."

Slowly, almost with reluctance, he pushed open the door.

It was James Hannin who came to meet him in the dim coolness of the room. There was weariness in every line of the American's broken body. Weariness had cut deep lines in his ravaged face. And even his voice was heavy with fatigue when he spoke.

" You were a long time coming, Hugh." It was almost the first time he had ever called Hugh Davin by his Christian name. " I was afraid I'd have to go without seeing you."

He moved nearer to the window and peered out into the street. He seemed not so much afraid as alert and cautious, with the alertness of the hunted.

" Maybe I waited too long as it is."

" What is it ? " Hugh made no effort to hide his gathering alarm. " What's wrong ? "

" They've a notion to put me behind bars again, lad. A dozen peelers pulled my lodgings asunder yesterday morning, not five minutes after I left it. When they found the bird flown, they swept down on the mill ; but I had the word they were on their way there in time, a bare two minutes before they came."

" What for ? What could they want you for now ? "

" I didn't wait to ask, lad. I got to Ballinrobe town last night, and down to Cong this morning before it was light. I was safe enough in Ballinrobe, but I've an idea that a patrol of horse police sighted me an hour ago from the bridge of Cong and rode in here on my heels."

The boys in the school-yard had given up whatever noisy game they had been playing, and the day seemed all the more heavy and oppressive for their sudden silence. Down the street the great booming voice of Sergeant Dempsey roared out an unintelligible order. There was a rumbling of wheel and hoof as the side-cars from the churchyard came bowling down the street. Hugh did not turn to look at them.

"In God's name, man, why did you risk coming here, of all places? Right into the heart of trouble. The place is swarming with policemen."

He was aware that the side-cars had rounded the long curve of the street and were drawing nearer. Rhythmic hoof-beats of ridden horses sounded now sharply against the rumble of wheels.

"I thought one of us was enough to be in trouble," the American answered with grim humour. "What trouble they have in store for me seems heavy enough and bad enough by all the signs. Aye! And big enough, too, for the pair of us to share if they were to catch you with the case of pistols I left in your keeping a while back. . . ."

He went on brusquely, as if to make light of the risk he had run and of his generous reason for running that risk.

"So we'll waste no more time about it, lad. Get me those wee tools of mine before some trouble-making peeler finds you with them—and my name stamped on the butts of them."

With one half his mind Hugh was aware that the sounds in the street outside, the rattle of wheel and thud of hoof, had ceased. But he paid no heed to that. His mind was aghast at the thought of the missing pistols. He was recalling the men who knew of that hiding place in Ahalard: Nalty; Haire; Foy; Michael Carroll's friend Heneghan. He was thinking, too, of Mark Killian, killed by pistol shot.

"Great God! Your pistols, man! I thought you took them away yourself days ago. They're gone out of the safe place I had them in Ahalard. They're gone this four days and more." He hesitated, reluctant even yet to put his suspicions into words. "They're gone this four days."

"Four days," James Hannin said very slowly. He, too, was remembering the man shot down three days before. "Four days."

He was looking past Hugh to the door, and suddenly his eyes widened. He drew himself up stiffly, squaring his shoulders into a stiff and exaggerated military swagger.

"All right, Sergeant," he called out loudly in a voice that warned Hugh to keep silence. "You want me?"

The windows darkened as a mounted policeman urged his horse past and pulled up, guarding the rear door of the school. The carbines of the patrol glinted over Sergeant Dempsey's shoulder as he stepped into the room.

"It's you I want, Hannin. For this time anyway, it's you I want." The Sergeant's voice boomed and rolled with satisfaction. "It's you I want; and 'twasn't hard guessing the place to find you." He regarded Hugh complacently. "It's a thing I noticed about you, Davin: you have a taste for the kind of company that isn't at all suited to a loyal and contented servant of the Crown and Government. 'Tis a thing I've often noticed."

He signalled to the leaders of the patrol to range themselves on either side of the American.

"It's a thing I've often noticed. And it's given up to me, Davin, to be a shrewd, noticing class of a man."

A side-car had drawn up so close to the school-house that its shadow fell blackly athwart the square of sunlight on the floor within the open door. Anne Killian had half-turned on the farther seat and was leaning across the well, looking down at the group within the door. The secret, apprehensive look was in her face most strongly now, Hugh saw. All colour was drained from her face; only her eyes were alive. Her live, stricken eyes held James Hannin in a moment's long regard. At Hugh she did not look at all.

On the nearer side of the car Ellen Killian sat huddled under a shawl that peaked forward in a dark cowl over a face ravaged by tears and desperate with purpose. The man who straddled in the driving seat, reins looped in beefy, raw hands against his massive thighs, leaned back to speak to her.

"Down with you now, Ellen. And don't be flustered." He was a florid, burly man with a stubborn, pugnacious jaw—a man Hugh had never seen before. "Don't be afraid or flustered now at all."

"A true word, Mrs. Killian. That's the true word your friend has. A man of sense, Mrs. Killian." The Sergeant stepped back over the threshold and lifted a hand to the woman to help her down. "There's nothing to be afraid of.

Nothing at all." He stepped back to allow her meet Hannin face to face. "Is this the man?"

"That's the man." Her voice was harsh and defiant. "I saw him many a time in the fields above at Killower and over west in Ahalard." She drew a deep, long breath. "I saw him the night my husband was killed on me."

"The same man." The Sergeant's voice boomed on its own deep, rolling note of satisfaction. "The same man. And the same man that owns the pistol found not a furlong away from the spot where your good man was murdered."

He stepped forward.

"James Hannin!" His voice crashed. "In the name of Her Majesty the Queen, I am about to take you into custody and charge you with the wilful murder of one Mark Killian of the townland of Killower. . . ."

CHAPTER TWENTY-TWO

THEY had talked and argued while the day faded and the last light paled behind the dark reef of the western hills. Long since their voices had become heavy with weariness and edged with strain. The newly-lit candles burned without flicker in the airless room, dull orange globes of light in the smoke-laden air.

"That's an end to it," old Martin Egan rapped out at last. "I knew James Hannin. Well I knew him in the old days." He came to his feet and moved stiffly towards the locked door between room and shop. "Aye! I knew him well. And I thought I knew the business that was bringing him here from Westport. And now this . . . this . . ." His red mouth twisted in disgust against his white beard. ". . . . this black, bad business. . . ."

"Hannin had no hand or part in the killing of Mark Killian." That was Steve Nalty's voice, passionate with conviction. "I know that. I know it, I tell you. In fair fight maybe, in the one fight he spent his life waiting for, Hannin wouldn't be slow to use that pistol of his. . . ."

"So! And that's the very pistol that *was* used, Stephen," Egan said patiently. "The very weapon. And 'twill go hard enough with James Hannin to prove that he had no hand in the using of it . . ."

"And harder on him to face the swearing of the woman that's informing on him," a voice ripped out of the uneasy quiet. "God's Judgment! Where's the use of all our talk if a man can be thrown from his farm and the grabber put under his roof; if a man can have his life sworn away for something he had no hand in? Landlord or agent, grabber or informer: it's all one; and the whip that beats one beats all of them."

It came as a shock to Hugh Davin that the man who had spoken, passion tearing his voice, had not been one of the wild few who had been drinking for nights past with Carroll and Heneghan, nor yet one of young Nalty's friends, boys restless and smarting under the memory of the race-day rioting. This was an older man, a dour, grizzled tenant of an outlying Erne farm who had lost his accustomed slowness of speech under the pressure of anger. And the men who mumbled agreement with him were older men, too, men slow to anger. They were angry now.

"Away out of this with us, Master."

Hugh felt the iron pressure of strong fingers on his shoulder. The fingers bit into bone and flesh, and hurt; and the hurt steadied the sudden, wild violence of his thoughts. Darby Haire went on quietly:

"Away with us." The smith's voice, as ever, was steady and deep. "The cool way is the only way; and the cool way stands little chance here to-night."

He did not move from Hugh's side, his arm hard pressed against the taller man's, until they had passed through the door which Egan had now unlocked, and until they had reached the empty street. They went silently down the street, the tall, lean man on his lounging stride and the small, squat man unhurrying. In the shadows before the forge they stopped.

"And now, what have you your mind made up to do?" the smith asked very quietly. "For if there's anything you intend to do, you must do it soon."

"Carroll! I'll have to find Carroll first." That was the thought that was uppermost in Hugh's mind. "He'll be in Kilmaine?"

"In Humphrey Gilfoyle's poteen shop. Leave him there. There is nothing you can do with Carroll."

"Nothing? Bar tear the truth out of his throat." For the first time the suspicion that had been in Hugh's mind was blurted out. "James Hannin will not suffer for trouble of Carroll's making."

The smith breathed deeply and heavily in the quiet. It was too dark to see his face clearly.

"Maybe that's true. Maybe Carroll was the one who did what Hannin is suffering for now. True enough, maybe. Heneghan . . . Bourke . . . Both friends of Carroll's. And both of them knew of that safe place in Ahalard. One of them, even Carroll himself for that matter, might have come on Hannin's pistols any day these weeks past. That's true enough and likely enough. But what good will that do James Hannin now?"

"It will clear him."

"Aye! Clear him! It would do that, Hugh Davin, if you could find a way of forcing Michael Carroll to tell the truth of what happened that night Mark Killian was killed. The truth." He gestured widely. "And remember, you, that the truth would put his own neck in a halter. You have no time for that now. No time at all."

It was quiet here in the village street. Far-away, towards Lough Mask, there was a dull glow in the sky, where the lights of the encampment were thrown against the low clouds. Every window of the police barracks was brightly lit, glowing orange squares, barred and crossed by grilles of black bars. A light sprang up in the window of Martin Egan's shop. The sense of secret, unguessable activity behind those lighted windows was suddenly terrifying.

"Time! There's time in plenty," Hugh said, but not with conviction. He knew well what was in the smith's mind. "The lads down there in Egan's—they'll argue and talk for hours, for days yet."

" Well you know they won't. Look! 'Tis said that Mark Killian had bargained with Connell to take the house and farm Michael Carroll was evicted from. Maybe that's true, maybe it's not. It's a secret the man took with him. . . ."

" Leave it with him. Let the man rest."

" Aye! Let him rest. But there are others will not be let rest. Look, you! Back there in Egan's, not ten minutes since, you heard it said that Mark Killian's wife had informed on a man, that she swore James Hannin into jail. . . ."

" Informer! What was she but a woman driven to distraction. . . ."

" True for you. A woman driven to distraction. There's few wouldn't do what she did if they were as hard driven, maybe." The smith was silent for a moment, staring down at the lighted windows. " Few enough, maybe, if they were driven as hard as she was driven," he said again. " And that's what was in the mind of the man down there in Egan's, Master: that no man of them would be safe where there was a danger of any other doing what Ellen Killian did to-day."

It was true. It was most damnably true. Fear of their own safety, fear of the informer's tongue that could ruin any man or any plan, would make these men in Egan's ruthless and pitiless. It would move them to action, wild and violent action, maybe, against Ellen Killian and . . .

He stopped short on that, remembering Anne's face; that guarded, watchful look of hers; her secret, apprehensive air. Slowly he fumbled out the heavy school key from his pocket.

" Wait here for me," he told the smith. " I have one small job to do."

That one small job, no more than the removal of his own papers from the schoolroom press, did not delay him long. He rejoined the smith, who waited for him in the shadows of the porch. He turned the heavy key in the lock and left it sticking there; he would not need it again.

" That's done," he said, with an assumption of easiness. " Whatever else I must do to-night I must do myself, Darby."

He said that easily enough, but his casual air did not

deceive the smith. In the darkness that small, squat man stretched out his hand and touched Hugh's hand lightly and briefly.

"You'll do what you must," he said quietly. "You did good work here in your day, good work and work that'll last after you. You did so." He paused. "And if you do what I'm guessing you have in your mind to do to-night, you'll save a girl from trouble and grief she did nothing to deserve," said the smith, "and that will be fine work too." He moved out of the shadows. "But it's work you must do in your own way."

At that he was gone, swinging down the street on that short, forceful stride of his. Hugh Davin watched him for a long moment; then he, too, turned away from the little school-house and went through the shadows towards the road that led to Killower.

He had no plan, no fixed purpose. And yet he felt, as he had not felt for many days, a live lift of hope and a confidence in his own ability to save Anne from the trouble that was darkly gathering. He would find a way, some way.

The lights of the village fell away behind him. Towards the lake, in the deepening night, the tents of the military camp glowed with colour, a clear orange radiance spilling through the taut white canvas. On a drift of the wind came a dull murmur of sound, a snatch of song and a burst of wild laughter, oddly threatening in the quiet. Nearby hoof clinked on stone, and Hugh slipped into the shadows until a mounted patrol of police had jingled past. He went on, more slowly and more cautiously now, until he came to the hill that overtopped the house that had been Michael Carroll's. Light glowed dimly in the windows of the house, the faint, flickering light of a turf fire; and in the angle between house and stable a bivouac tent had been set up, the 'protection' tent of a police guard set to protect whoever had taken possession of the house and relit the fire that had been stamped out when Michael Carroll had been evicted.

He quickened his step, skirting the house and tent, hurrying in a stumbling rush across the hill-side to Killian's house. The sight of the 'protection' tent and of those armed guards had filled him with alarm and haste.

He hammered on the closed door of the house, rapping again and again in a gathering storm of impatience, as slow feet came across the floor within and the heavy locking bar was fumbled open with maddening slowness. When the door opened a cautious inch, he threw the weight of his shoulder against it and pushed it open against the man who held it.

"You took your own time opening." Hugh's temper was wearing thin. "Didn't you hear me?"

He slammed the door shut behind him and leaned his shoulder against it, a tall, lax man in a mood that was driving him in its own fashion and its own dark direction. There was no warmth of friendliness or welcome in that room, for all the light and heat that flooded it. And now, in the pause after Hugh Davin had spoken, there was no sound save the remote, hushed whisper of the turf fire.

Ellen Killian huddled over the fire, hunched and angular in the stiff, creased folds of her dress. The light and heat had brought no colour to her face. She looked from Hugh to the man who had opened the door. It was the man who had sat on the high driving seat of the car earlier in the evening, a great-limbed, deep-chested, slow-moving man, with the glow of rich, violent blood in his dark face and a smouldering darkness in his eyes.

"Haven't we cause? Hasn't the decent woman her cause, and cause in plenty, to be slow opening her door?" His voice was deep and rolling. It had a rich, ripe vitality in it; but there was a faint echo of uncertainty beneath all that crude strength. "How quick she should be opening doors, and her husband not cold in his grave."

Hugh pushed his shoulder more firmly against the door and considered that burly, uneasy man from under level brows. It would be well to know who this man was. He listened for a moment, but there was no sound of Anne's presence in the empty house.

"What would she have to fear?" he asked, "and you minding her. And no one else in the house."

Ellen Killian looked back at him over her hunched shoulder, her lined, vindictive face as sharp-set as it had been earlier in that day when she came face to face with James Hannin.

"I have plenty to mind me, Master Davin," she said. "Sergeant Dempsey below has three policemen outside, watching the house day and night. Day and night. But I'll have no need of his policemen or his protection." She turned back to the fire, huddling towards the heat, mumbling her words: "What need would I have, an' my own cousin here, Malachy Bourke, of Tullycarne, to see to me? That's something for you to remember, Master Hugh Davin! Something for you an' your likes to remember: the Bourkes of Tullycarne look after their own. They look after their own and stand by their own. They do so."

So that was who the man was, a cousin of Ellen Killian, rallying to her aid. But why the evident unease under all the man's rough strength? Hugh pondered that question. The night had fallen still again, and the house was empty and echoing. There was something here he did not understand. Before he could speak, the woman went on, mumbling vindictively:

"If that's the height of what you came to know, you have your answer. The Bourkes will stand by me." Colour crept up under the drawn skin of her cheeks. "There's your answer for you; and let you be going with that answer."

"I'll not be going for one minute more." Hugh was more than ever conscious of the silent, empty rooms beyond the kitchen. "I'll talk to Anne before I go."

There was no mistaking now the lack of ease under the big man's bluster. He leaned back against the chimney breast, his massive legs straddling the hearth. The firelight redly outlined his great bulk. It was the woman who spoke.

"You'll not find her here," she said in a hard, rasping tone. "She's gone out of here. Gone this half-hour and more."

"Gone? Where?"

Into Hugh's mind flashed a picture of the angry, flushed faces in the smoky light of Martin Egan's room. He was seeing, against the screen of his mind, the closed doors that would be bolted and barred to-night against anyone from Ellen Killian's house.

"You hear me ?" he said. "Where ?"

"I don't know. I tell you I don't know."

The woman's voice was broken and crushed beneath all its harshness ; but he had no pity on her, no thought of the tragedy and misery that had broken her and might well crush her again before many hours were past.

"I don't know," she said again. "There's cousins of her father's live over beyont Ballinrobe. Maybe it's to them she's gone."

"Beyond Ballinrobe ? To go so far at this hour of night ? And in this night, of all things, with the country storming with trouble. . . ." He turned to Malachy Bourke. "And you let her go ?"

He did not raise his voice, but the rage that was in him must have been most evident in every shade and stress of tone, for the last spark of courage in the big man dimmed before it, spurting in a last flare of bluster.

"Could I help her going ?" he protested loudly, too loudly. All pith seemed sapped out of that mighty frame of his. "Hadn't she her own mother's house here, a grand snug house and a grand warm home ?"

Those hot, smouldering eyes of his faltered a little under Hugh Davin's level stare, but he went on loudly :

"And if I am her cousin itself, hadn't she a match and a marriage in me that'd make her snug and warm to the last days of her life ?" Something in Davin's eyes checked him ; his voice lost all its certainty : "Maybe I'm not the marrying kind. And I'd force myself on no woman." His lustrous, soft eyes gave the lie to that saying. "But 'twould be suitable. No one can deny that 'twould be grand and suitable. The girl in her mother's fine farm here ; and myself in the farm across the hill—a farm that'll be a good farm when I'm a while labouring it. . . ."

"The farm across the hill ?" Hugh asked quietly. "Michael Carroll's farm ?"

The great burly frame seemed to gather strength and

courage again from some source greater than the source of his fear.

"And why not, man? Is it let a grand place like yon run idle? Why would I not take the farm, and it there for the taking? That's the very thing I said to Ellen, the day she came to Tullycarne a month ago and brought me the word that the farm was wanting a tenant. The very words I said to Boycott's bailiff, an' him fixing the lease for me."

His voice was gaining confidence and courage, as if he was drawing strength from the thought of those idle acres that would soon be under his hand.

"Why wouldn't I? There'll be trouble and bother, maybe. But 'twill blow over. 'Tisn't the first evicted farm a man went in on," he said. "'Twill blow over. The men that put their heads in a noose three nights ago when they did away with Mark Killian, an' him having no hand in the business—them fellows 'll be glad to keep quiet now. Enough trouble they'll have on their hands. . . . They'll keep quiet enough. . . ."

"Will they?" Hugh asked very quietly, and watched the colour darken in the man's dark face.

"My soul they will. And the others 'll keep quiet enough. And then, in a wee while, 'twill all blow over. People have a short memory for another man's troubles and another man's lands. 'Twill all blow over. Them's my words. The very words I said to the girl before she walked off her mother's floor."

Hugh Davin said nothing at all. There was nothing to be said. He looked from the man's flushed face to the girl's mother; but Ellen Killian had huddled over the fire, sunken and withdrawn into whatever mood of grief would drive her to mourn Mark Killian now with a force that was part fear, part loss, part sense of the wrong she had done the dead man.

He slid his fingers down along the door frame until the cold metal of the locking bar touched against his hot hand. For an instant he felt, horribly, that the room held yet all the horror of the moment earlier in the night when Anne had learned that her father had been shot down for something this man and woman had done, for an offence that was all theirs and in no smallest part his. He could feel, only too sharply, the revulsion of disgust in which she must have turned from Bourke's crude offer to share the roof and hearth that had caused her father's death. The horror of that thought struck him like a blow. He felt the sweat bead on his hand against the cold metal.

Very slowly he pulled open the door. Into the room poured all the dark silence of the night and all the night's hidden perils.

CHAPTER TWENTY-THREE

THE moon had not yet cleared the dark reef of the hills, but already land and lake were palely touched by the first faint light of moonrise, a radiance that burnished the lake to silver and lined hedge and tree and hill with an ashen glow.

Hugh Davin made his way with caution through that lighted land ; for the night was no longer still. From the encampment came the clamour of voices in excited uproar, and all the nearer roads between Killower and Lough Mask and back to the village of The Neale itself, were now loud with the clopping of hooves and the heavy tread of marching men, as patrol after patrol moved out in a wide circle above Lough Mask House.

Once Hugh was forced to shelter in the shadows of a hedge as a party of troopers, a dozen strong and far gone in drink, came crashing out of the woods beyond the demesne wall. On the lower road he found his way blocked by two police patrols linking up at the ends of their beats. He waited in the shadows, watching the glint of light on cap badge and gun muzzle and listening to the complaining voices.

" If it's a thing you ask me," a voice was saying in a high southern lilt, " I'd say 'tis no more than a notion of that new County. County Inspectors is all one bag, one sample," the soft, lilting complaint went on. " Leave them think of something to keep the men marching the feet off of themselves, and they're as happy as the day is long. . . ."

" No ! No ! 'Tis more than that, Dwyer." Hugh could see

the stout, pompous speaker. " I'm told by one of the sergeants that had it straight from Sergeant Clerk in the County's office, that the soldiers in the camp above are getting out of hand. Kicking up hell's delight they are, I'm told. Breaking camp and thieving and looting and stealing, and heavens knows what else. . . ."

" That's more the class of talk I'd like to hear." Again it was the soft southern tilt. " I'd give me chance of a stripe to get a belt at one of them red-coat fellows. . . ."

" You'll get no chance to-night." A strong, hard voice cut short the other's talk. " The work we're out for is more nor the trimmin' of a few soldiers and learning them their manners. My sowl ! 'Tis so ! " A murmur of agreement arose, that strong voice lifting out of it. " The arrest of yon Fenian and the murder of the grabber fellow has the country all stirred up. There's a power of men, Fenians and Land Leaguers, and the devil knows what else, gathering all evening in the village below, and there's no telling at all what mischief they're ripe for. The patrol over on the bog road sent in word that a man got apast them in the dark, heading down for Lough Mask House. . . ."

The squads were reforming, preparing to go back along their separate beats. A grumbling voice was growling in the quiet :

" The patrol on the bog road ! Is it Hargadon and MacCarthy ? Devil a much pass or heed I'd put on what them fellows saw or think they saw. . . ."

The voice drifted away into the night. Hugh waited and watched in the shadows until the last footfall had faded into silence. Hurriedly he considered his position. Between him and the village was spread now a cordon of policemen. To venture back that way would be to invite actual arrest or, at the very least, long and tedious delays while he was being brought from patrol to sergeant and from sergeant to inspector for questioning. He could not risk that, not until he had seen and spoken to Anne.

And Anne herself ? It was not likely that she would attempt to pass through the lines of policemen on her way to Ballinrobe, risking constant haltings and questioning. No! She would not risk that. Her whole wish would be for secrecy; she would not desire to call attention to her going. She would take the quiet road.

That road would be easily chosen, it was the only road now open to her: the road that led away from the village and skirted the lake shore to link again beyond the river with the road to Ballinrobe. It led through the grounds of Lough Mask House, to be sure, and too close to the house itself, but that would seem a small matter to a girl anxious to get away quickly and quietly.

"There was no other way she could go." Hugh turned his back on the village and on the roads and lanes now lined by watching men. "No other way."

He took his bearings by the broken tower of Ahalard and made his way with caution through the low-lying fields. The night had brightened. The hills were sharp and clear against the brightening sky. He went swinging down the grassy lane past the castle and up over the rise of ground that looked down on the lake and the grounds of Lough Mask House. The soft, timeless babble of running water heightened the stillness. And then, from out of the dark and silent woods, sounded suddenly the loud pealing of raucous laughter. Loud and long the laughter echoed from some dark side of the woods. Over at the military camp a voice volleyed loud orders and hoarse voices rose in wild clamour. Again, from the nearer woods, came the raucous, wild pealing of laughter.

On the lift of the hill Hugh Davin paused, listening to that laughter which seemed to toss and echo bodilessly through the dark trees of the woods; listening and remembering the troopers who had gone roystering through the woods a few minutes ago. Somewhere in those woods, along that road which had once been quiet, Anne was. He paused for one moment more to take his bearings from the stream that thrust its live head into the still waters of the lake and from the wicket gate leading into Captain Boycott's grounds. He went quickly across the bright hillside and into the shadows under the trees.

The road, quiet again, led him in a wide half-circle along the rim of the house lawns and past the uncurtained windows of the room in which Caroline Boycott was moving restlessly to and fro, talking to a man vaguely seen in the shadows. Hugh slipped past that staring window and began to move cautiously from shadow to bank of shadow along the hedge of laurels that carried the road in its wide curve from house to stable yards. He made his way silently through the thick gloom, a hand outstretched before him. A twig crackled underfoot, and so near that he could feel the faint, warm pulse of breath against his cheek, a voice gasped in strangled fear. His groping hand closed on a hand that was cold as death.

" Anne ! " His voice did not rise above a whisper, but there was in it an explosive force of relaxed tension that stirred them both. " Thank God I've found you."

" Why did you come ? " Her voice, too, was a whisper of sound. " You had no right to come. You had a right to let me go. It was the only thing to do. The only thing. Don't you see that, Hugh. I must go."

" You'll not go alone." Her hand had grown warm in his. He could feel the soft rise and fall of her breast against his arm. " I was no more than in time."

" No ! No ! " Her voice was low still, but stormy and urgent. " No, Hugh! No! Can't you see. My father . . . your friend. James Hannin . . . All your other friends . . . All that happened to-day. All that will happen when Malachy Bourke takes Michael Carroll's house. All that will happen when James Hannin is made pay for what he did." Her voice did not falter. It held firm, unshakeable and unwavering, to an inner strength. " All that would be between us, Hugh. It would be for ever between us. Now and for ever."

There was no time now to argue with her about James Hannin's innocence, about his own innocence of any part in the crime that had cost her father's life. On the rising wind drifted the deepening uproar from the camp and nearer, on the gravelled drive, the dull thud of marching feet. He held her wrist firmly.

"Listen!" he whispered. "We must get away from here now. There's no time for talk. No time for anything except to get away. Quickly."

She did not speak, but drew him nearer, so that he, too, could see the man and woman who were pacing restlessly back and forth across the only path that led away from the house, a tall, rounded woman and a man as tall, whose lean, sun-roughened face over the unhooked collar of his tunic was blanched now in the ashen moonlight.

The quick, nervous pacing brought them nearer, and for a fleeting moment their voices rose and fell in a passion of argument.

". . . . fail me and fail me again, Harry. And now I'm tired, tired of failure . . . of promises . . . of disappointment." The clear, lovely voice, true as a bell, was brittle with tears. For an instant only that voice faltered as the girl made her choice. "So you mustn't blame me if I give up all the hopes and disappointments and catch at safety and security with both my hands. You mustn't blame me, Harry. You mustn't. . . ."

The brittle voice was near to breaking now. In a swirl of skirts and a flutter of caped coat, the tall girl turned and came running back blindly towards the house. She passed so close to Hugh Davin that he could hear her stifled sobbing. A house door slammed shut behind her, and down in the pathway the tall soldier turned away in the shadows, slowly and reluctantly.

"Wait!" Hugh held his hand over Anne's hand. He watched the deep bank of shadow in the curve of the hedge near the stable gates. "We'll give him time to get clear away."

At the encampment a trumpet had begun to blare, and blare again, a brief, brazen call. Twice again the call was blown, and the urgent, sharp rolling of kettle-drums began to echo through the night. Then bugle and drum fell silent again. All at once the night seemed oddly and ominously still.

"Don't move till you see me lift my hand and signal to you," Hugh warned. He brushed aside the unvoiced argument that still lay between them. They must lose no time now in winning clear from the danger all about them. "I'll make sure he's gone."

He had reached the shelter of the stable wall and was stooping to peer more closely into the farther shadows, when the stillness was hideously rent by the shrill, screaming whinny of a horse. A pistol shot rang out in the echoes of that rasping scream.

Hugh lifted to his full height and showed for a moment clear in the moonlight. He turned towards where he had left the girl. In that moment disaster came. A hurtling body crashed against him and lean, muscular hands caught him in a strangling grip. He fell, crashing under the lean, lithe weight of his attacker, and the world swam into darkness in a moment's brief oblivion.

CHAPTER TWENTY-FOUR

THEY lifted the still living body of Michael Carroll from where it had been hurtled, maimed and broken, by the flaying hooves of the horse he had shot down. They carried him from the stable and laid him down in the shadowed arch of the gateway. And there he died.

It was Sergeant Dempsey, working clumsily and with a surprising gentleness, who prised open the dead man's hand and took away the heavy cavalry pistol Michael Carroll had used to kill the horse. He put the pistol away in the leather case that had fallen from the dead man's pocket and handed pistol and case to one of the constables who had come running with him from the patrol before the house at the sound of the shot.

"Take good care of these, Matthews," he ordered, his normal pomposity still shadowed by the violence of the deed he had stumbled upon. "There'll be a deal of investigating to be done here."

But there would be little enough need for investigating, Hugh Davin thought dazedly. A trickle of blood burned his eyes and his head still swam in a mist of pain. He eased his aching shoulder against the grip of the tall, lean soldier and of the policeman who now helped to hold him. There would be little need for investigation. It was only too plain that Michael Carroll had come here, driven by the wild, mad mood that had held him for days, and inspired by some crazed plan to destroy the horse that Boycott had taken from him. And in killing the horse Michael Carroll had come horribly by his own death under those flaying hooves.

Dazedly, a little sick with horror. Hugh watched the Sergeant spread his cape reverently over the dead body and come stiffly to his full height. Beside the Sergeant, the constable was gaping down at the pistol case and at the heavy cavalry pistol. Hugh could see, even at this distance, that it was one of the brace of pistols James Hannin had entrusted to his care ; one of the pistols that had been stolen from Ahalard and used to kill Mark Killian. Somehow, he felt no shock of surprise at the certain knowledge that it must have been Michael Carroll who had shot Killian down. He watched the gaping, slack-mouthed face of the constable in the light of the lantern that Watty Connell had at length succeeded in lighting.

" Sergeant ! Look here one minute, Sergeant." The constable's voice was touched with excitement. " The pistol here is the twin and companion of th' one was used to shoot the man at Killower. Look ! The name and all cut in the butt of it." The heavy, excited face hung like an October moon in the misty lantern light. " Dambut, Sergeant ! I'd swear me davey, 'twas this lad did the shooting, not Hannin. D'ye see what I mean, Sergeant ? 'Twas Carroll, here, did it all the time."

The Sergeant had recovered his authority, and his pomposity. He stretched out a massive hand and seized pistol and case.

" Matthews," he thundered. " Constable Matthews ! When you have been appointed Lord Chief Justice of Ireland, it will be time and time enough for you to be delivering judgments and verdicts. I'd go so far myself," he added with great solemnity, " as to say that the discovery may prove helpful to the prisoner, James Hannin. But when your opinion is required, Constable Matthews, it will be asked for. It will be asked for.

" And now . . ." He looked for the first time at Hugh

Davin. " And now, Captain Boycott, we will leave Matthews and Thompson in charge here, and if you will place a room at our disposal, we will question the prisoner."

Charles Boycott, who had said no word since he had come hurrying from the house, spoke no word now. He led the way towards the house door, down past the dark laurels, and so close to them that Hugh Davin could nearly see that darker patch of shadow within sight and hearing of the gateway where he had left Anne Killian a few moments ago.

She would be gone from there within a very few minutes ; gone on whatever dark road she had chosen; gone with all that shadow of distrust still lying between them. For the first time in all that night of danger a sick sense of loss and of despair seized him. He went on, plodding heavily, urged by the grip of the men who held him, the striding policeman and the tall, lean soldier.

The room to which Charles Boycott led them was the gun-room at the end of the passage. They crowded into that room, not hurrying, yet jostling one another in their eagerness to pass from the darkness into the light of the table lamp that Caroline Boycott had lit.

The old woman stood beyond the table, within the circle of light. The mellow light struck upwards in a soft, golden flood, touching the hollow of cheek and eye and throat with shadow. Beyond the older woman, no longer wearing the cloak that had swung about her like a cape, was Judith Wynne, and now her eyes were dry and her face was not eager but resolute.

The soldier's fingers crushed Hugh Davin's shoulder in a sudden intensity of pressure. Then he, too, came to a halt within the door. Watty Connell crowded past them and took up a place just beyond the doorway.

" We'll not be wasting time, Captain. Your time and mine." The Sergeant had won back all his old air of authority. " 'Twon't take us long to find out what everyone knows."

" It certainly won't take you long to find out all *I* know, Sergeant," Boycott answered shortly. The tired, strained lines had drawn down his mouth in a droop of weariness. " I'd just walked back here from the military camp when I heard the shot. You had reached the stables yourself just as soon as I did."

He crossed the room to the desk which stood within the circle of light and began to pull out drawer after drawer, tossing the contents aside. There was a jerky, badly-controlled energy about all his movements, as if he were holding himself above the engulfing weariness of nights of sleeplessness. He spoke back over his stooped shoulder, harshly.

"What happened out there? . . . That young madman and the horse . . . It was a bad business, a mad business, Sergeant. I know that. But there's nothing I can do about it. Mad things are happening all about us . . . To all of us . . . To me . . ."

He turned from the desk, a bundle of papers in his hand. Nervously, jerkily, he ripped the papers into shreds. The tearing of paper rasped in the stillness.

"Worse things! Things that'll make work, plenty of work, for your fellows, Sergeant. The commission of the military party ends at midnight to-night. At midnight! That's right, Captain Levinge, isn't it? At midnight to-night."

He threw the torn papers aside and watched them flutter to the floor. A scrap of paper was blown against his trouser leg; he brushed it off with a quick, nervously jerky movement, as if it had been some repulsive, crawling thing.

"At midnight," he said again. His voice lifted. "And Major Osborne tells me now that he'll not wait one minute here after the fixed hour. His men are out of hand, mutinous. But he won't admit that. Gad! He won't. He's got a score of excuses. But one excuse is as good as another—or as bad. They're blowing 'Boot and Saddle' in the camp square now. Inside an hour, they'll be on the march to Ballinrobe. Inside an hour . . ."

Hugh felt the fierce grip of the hand on his shoulder relax. He leaned back against the wall and lifted a hand to touch the trickle of blood that had clotted across his face.

With every passing moment the realization of his own danger became more and more clear. The finding of the pistols would help to shift the suspicion of killing Mark

Killian from James Hannin ; it would shift the suspicion to Michael Carroll, but the law might well claim, Hugh thought, that the man who had been found to-night so near Michael Carroll's dead body might be Michael Carroll's accomplice. It would be a suspicion after Sergeant Dempsey's own heart ; it was a suspicion that would conveniently supply a new prisoner when James Hannin had to be freed. Yes! The law might well think that. Another thought struck him: Anne Killian might think it. He pressed his hand against his face, and his hand was damp with sweat.

" Inside an hour," Charles Boycott was saying in that harsh, hard-held voice of his. " And inside an hour I go, too. You hear that, Sergeant Dempsey? Inside an hour I'll require protection, full police protection, to take me . . ." He paused, and it was not at Caroline Boycott he looked, but to the girl who stood beyond her in the lamplight, " . . . to take us safely to Ballinrobe."

" Going, Captain? " It was Watty Connell's voice that fell dully into that sudden, leaden silence. " Why for would you go, Captain? Why for? "

" Because I'm beaten, Connell. Beaten." For an instant there was a new and kindly note in Boycott's voice, as if he found himself suddenly surprised by the bailiff's loyalty. " Yes, beaten. Oh! Yes! I know we did all I promised to do. We saved the crops, every penn'orth of them. Every penn'orth."

He picked up papers from his desk, crumpling them in a nervous grip.

" Crops to the value of three hundred pounds, Connell. Three hundred pounds." He tossed the crumpled papers aside. " And they tell me now that the cost to the Government and the Orange Order will be every ha'penny of four thousand pounds.

" Four thousand pounds! Think of it," he said savagely. " Four thousand pounds spent to save three hundred pounds' worth of crops."

He swept the last of the papers from his desk and slammed shut the drawer.

"A fine joke. But I'll not stop here to listen to them laughing at it. A laughing stock for Land Leaguers and Moonlighters! I'd sooner have them shooting at me."

He walked slowly across the room to where Judith Wynne was standing in the lamplight, her face and shoulders bathed with brilliance. Her live, stormy eyes lifted to meet him, and if there was not in them any real warmth of welcome, there was, at least, an answer to his unspoken question.

"That's all the help we can give you, Sergeant." Boycott's voice had something of its old strong ring in it. "You know as much yourself as I do"—he looked down at the girl—"as we do, of Carroll's death. You can make your own arrangements for Coroner's Quest and Enquiries and the like, but you'll have to see to it immediately that I have the protection I've asked for, within the hour. Connell here may be able to help you with your questions . . ."

"Is it me, Sergeant? The devil a news I can give you."

The bailiff's sidelong glance swept Judith Wynne's guarded face, and that glance was not brightly derisive now, but bitterly vindictive. He went on, stirred to venomous hope by his memory of the bitterness that lay between those two women. He would give the older woman a weapon ready to her hand against the other.

"The devil a thing I can tell you, for the devil a thing I saw or heard. It's how the mistress herself here sent me looking for Miss Judith an hour and more ago. Inside the house and outside the house, up and down, upstairs and downstairs I looked, and devil an eye I laid on her, wherever she was . . ."

It was odd, Hugh thought with weary detachment, how strong and forceful the tall girl's gestures were. She pressed her hand back over her hair, and her hair under that passing pressure gleamed with a new golden radiance in the lamplight.

"How stupid of me, Watty." Her voice was smooth and clear and utterly at ease. "How stupid not to have told you where you could find me." She smiled back at Boycott, a wide-eyed, candid smile that lightened his air of doubt. "It was so very, very warm and oppressive, I walked down to the boat-house," she lied, "and walked up and down under the trees, watching the moon come up over the lake."

"So I'm afraid, Sergeant," she smiled, "that I can't tell you anything of what happened away on the other side of the house, at the stables."

The older woman was looking down at her hands in the lamplight, at the faint, warm glow on the cold skin. The cold, bitter hatred on which Watty Connell had counted had not waned. She lifted her head.

"But perhaps Captain Levinge can help the Sergeant," she said gently. "Perhaps he saw more than the moonrise?"

The thin, clear voice and the darkening of Captain Boycott's face were the things Hugh most clearly remembered of that moment. The room smothered in the taut instant of unease. The soldier's hand closed again on his shoulder, as if asserting his rights over this prisoner.

"Lucky for you that I did, Sergeant," Levinge said lightly. "Lucky I did see more than the moon. If I'd come by the lake, I might quite well have met Miss Wynne and missed picking up your prisoner here."

A smooth enough lie. Hugh let his shoulder go lax under the urgent pressure of the man's hand. A smooth, convincing lie. Out of his own narrow code of conduct the soldier would lie stoutly and unshakeably to aid this woman, even though he was aiding her to leave him for another man. He would do that, Hugh thought bleakly, with little thought one way or the other of the good or ill it would do to others. He felt the firm pressure harden on his shoulder.

"Over at the woods on the other side of the stables I sighted this fellow, an hour and more ago, when I was walking over to make my adieus to the ladies," the smooth, lying voice went on. Easy and smooth and with its own certainty of belief, Hugh told himself, not yet sure how much or how little the lie would help or hurt him. "More than an hour ago, Sergeant. I got to wondering what the fellow was up to, and I've kept an eye on him ever since."

The tight grip loosed on Hugh's shoulder. A lean hand slapped him lightly. The high, clear voice drawled on.

"I've had my eye on him every minute since, Sergeant. And you can take my word for it, this lad hasn't been up to any mischief in that hour. I never lost sight of him."

The lean, sun-roughened face creased and wrinkled briefly in its own ironic humour.

"Fellow might have had a bit of poaching or thieving or general blackguardism in mind, Sergeant, but he's had nothing to do with the other—he's been doing nothing worth arresting him for. Afraid you'll have to turn him loose."

So that was it. Hugh's eyes were dark with a humour that was savage and ironic. The last lie was told. The last evasion planned. Levinge had used his to uphold Judith Wynne's lie. Just that.

Just that, he thought with sudden bitterness. He was being contemptuously offered the reward of freedom at the cost of a shut mouth. This lean, cool soldier's lie could be his passport to freedom. Well so! He could play that game to the last throw. He met the Sergeant's baffled, unsure stare and could read the man's slow uncertainty in his flushed face. It was on Dempsey's slowness of thought they must all trust now.

"True for you, Captain Levinge," the Sergeant was saying. "True for you, of course. If you had your eye on him, devil a much mischief the boyo here could be up to. That's true enough."

He floundered, pulled this way and that, divided between suspicion and the long habit of discipline. He blinked unhappily at the uniformed officer.

"If you had him in sight and under observation for an hour he couldn't have been in the company of the deceased, Carroll, for," intoned the Sergeant, "the said Carroll is believed to have slipped past the patrols on the bog road not more than fifteen minutes ago."

He held up a hand to check Levinge's impatient interruption.

"But there are other matters to be taken into consideration, Captain. Other matters entirely. There's the matter of breaking and entering. And there's the matter of entering with intent. And there's the matter of illegal trespass. . . ."

"Quite so! And the matter of getting on a special parade in good time, Sergeant. An infernally important matter for me, what?" The soldier picked up his cap. He twirled it jauntily in his fingers. "Well! I'm afraid I shan't be able to help you with your trespass and all the rest of this business. Not likely that my Adjutant will grant me special leave to come back here to give evidence in a petty trespassing case. What?"

He turned smartly to the others. The cap twirled in his fingers, the badge glinting in the light. He bowed stiffly, very formally.

"And now I simply must get away. It's been so pleasant knowing you all. You've all been so kind."

The lean, reckless face was hard and tight-lipped in the lamplight. The light eyes flickered over Judith Wynne's face; they darkened before the resolute purpose he saw there.

"Too bad it's so unlikely that we'll meet again." He made no move to hold out his hand, nor did Boycott, puzzled and as yet unsure and slow to make up his mind, make any move. "And now I'll leave you to get rid of this poacher fellow in your own way."

It was Judith Wynne for whom those last words were meant. Hugh watched her as the soldier's quick footsteps faded away across the hallway. He watched the hard, controlled misery in her face and the bleakness in her eyes. In that moment he saw a gleam of hope. She could not risk, now, having the lie that Levinge told contradicted. For her own sake, she must back up that lie to the last breath. He turned to the policeman.

"Are you satisfied, Sergeant?" he asked. "If you're not arresting me, I'll be on my way now. . . ."

"Oh, faith you won't."

The Sergeant took a great stride towards the door. His slow-moving mind had seen a way of accepting Levinge's story and of holding Davin prisoner at the same time.

"The Captain's story might have cleared you of having anything to do with Carroll's business, but you still have to answer to Captain Boycott for trespass on his grounds and policies." He hooked his thumbs in his belt. "We'll hold you now for Captain Boycott to prosecute; and you'd never know what else we'd find against you while we have you safe under lock and key. For you're a man, Davin, I have an eye on this long while past. This long while past, surely. . . ."

Across the hallway the door clanged shut behind the soldier, and that sharp clanging seemed to rouse Judith Wynne from her rapt misery. She dropped her hand on Boycott's arm, but it was to Hugh Davin she looked across the room.

"Charles!" Her voice was very low. "If we go, we must go now, at once. . . ."

"But, of course. . . ."

"At once. Without all this wasting time. . . ."

Hugh drew a deep breath of relief. He saw now that he was right. The girl would not risk his spoiling Levinge's lie; and if he were held a prisoner now that lie might most easily be spoiled.

"Without wasting time on all this stupid talk of courts and arrests," she went on. "What does all this silly, petty business of trespass and arrest matter now? What does it matter when there's murder and madness at our door? Don't you see, Charles? We must go now. Now, I tell you. Now. . . ."

Out of his own dark mood Hugh watched them—the girl whose way was now clear to her and who would hold to that way without scruple or weakness; the man who would for ever now be moulded in that girl's strong hands, as he was being moulded at this very moment.

"Have done with this nonsense, Dempsey," Boycott rapped out. "I'm still waiting for that escort to Ballinrobe. You hear me? I'm waiting. Now."

"But the prisoner, Captain. What about the prisoner? Aren't you going to prosecute? 'Tis important to hold him now. . . ."

"The thing that's important now, Dempsey, is to get me a safe escort. D'you think I'll waste time talking about trespass and petty prosecutions when there's murder at my very door? D'you think I'll give them one more reason to laugh at me?

Gad! I've proved myself the world's fool; but I'll not be your fool too."

He fumbled open the door and laid a violent hand on Hugh Davin's shoulder.

"You!" The violence was in his voice, too. "Get out! When I come to deal with moonlighting savages, I'll deal with them for more than trespassing or loitering. Out with you while you're safe. Out!"

CHAPTER TWENTY-FIVE

WITH that casual, contemptuous dismissal rankling in his mind, Hugh Davin went down the steps of Boycott's house. He was free, but he knew that he could not risk putting his freedom to the test. Only too well he knew how readily Sergeant Dempsey would find some new charge to level against him. By morning, sooner perhaps, if he stayed within reach, the policeman would have found some new excuse for an arrest that would link his name with Michael Carroll's and with the dead man's crime. He went on down the steps and into the shelter of the trees.

It was a night heavy with foreboding, a night that had not yet rung with the bravado of marching bands and the tramp of feet and rumble of wheel as infantrymen and gunners swung away from Lough Mask and went marching down the road to their barracks at Ballinrobe. It was a night that was yet to see Charles Boycott and the tall, rounded woman by his side turn their backs for the last time on Lough Mask House and go bowling through the night under guard and escort on the first miles of the long road that was to lead them to England and their own place of safety. It was a night that was to see, too, the defiant air of Caroline Boycott as she drove with no other guard or escort than Watty Connell to seek the hospitality of Robert Browne's house at Kilmaine.

But the night and the night's happenings still lay ahead as Hugh paused in the shadows, undecided.

The night was brighter now in the full moonrise. All the

high hollow of the sky swam in a milky mist of light, and tree and hill stood out redly dark against the wan glow. The uproar from the military encampment had died away, and now there was a steady hum of sound, a muted echo of disciplined activity from the tented square. Nearer was a wilder clamour, and from the shadows Hugh saw now a dark knot of men crossing the moonlit side of Killower Hill and sweeping in an angry flood along the road that led to the house that had been Michael Carroll's and was now lit and warmed against Malachy Bourke's homecoming.

For a moment he watched the dark mass of men, the men who had gathered in Martin Egan's room, surge forward, bent on whatever plan of vengeance they had made against Malachy Bourke, and also—who knew?—against Ellen Killian. He watched them round the last bend of the road, and saw come towards them, hastening and alone, a broad, burly man, striding strongly. Even at that distance he knew Father John O'Malley's carriage, and the abrupt, forceful gesture with which he threw up his hand to halt the surging crowd.

He watched that surging crowd of men and the lone man who was endeavouring to stop them. He watched, suddenly chilled with fear. If Anne had found her way cut off, she might well have turned back to Killower. And in Killower to-night there would be danger from maddened men whose tempers would not be held or curbed. The thought of his own danger went from his mind, and he stumbled through the shadows heedless of a loud shout from a policeman who was standing guard on the front avenue.

He slipped past the lighted windows and, with silent caution, made his way through the gloom under the laurels. Step by step he made his way towards the archway, where the guarding police still stood over the body of Michael Carroll. Back towards the house a voice called out, the voice of the policeman who had hailed him; and Sergeant Dempsey's voice boomed back in answer:

"That was Davin. Stop him and bring him back here. I have a word or two yet to say to him." The voice slipped down into a deep, rumbling grumble: "Too easy he was let go. Too dam' easy." Again the voice rose: "Stop him and bring him back here. Pass the word along."

The voices, calling from guard to guard, came echoing down the night. Beyond those calling voices sounded the deeper, angry voices of the men on Killower Hill. The night stifled with danger.

"Bring him back here!"

Hugh moved softly into the deeper shadows. He would not seek safety yet. He must first be sure that Anne had got safely away, that she had not gone back to Killower into the danger that threatened there. He moved on into the gloom, a hand outstretched to guide him. His outstretched, groping hand touched the shoulder of the girl who had made no attempt to win clear from the place he had left her. He felt her shoulder go taut with shock, and then she knew him.

"This way, Hugh." Her hand slipped down and caught his hand. She drew him back under the laurels to a low, arched passage between the twisted stems. "I found a way here. A safe way. A safe way down to the lake. . . ."

"In God's name, why didn't you take that way yourself? Why didn't you go while it was safe?"

He was thinking, with horror and pity, of the long, long minutes she had spent here in the shadows close to the dead body of the man who had caused her father's death, within hearing of the police guards' coarse gossip.

They moved forward, step by cautious step, until the arched pathway gave place to a narrow, grass-grown ride between the trees. They went on more quickly now, the faint, wet wind from the lake blowing in their faces. His hand closed tightly about her hand, and life pulsed to life at their hands' touch.

"Why didn't you?" he said again.

"Well you knew I couldn't go till I knew you were safe." The faint, dark fire that he had once known so well was in her voice again. "Well you knew I wouldn't go." He heard the deep, shaken murmur of her breath. "We can go now."

He knew that there was no need now to protest his

innocence of Michael Carroll's crime, to protest James Hannin's innocence. The girl had come to the truth in her own way here in the dark, lonely minutes of waiting.

"We can go now," he said, and the lift of his heart was in his voice. "A long road and a hard road, maybe; but we can go that road together."

"We will go together," she said very quietly.

At that the desperate courage and resolution that had for so long upheld her wavered. Her face crumpled and broke like a child's. She turned towards him, her mouth pressing against his breast. His hand passed back in a smooth, caressing gesture of reassurance over the dark, sleek wings of her hair.

"Together," he told her again.

They went on then into the moonlight. Behind them the clamour of angry voices slowly died away, and a single, strong voice triumphed against the clamour and came clanging through the night:

". . . so you can go back now to your homes and leave violence be." That deep, strong voice of Father John O'Malley filled the night. "You have no more need for violence. Here on the shores of Lough Mask you have forged a weapon that is stronger than violence. You have that weapon now to use against the grabber and the rack-renter, a weapon that'll strike terror into the heart of any man that levies an unjust rent or into the heart of any man who seizes a farm from which his neighbour has been unjustly evicted. You have that weapon in your own hands. You can punish the rack-renter or the grabber. You can ostracise him . . . you can isolate him . . . you . . . you . . ."

The deep voice checked, hesitated, seeking for a word that would be readily understood and easily remembered by the men who now listened to him silently. He hesitated for a long moment. His voice crashed again in the quiet:

"You can Boycott him!"

[THE END]

By the same Author:

NORTH ROAD

SINGING RIVER

RED SKY AT DAWN

ALL OUT TO WIN

DARK ROAD

GOLDEN COAST